PUMPED

MARS FITNESS
BOOK 3

LINDEN BELL

PUMPED

Love is co-parenting with my worst enemy.

OWEN

Everest is an irresponsible, delinquent, attention-hungry man-child.

Ever since my brother married his sister, we've hated each other with an unrelenting passion. It was bad enough when I had to see him at occasional family gatherings, but now I'm living in a nightmare and he's right here with me.

EVEREST

Owen is arrogant, uptight, snobby, and cold-hearted.

I don't want to have anything to do with him, but I don't have a choice. After a tragic accident, we're forced to raise our niece together, but our grief and mutual animosity is turning the house into a pressure cooker. We have to make peace and learn to work together, if not for our sake, then for the little girl who's already lost everything.

PUMPED is an enemies to lovers, forced proximity, grumpy/sunshine, opposites attract MM romance between a free-spirited personal trainer and his overbearing veterinarian brother-in-law. Expect reluctant cuddling, teasing as a love language, annoyingly hot backwards caps, pillow chastity barriers, pool wrestling, begrudging I love yous, and a little girl who has them both wrapped around her little finger. PUMPED is the third and last book in the Mars Fitness series and can be read as a standalone.

CONTENTS

EVEREST

Vegas, baby!

We're at the blingy-est club I've ever stepped foot in, and we've got fucking *bottle service*. Bachelor parties are the fucking best, and I've seriously gotta find myself more friends who are getting married.

Except, this isn't my friend's bachelor party. It's my future brother-in-law's, and he didn't technically have to invite me. Jeremy's cool, though. He's super chill and even offered to pay for my trip without me asking. Don't worry. He can afford it—he's some fancy banker dude on Wall Street.

Me? I couch surf from one beach town to the next, searching for the next big wave. The whole staying in one place and holding down a job thing isn't really for me. Who wants that kind of responsibility? Not this guy.

The other dudes in our group are alright. They're all Jeremy's friends from work or school. All older and loaded, which means I've barely had to pull out my wallet since we stepped off the plane.

The only guy here that I can't fucking stand is Jeremy's brother—Owen. See, even his name is so fucking pretentious. *Owen*, ugh. He's uptight, arrogant, and just fucking rude. I don't know what the hell I did to him, but Jesus, if looks could kill, I'd already be six feet under.

The fucked up thing is, the guy hates my guts, but at the same time, I keep catching him staring at me. Like, it's not enough for us to just ignore each other for the weekend. Nope, he wants me to know that he hates me. He wants me to *feel* how much he hates me.

Like right now. In the middle of the club, the champagne's flowing, everyone's hyped up, the music is pumping, and we're here to *celebrate*! But Owen's sitting in his little corner, glaring at me like it's my fault he's not having a good time. What-fucking-ever. His idea of a good time is probably sitting at home reading a fucking textbook.

About animal parts. *Snort*. Yeah, he's in veterinarian school. Gonna be an animal doctor. He's already got everyone calling him "Doctor Owen."

Doctor Owen, my ass.

"Ev-er-est! Ev-er-est! Ev-er-est!"

I chug down the pint of beer and slam the heavy glass on the table in front of me. Jeremy and his friends explode into cheers as I wipe my mouth with the back of my hand. I can feel the heat of Owen's stare on the side of my face, like he's trying to burn through my cheeks with his laser eyes. I ignore it and reach for another pint.

"Not so fast." Jeremy grabs the glass from me. "I promised your sister I'd look after you."

"What? It's only my third pint!" I try to snatch the glass back, but he holds it out of my reach.

"Yeah, and the night is young. Besides, you're only twenty-one."

I roll my eyes. "Right, and I haven't had a drop of alcohol before this," I say, voice dripping with sarcasm.

Jeremy pushes me toward the edge of the booth. "Go dance for a bit. Then come back and you can have another."

I give him an unamused look. "And here I thought you were kinda cool."

He laughs and takes a sip of *my* beer. "I respect your sister too much to care about cool."

Well, fuck if that's not sickeningly sweet. Ugh.

I let Jeremy shoo me out onto the dance floor. The music is thumping and the bass is so low and loud that the floor reverberates with each beat. I slip into the crowd, and the temperature rises a couple degrees with sweaty bodies pressing in on all sides. An arm brushes against mine, an ass presses against my hip, a pair of boobs graze my back.

Someone drags a hand down my front, but in the flashing lights of the club, it's hard to see who it is. Another hand palms my ass cheek, but it's there and gone so quickly, I barely have time to turn my head.

Blood pumps through my veins in time with the music and my head grows a little fuzzy with the high. I raise my hands into the air and drop my head back, letting out a whoop as the beat drops and the dance floor erupts.

The entire time, I can feel the steady, unwavering focus of a pair of eyes on me. The hair at the back of my neck lifts and goosebumps break out across my skin. It's fucking creepy, the way he watches me like he wants to hunt me down and—I don't know—tear me apart or something. And yet, there's something tempting about it, like a giant wave I know is too dangerous, but I'll still paddle out on the off chance I'll be able to ride it, to tame it.

The spotlight tracks around the club and for a split second, it lands on Owen. He's sitting at the edge of the booth, one ankle propped up on the opposite knee. A glass tumbler is balanced in one hand and the opposite arm is slung across the back of the booth. His eyes are shaded, but I know they're trained on me. His lips are pressed into a straight line. Arrogance pours off him, fueling this strange itch that's been growing inside me.

It's like there's something restless expanding in my chest, reaching out through my arms and down into my legs. It's pressing on my insides, seeping into every nook and cranny, looking for a way out. It's weird. I've never felt anything like this before, and honestly, I'm not sure I like it.

The spotlight swings across the spot where Owen's sitting, except now the booth is empty. He's not there anymore. He's gone.

Where is he?

Lights flash in my eyes and white spots appear in my vision. Bodies press into me, pushing me left and right, farther and farther away from our booth. Music blares in my ears, so loud it's disorientating.

Where did the fucker go?

I struggle through the mass of elbows and shoulders and toes, feeling like I'm swimming against the current just to get to the edge of the dance floor. When I finally get there, I scan the club, looking for that head of dark, neatly trimmed hair, shoulders clad in a perfectly tailored white dress shirt, narrow hips filling out a snug pair of dress pants. I don't see him.

I start toward the restrooms. I don't know why I'm doing this—looking for fucking Owen. I don't care where he is or what he does. It has nothing to do with me, and seriously, the less I know the better. But still, my feet take me down the narrow hallway, lit only by a weak line of light running along the middle of the floor.

The men's room is at the end of the hall, and I weave my way past the line of girls waiting for the ladies' room. I'm halfway down the hall when a hard body crashes into me from behind, plastering me face-first against the wall.

"Are you following me?" a voice growls next to my face.

Owen's lips brush the shell of my ear. His breath is hot against my cheek. A shiver runs down my spine and every drop of blood in my body rushes to my dick, leaving me lightheaded and at a loss for words.

He's a couple inches shorter than me, and I thought he was kind of scrawny, but the body pressed up against mine is hard and solid and strong. He has no trouble keeping me pinned against the wall, and for some crazy reason, my groin tightens with arousal. That itchy, too-big-for-my-skin feeling melts away, leaving me soft and pliant as the heat of Owen's body seeps into mine.

He shifts and something long and stiff pokes me in the ass—his cock. Owen's hard cock. The realization makes my dick throb in my jeans and a whimper escapes my mouth.

A hand slides down my back and around my side to my hip. Without thinking, I cover it with my own. Then taking ahold of it, I drag it around and curl his fingers around my aching bulge.

"Fuck." Owen drops his head forward onto my shoulder and his hips buck, grinding his cock into my ass. "What are you doing to me?"

Before I can ask him what he means, the weight on my back vanishes. Disappointment hits me hard, like an unexpected wave, then suddenly, I'm being dragged back through the club toward the exit.

"What are you doing?" I yell at Owen's back, but he doesn't hear me over the loud music and screaming crowds. Or maybe he does and he's ignoring me. "Where are we going?"

Owen's grip on my wrist is so tight I don't think I'd be able to break out of it. But instead of trying, I let him lead me out of the club and along the crowded sidewalks toward our hotel.

My heart is racing just as quickly now as it was in the middle of the dance floor. If anyone looked, they'd see the obscene bulge in my jeans. I feel like I'm adrift in the middle of the ocean, at the mercy of the wind and the currents. And the only thing keeping me from floating away is Owen's fingers curled around my wrist. If he lets go of me now, I think I would drown.

How messed up is it that I'm happy he doesn't let go? Not when we get back to the hotel. Not while we ride the elevator up to the twenty-ninth floor. Not when he pulls out his keycard and unlocks the door.

The door isn't fully shut before Owen pushes me up against the wall again. Facing him this time. We're nose-to-nose, lips an inch apart. He smells like old, worn-in leather, rich and earthy and just a bit sweet. The scent fills my senses and wraps around me like a deliciously weighty hug. My eyes flutter shut and my lips part as I sink into the feeling.

"Motherfucker."

That's all the warning I get before Owen crushes his lips against mine so hard I think I cut my lip on my teeth.

The shock of his attack makes me gasp and he takes the opening, plunging his tongue into my mouth. The invasion ripples all the way down to the soles of my feet.

Someone moans. Someone whimpers. I think that someone is me.

His body is hard against mine. He grinds his erection against my hip. My fingers dig into his waist as I hang on for dear life.

At the back of my mind, I know this is Owen—annoying, uptight, thinks he's better than me. I'm supposed to hate him and he's supposed to hate me. My sister is about to marry his brother and we're technically going to be related.

But knowing all that only makes what we're doing better. Hotter. Like we're breaking the rules or going behind someone's back, doing the thing we've been told not to do.

Owen grabs the front of my shirt, pulling me away from the wall and pushing me farther into the room. I stumble backward, just catching myself at the edge of the bed.

He stalks toward me, eyes dark and laser-focused, jaw set and determined, every muscle primed to pounce. He looks dangerous. Like he wants to tear me apart. Like he wants to hurt me. And all I can do is stand here and take it.

"Strip," he growls and my body reacts to the order before my brain can process what it means.

My hands fly, ripping at my clothes and tossing them all over the room. Owen moves more slowly, unbuckling his belt and yanking it out of the belt loops. He winds it around and around his hand, then sets the coiled belt on a chair before reaching for the buttons of his shirt. One by one, he unbuttons them, revealing the dark hair covering his chest. He slides the shirt off his shoulders, shakes out the fabric, and carefully folds it into a neat little rectangle. It joins the belt on the chair.

Owen bends down to untie his shoes. He sets them off to the side, perfectly aligned, then takes off his socks and folds them into a ball. When he straightens, my breath catches in my chest. Jesus, he's hot. Did I know that? How did I miss that?

He's trim, not like, in a twinky sort of way, but like one of those guys who wouldn't gain an ounce of fat if they ate bucketloads of ice cream. He's not muscular, but he is all muscle.

Dark chest hair narrows to a thin line on his flat stomach, and it trails all the way down, disappearing under the waistband of his pants. My eyes are glued to his fingers, long and strong, with a dusting of hair across the tops of his knuckles. They pop the button on his pants, then drag the zipper down one tooth at a time. My breath hitches with each subtle *tick* of the zipper until I feel like I'm hyperventilating.

Owen steps out of his pants—and folds them neatly— leaving him in only a pair of black boxer briefs. His dick print is clearly visible, and there's a growing wet spot around the head I want to suck on. His thighs are thick, his calves are toned, and there's more hair dusting the tops of his toes.

I gulp.

Owen is older than me, but I don't think by much. Except seeing him now, all dark and dangerous, he feels so much older, more in control, more put together, more of a man.

"Get on the bed."

I don't think. I just scramble to obey.

Owen grabs the complimentary condom and lube from the tray of miniature-sized snacks and drinks provided by the hotel and tosses them onto the bed next to me. Then he hooks his thumbs under the waistband of his underwear and pauses. He waits. Like he's hesitating, like he's not sure this is a good idea anymore, like he might want to put his clothes back on and tell me to get the hell out of his room.

Fear makes my gut clench as everything inside me screams, "No!" That can't happen. Not now. Not when we've already come so far.

I crawl to the edge of the bed and put my hands on top of Owen's. Then together, we push his underwear down past his hips until they drop to the floor. His cock springs up, close enough for me to see the veins running along its length, to smell the dark, rich scent of his pre-cum.

I take it in my hand, marveling at the velvety smoothness of the skin and the steely hardness underneath. Owen sucks in an audible breath and his hands curl into fists by his sides.

Satisfaction surges through me knowing that I'm affecting him as much as he's affecting me. This isn't just a one-way thing. I'm not the only one completely thrown by what's happening to us.

I lean forward, opening my mouth and reaching my tongue out to lick the bead of pre-cum forming at the tip of Owen's cock. The potent, bitter flavor explodes on my tongue and I immediately want more—*need* more. I seal my lips around the head of his cock and suck, desperate to drink him down.

Owen hisses, his hand coming to the back of my head. His fingers slide through my hair, possessive and controlling, and something inside me breaks open.

God. Fuck. Yes. This—whatever this is—this is what I've been searching for my whole life. The spark of something new and scary, the thrill of being in over my head, the release from going with the flow because I have no other choice.

Owen pushes my head down and I don't resist. I let him hold me there, with his cock stuffing my throat so full I can't breathe. My lungs burn and my vision goes blurry, but still, I don't push him away.

When he finally lets me up for air, I'm panting, barely able to catch my breath. I roll to the side and collapse onto my back. My cock throbs with my every inhale and pre-cum gushes from me with every exhale. I swear to god, I think I could come like this. If he'd kept me there a second longer, if he'd tugged on my hair a bit harder, I would have come with nothing more than Owen's cock in my mouth.

Owen grabs the lube and tears it open. He squeezes almost the whole thing out onto his fingers, then hikes one foot up onto the bed. With one hand, he strokes himself in long, lazy pulls. With the other, he reaches between his legs and past his balls.

I watch with half-lidded eyes as he preps himself. His body tenses and he shudders. He squeezes the base of his cock and lets out a slow, deliberate breath.

His eyes flash, blazing almost like there's a light shining behind them. They're amber, golden brown with a hint of red. I've never seen eyes like that before. I didn't know eyes could be that color.

I stare into those eyes, caught by the intensity I see in them. Emotions so strong and yet so tightly reined in. A flurry of thoughts racing faster than I could possibly follow. There's a world inside Owen's mind that I don't understand—that I'll never understand.

I'm entranced as Owen climbs onto the bed and straddles my hips. He rips open the condom packet and rolls the latex over my aching, sensitive cock.

"I knew you'd be fucking huge," he mutters more to himself than to me. Then he lines himself up and guides me into him.

Jesus H. Christ. My eyes roll toward the back of my head as I'm swallowed into his body. It's heaven. It's paradise. I've never felt anything so good, so perfect, so right.

Owen sits on my cock, hands braced against my stomach, every muscle flexed and taut. I fist the sheets under me, not daring to move, barely able to breathe, hovering right at the edge of an orgasm.

I don't get it. It doesn't make any sense. It's just an ass, a hole, a dude I don't even like very much. We haven't done anything weird or kinky or new. And yet, I feel like a fucking virgin getting his first taste of sex. I feel like my body isn't mine anymore, that it belongs to Owen to do with as he pleases.

When Owen finally moves, I have to squeeze my eyes shut. I can't watch him ride me, his body rolling as he bounces on my cock. I don't want to see the look on his face, the pleasure mixed with something harder, darker. If I see any of that, I'll come and I don't want this to end just yet.

Owen is relentless. He doesn't start slow and easy and work his way up. He lifts himself up and slams himself down, like he's trying to punish both of us with his fucking. Each time he bottoms out, he makes this deep, guttural sound that's half grunt and half growl.

His cock slaps against my stomach, hard enough that it stings a little, and the sound of skin hitting skin sends goosebumps racing across my flesh. His fingers find my nipples and I can't help crying out when he pinches them and twists. The delicious pain shoots straight to my cock and my hips come off the bed. Owen slams himself down on me and the pleasure radiates out from my groin to the outer extremities of my body.

Every cell is on fire. Every nerve ending is fried. I'm consumed, head to toe, in the pleasure Owen is wringing out of me. I never want this to end. I want to live here forever. Under Owen. At his mercy.

"Fuck. Fuck!" Owen yells, his hand flying over his dick as his ass clenches vise-like around me. Creamy white cum shoots from his cock, landing scalding hot on my stomach and chest.

His eyes are squeezed tightly shut, brows bunched together, jaw hanging wide. The sight of him coming, the splatter of his cum on my skin, together they send me over the edge.

I punch my hips up into him as I hit climax and my balls turn themselves inside out. As I empty myself into the condom, one single thought filters through my brain. *I love the way he looks when he comes.*

I don't remember what happens next. Taking the condom off and throwing it away. Crawling under the covers. Falling asleep next to Owen.

The next time I open my eyes, sunlight is streaming in through the window.

I'm alone.

EVEREST

"Who's the bestest uncle in the whole wide world?!" I crouch down, arms outstretched as Ivy barrels into me.

"You are!" she screams directly into my ear.

"Don't let Uncle Owen hear you say that," Eden says, a few steps behind her six-year-old daughter.

I scoff at my sister. Me versus Owen? Pssh. There's no competition. I'm a way better uncle than he is. I bring gifts for my niece every time I come over. I play make-believe with her and carry her around on my back as I run through the house. I even let her paint my face with her mom's makeup.

Would Owen do any of that? I'd fucking pay to see it.

"What did you bring me? What did you bring me?" Ivy jumps up and down, holding out grabby hands in front of her.

"Ivy," Eden scolds. "Uncle Everest doesn't have to bring you anything."

"Oh, but I did!" I unzip my duffel and pull out a

coloring book I picked up on the way to Eden and Jeremy's house. Fine, it might not be super impressive, but Ivy goes through her coloring books lightning-fast, so she can always use new ones. This one has pictures of baby animals in them.

Her eyes light up like I brought her a real-life unicorn. She grabs it and hugs it to her chest. "I love it! I love it! I love it!"

That's the great thing about kids, so easy to please. Not like *some* adults I know. Mentally, I give an imaginary Owen the middle finger.

"Ivy, what do you say?" Eden prompts.

"Thank you! Thank you! Thank you!" Ivy throws her arms around my neck again in a hug and I squeeze her back before letting her go.

"Can I go color, Mommy?" Ivy turns big pleading eyes onto Eden.

"Yes, fine, go color," Eden sighs in resignation. "You're going to have to pry her away from that thing when it's time to eat." She points at me in warning.

I stand and pull Eden into a quick hug, giving her a kiss on the cheek while I'm at it. "No problem. Ivy's an angel. It'll be a piece of cake."

Eden holds me at arm's length and examines me like she's checking for changes since the last time she saw me. Which was last week. But that's how she is—my big sister, always looking out for me, always on my side. She was the only reason I didn't get into more trouble when I was a kid, always covering for me with our parents, with the teachers. She even perfected Mom's signature so she could sign notices from school for me.

Now that we're both grown up, she's still looking out for me. She sends me home with frozen meals and reminds me to call Mom and Dad every couple weeks. Even during my nomadic days when I couch surfed from one beach town to the next, she called me every other day to make sure I was okay, that I had enough money and a place to stay. She even paid for motel stays when I told her I was sleeping in my car.

It's no exaggeration to say that I wouldn't be here if it wasn't for Eden always watching my back. I don't know what I would do without her.

Eden slaps me lightly on the arm and leads the way into the kitchen where Jeremy is mixing up drinks for brunch.

"Hey, Jer." I give him a bro hug before hopping onto a stool in front of the kitchen island.

"Hey, what did you bring Ivy this time?" Jeremy asks suspiciously.

I throw my hands up in innocence. "Just a coloring book. It's no big deal. It's not like I bought her a castle or anything."

Jeremy shakes his head. "No, that's more Owen's style."

I huff quietly. Why do they have to bring up Owen all the fucking time? "He bought Ivy a castle?" I can't keep the sneer out of my voice. That's just like Owen, though, always trying to one-up me to prove he's better than me.

"No, he didn't buy her a castle. He took her to an exhibit at the Brooklyn Museum last month, and they had a fake castle for kids to play in," Eden explained.

I roll my eyes. Museums. Boring. I'm definitely the cooler uncle.

Jeremy sets a mimosa in front of me and I take a healthy swig of it just as the doorbell rings.

Wiping my mouth with the back of my hand, I ask, "Are we expecting anyone else?"

Jeremy and Eden exchange a look—one I've seen before, unfortunately. A little embarrassed. A lot scheming. I don't like it, because I know what it means.

"No, you didn't." Dread fills me, immediately ruining my perfectly happy mood.

Jeremy goes to answer it while Eden steps in closer to give me a look, warning me to behave. Ivy's footsteps stomp down the stairs as she races to the front door.

"Why?" I whine. "You know we hate each other. He's going to ruin my whole day."

Eden lowers her voice. "No, he's not. And you aren't going to ruin his either. You're both adults. You can be civil to one another for a couple hours."

"But why? Why bother when everyone would be so much happier if we weren't in the same room at the same time?"

Eden pins me with a stern look. "Ev, you're family now. You're both important to me and Jeremy. You're especially important to Ivy. We're not saying you have to be BFFs. But at the very least, you do need to learn how to get along."

I huff in annoyance as voices filter in to the kitchen. A moment later, Owen strolls in, holding Ivy's hand while she skips along, telling him about dinosaurs. Guess she's forgotten about my coloring book already. Traitor.

"They're sooo biiiggg!" She swings her free arm through the air.

"They are. Would you like to see them in person?" Owen asks.

Ivy gasps. "Can we? Real live dinosaurs?"

Owen laughs, the sound low and throaty, and heat settles low in my stomach. I push the feeling away, irritated at how my body responds to Owen. No matter how annoyed I am, no matter how much I can't stand him, it's like my body hasn't gotten the message that, hey, we *can't stand each other*. Nope, without fail, something inside me perks up in anticipation of a reenactment of Vegas.

Not gonna happen.

"No, not live dinosaurs. But scientists have found their bones and recreated what they look like," Owen explains like he's giving a fucking college lecture or something.

"Sooo cool!" Ivy claps her hands in excitement.

A smile spreads across Owen's clean-shaven face. Jawline ridiculously strong, lips naturally pouty. He steps into a ray of sunshine that glints off his perfectly combed dark hair. His amber eyes twinkle like he's got a secret he's not willing to share.

The heat in my stomach grows.

Then he looks up and spots me. His eyes narrow, the twinkle disappearing as they harden. "Everest." His voice drips with arrogance and hostility.

"Owen," I say back, just as mockingly.

"I didn't know you were going to be here," he says, gaze flitting accusingly to Jeremy.

"I didn't know you were going to be here either."

"Surprise!" Ivy shouts, throwing her arms in the air as if she had fistfuls of confetti.

I lift an eyebrow at Eden. Are we seriously going to do this? Sit across the table from each other and pretend we don't hate each other's guts? Why in god's name did she think this was a good idea?

Eden gives me a helpless shrug.

Rude.

It's awkward as we settle around the large kitchen table. The only person who seems oblivious to the tension in the room is Ivy, who's still chattering away about dinosaurs. Owen's listening intently, spouting fact after fact like he's some sort of dinosaur expert. Who knows that much about ancient dead things anyway?

"Do you think there's a dinosaur unicorn?" Ivy asks, hopefulness written all across her face. Unicorns are her favorite animal of all time—yes, I know they're not real animals, lay off me—and her entire bedroom is decorated like a unicorn took a shit in it. Pink everywhere, with rainbows and sparkles and every kind of unicorn you could possibly imagine.

Owen pretends to think. "Hmm, I don't know. Scientists haven't found any creatures that resemble a unicorn, but that doesn't mean it didn't exist. Perhaps they just haven't found it yet."

Ivy bounces in her seat. "Did you hear, Uncle Ev? There might be unicorn dinosaurs!"

Owen shoots me a smirk, almost daring me to contradict him. I let myself glare at him for a second before turning to Ivy.

"Really? That's awesome! How big do you think they'd be?"

Ivy laughs. "They're horse-sized, silly!"

Owen drapes his arm across the back of Ivy's chair, smug satisfaction radiating off him like an obnoxious cologne.

"Right. Of course. Horse-sized. My bad. But do they have wings?" I ask.

Ivy scrunches up her face as she thinks. "I think they should have wings. It'd be cooler if they could fly. And safer too, right? In case the larger dinosaurs want to eat them? They can just fly away."

I wince at the idea of extinct dinosaurs eating imaginary unicorns. That's just a little too circle of life for me.

"That's right," Owen says. "They could have evolved to have wings for survival."

Fuck this. I'm bored with the dinosaur talk. I shoot Eden a pleading look to please save us from Owen's nerdery.

"Jeremy and I are going to the opera in a couple weeks," Eden jumps in.

Great. Opera. So much more exciting. I stab at the hash browns and shove them into my mouth. Then wash them down with the rest of my mimosa.

"At the Met?" Owen asks, perking up. Which, of course he would. Snob.

Jeremy nods. "My company got tickets to *Carmen*."

"I heard that got great reviews," Owen adds. "Let me know if it's good. I'll have to go see it."

"Do you guys need a babysitter for Ivy?" I ask. I've done it before when Eden and Jeremy go on their monthly date nights. I know Owen has too.

But given today, I wouldn't be surprised if Eden and Jeremy asked *both* of us to babysit. At the same time. Without telling us ahead of time. They'd get some perverse pleasure out of our misery, I'm sure.

"No, we've already got a babysitter scheduled," Eden says. "You guys are off the hook." She gives us both a pointed look that makes me squirm in my seat a little. Then she catches Jeremy's gaze and they smile at each other.

The look in her eyes starts out mischievous, like the two of them are sharing some unspoken joke. Then it softens to something warm and tender. Jeremy's wearing a matching expression.

They really are great together. A perfect match. I've never seen them arguing or fighting. Not over big messy things, or even small silly things. Not when the basement of their brownstone flooded the year before or when Ivy got a bad flu last winter. They just dealt with it all as if it were nothing. They make marriage and raising a kid look so damn easy. Like anyone could do it.

A little ache lodges itself in the middle of my chest. It's not that I want their life—I definitely don't. Marriage and kids? No, thank you. But there's something magical about the way they are together that fascinates me.

Eden never complains about Jeremy staying out too late or working too hard or not pulling his weight at home. She never complains about being tired or frustrated or angry. Whenever I ask, she gets this dreamy look on her face like she's living in a fairy tale and she's found her happily ever after.

That must be nice. Being that happy. I wonder how that feels.

A weight, heavy and hot, bores into me, and I glance up to find Owen glowering at me. His brows are furrowed and his lips are pressed into a firm, straight line. Jesus Christ. What is it now? Am I breathing too loud for him? Am I not sitting up straight enough?

I slouch down in my chair, take a deep—and noisy—

breath, and glower right back. Sometimes it's hard to believe Owen and Jeremy are related. Like, I get along great with Jeremy and with their parents. I have from the first time I met them. But except for that one night in Vegas, Owen's always had it out for me. In fact, I think he hates me more now than he did back then. I just don't know what I did to get put on his shit list.

Most of the time, I don't care. He can think whatever the hell he wants. I've got plenty of friends. I don't need him. But sometimes, there's a part of me that really, really wants to know. Sometimes, I want to peel back all those layers and see if there's actually a human being hiding inside.

OWEN

Soft violin filters through speakers hidden around my study, and I settle into the plush armchair by the window. A glass of red wine sits next to me on the side table, and the latest issue of *JAVMA* is cued up on my iPad. Ahead of me stretches two full days of uninterrupted time. No shifts at the animal hospital where I'm a veterinary surgeon. No chores or paperwork to get caught up on. No plans to drive up to Westchester to see my parents or to head out to Brooklyn to see my brother and his family. I've got nothing but time to read, go for a few walks, maybe try out a couple new recipes I've bookmarked. Total bliss.

I take a sip of the pinot noir from an up-and-coming vineyard in Napa Valley and scroll to the article that piqued my interest: new procedures for treating cleft palates in canines. I'm only halfway through the introduction when the screen on my phone lights up.

Unknown Caller ID.

I stare at it for a second, debating whether I should ignore the call and let it go to voicemail. It's probably my hospital. I'm not supposed to be on call, but there could be an emergency they need me for.

I swipe to accept. "Hello?"

"Is this Owen Lambert?"

My entire body snaps into high alert at the dry, official tone of the unfamiliar female voice. "Yes, this is he."

"I'm calling from New York-Presbyterian Hospital. You're listed as the next of kin for Jeremy and Eden Lambert?"

Her words are a bucket of cold water right in my face. The chill soaks straight into my bones. "Yes? Are they okay? What happened?"

"I'm sorry, Mr. Lambert, there's been an accident. You need to come to the hospital."

I don't hear the rest of what she says.

For a moment, I'm frozen. Sitting on the edge of my armchair, holding my phone to my ear, I disassociate. Whatever this is, it isn't real. This phone call isn't real. The person on the other end isn't either. Any second now, I'm going to snap back to reality and continue with my evening as planned.

But I don't. And it doesn't. I'm still holding my phone to my ear and the woman on the other end is still talking.

"Mr. Lambert? Are you there?"

I give myself a little shake. *Snap out of it, Lambert.* "Yes, I'm here."

"Do you need the address of the hospital?"

"No, I know where it is."

The call disconnects and I jump into action. This is not the time for emotions, for shock or fear or anything other than taking decisive steps forward. My brain races, throwing thoughts at me a mile a minute: make sure I have my phone, my wallet, my keys; pull out the file folder with all of Jeremy and Eden's emergency information; grab the phone charger from the bedroom, and a bottle of water from the kitchen; double check the stove is off.

And while my conscious mind is assessing the situation, creating a game plan, and executing it, a ball of unease grows in the pit of my stomach. There was something off about that woman's voice over the phone, something not quite right. A touch too much sadness, perhaps. A noticeable lack of urgency. I don't like it. I don't like what I think it means.

The trip from my apartment in Alphabet City up to the hospital in the Upper East Side takes almost twice as long as it should. I swear to god, the taxi hits every red light along the way, and pedestrians keep darting out onto the road like this is some fucking obstacle course. My leg won't stop bouncing the entire ride.

When the cab finally spits me out in front of the hospital, I'm itching to run inside, but I force myself to walk instead. Stay calm. Stay focused. Stay in control. I put a stranglehold on the emotions that are building inside me and force them down. This is *not* the time.

"I'm Owen Lambert. I got a call about my brother and sister-in-law. Jeremy and Eden Lambert." I can hear myself speak. It's flat and rigid, cold and distant.

The receptionist directs me up to the eighth floor and I

jab at the elevator buttons, convinced that pressing them multiple times makes the damn thing move faster. A doctor is waiting for me at the nurses' station, and from the apologetic expression on her face, I know I'm not going to like what she has to say.

"Mr. Lambert?"

"*Dr.* Lambert." The correction slips out before I'm able to stop it, landing just shy of harsh and demanding. I'm not sure why I do it. It wasn't a conscious choice. But that small change in address keeps the floor under my feet just a little bit firmer. "I'm a veterinarian."

She flashes a quick, understanding smile. "Dr. Lambert, let's sit down over here."

It takes a second for me to move. I don't want to sit. I want her to tell me what happened. I want to go see my brother. My big brother. My hero. My best friend. Because if I can just see him, then everything will be alright. Everything *has* to be alright.

Stiffly, I sit where she's indicated, hands braced on my knees to keep them from bouncing.

The doctor pulls a chair over and sits down across from me. In the same even-keeled tone I use on my own clients, she explains the situation. "There was a multi-car accident. They were in the backseat of a cab and weren't wearing seatbelts. The car flipped over and was hit multiple times."

A choked sound claws at my throat, but I swallow it back down. *Keep it together, Lambert. Lock it down.*

"I'm afraid Jeremy didn't make it."

Air rushes from my lungs as the doctor's pronouncement punches me in the gut.

"Eden's on life support, but there's no brain activity."

My diaphragm spasms, unable to contract and draw in oxygen.

"I'm so sorry."

My lungs burn. The room tilts. My ears ring. I'm *this close* to passing out before I'm finally able to force myself to breathe.

This can't be right. I must have heard her wrong. But the doctor's watching me with a wary look in her eyes, like she's waiting for me to break down into sobs or to freak out in a rampage.

I'm not going to do either. Because neither will make this situation any easier. Instead, I nod, the movement abrupt and jerky.

"I'll give you a moment and get someone to take you to see them. Eden's room is on this floor, but Jeremy is down in the morgue."

I flinch at the word. The morgue—but that's where they put the corpses. If Jeremy's down there, then that means… No. Don't go there. Don't feel. Don't succumb to emotions. This isn't the time.

"I'd like to see him first."

The doctor hesitates like she's not sure she should let me.

"Please, I need to see him." The words come out rough. I clear my throat and shove my emotions back down.

An orderly leads me down to the morgue, and the entire way, a stray thought dangles at the back of my mind. *Maybe they got it wrong. Maybe it's not Jeremy. Maybe this whole thing is just a big mistake.* I don't let myself reach for the thought, but I don't bat it away either. I can't afford to cling to false hope, but I also can't quite give it up altogether. I balance precariously in the in-between until the coroner's assistant leads me to a body covered with a white sheet.

My hands curl into fists, my nails dig into my palms. *Don't let it be him. Don't let it be him.*

The coroner's assistant waits for my nod before lifting the sheet and folding it back.

I stare.

It looks like Jeremy. The hair is dark like mine. The same nose, same chin. He has a scar above his left eyebrow from playing basketball. He looks... normal. Like he's asleep. Like I can reach out and shake him and he'll open his eyes. He barely has any scratches on his face.

But— I don't— He can't— I just saw him earlier in the week. We grabbed coffee after the meeting he had in my neighborhood. I'm supposed to go over for brunch next weekend. How— What—

"Mr. Lambert suffered massive internal bleeding," the coroner's assistant reads from a chart. "The paramedics rushed him to the emergency department, but he'd already lost too much blood. There was nothing the doctors could do."

My control slips and a riot of emotions surges forward. Bile shoots up from my stomach, burning my esophagus. I spin and race out of the room, away from the sharp, stinging odor of formaldehyde. I gasp as I burst into the hallways, trying to breathe past the sudden bout of nausea.

Fuck. FUCK.

I slam my fist into the concrete wall and the pain radiating through my hand and up my arm helps to clear the nausea from my stomach. I shake out my hand and slump back against the wall, banging my head against it a couple times when the nausea threatens to return.

It's true. I don't know how, but it is.

Jeremy is dead.

"Mr. Lambert?"

Taking a deep breath, I squeeze my eyes tightly shut until the stinging fades. Only then do I straighten and open my eyes.

The coroner's assistant holds out a clear plastic bag. "The clothes and other belongings your brother had on him when he arrived at the hospital."

I stare at the bag. The folded clothes look like a suit and shirt. The dress shoes look like the pair I got him for Christmas last year. Wallet, keys, phone. It's so normal. Like he folded it all up and placed it neatly inside the bag before climbing onto the table.

I reach for the bag, bracing myself for the weight. But it's surprisingly light. Too light. It should be heavier, shouldn't it? Considering it contains the last bits of life my brother lived. I clutch it to my chest as I make my way back upstairs.

A nurse shows me to Eden's room and I stop just inside the door, afraid to go any farther.

Somehow, seeing her like this is harder than seeing Jeremy downstairs. The sheets are arranged neatly around her and her hands are clasped gently on her stomach. Someone took the time to brush out her long blond hair, pulling it to the side to lay across one shoulder.

She looks peaceful, serene, like she too could wake up if I reached out and shook her. She's breathing steadily, her chest rising and falling in time with a whooshing sound coming from the machine. But it's not actually Eden who's breathing.

She's alive. But she's not. She's here. But not really.

Reluctantly, I inch forward until I'm close enough to grip the guard rails on the side of her hospital bed.

The nurse does a quick check of the monitors. And even though I know it makes no difference, the charade is strangely comforting.

"What's her condition?" My throat is tight and my voice is coarse.

The nurse shoots me an assessing look, and I return it with as much steely confidence as I can muster. Solemnly, he picks up Eden's chart.

"She had—has a severe concussion and several broken ribs. There were also some internal injuries. She was taken into emergency surgery and they were able to repair the damage. But then her heart stopped beating. The team was able to revive it, but by then her brain had already been deprived of oxygen for too long."

In slow motion, my legs give out under me and I sink into the chair next to the bed. The bag of Jeremy's belongings lies in my lap. A similar bag sits on a table beside me. The fabric inside is dark purple, along with nude pumps and a small, sparkly clutch. I glance from it to the bag on my lap.

They were dressed up. They were on their date to the opera. *Carmen.* The show's gotten good reviews. They must have enjoyed themselves.

And now they're dead.

A hollowness opens up inside me, a deep, yawning cavern that wants to swallow me whole. I wrap my fingers around the wooden armrests of the chair and hold on tight, willing myself not to fall in.

The nurse quietly closes the chart and replaces it. "The doctor will stop by in a bit to answer any questions you have. Would you like us to call anyone for you?"

It takes a second for my brain to process the nurse's question. Call? Call.

Fuck. I'll have to break the news to the rest of the family. Mom and Dad. Eden's parents. And—

I shoot to my feet. "Ivy."

Jesus, Christ, how could I forget about Ivy? Why wasn't she the first thing that popped into my mind?

"Do you have her number?" the nurse asks helpfully.

"No…" I shake my head. Ivy doesn't have a phone number. Because Ivy is only six years old and in her first year of big-girl school. Ivy… who must still be at home with a babysitter. Shit. "No. No, I've got it."

Placing Jeremy's belongings next to Eden's, I pull out my phone.

The time for shock is over. Grieving will have to come later. Right now, there are things I need to take care of.

EVEREST

The music is thumping, I've got a good buzz going, and I'm *this close* to bringing this cutie home with me. We've already been eye-fucking each other all night and I just need his friends to stop sucking tongue so he can tell them he's leaving.

I wrap my arms around his waist and nuzzle the sweaty skin of his neck. My chubby is pressed nice and snug against his bubble butt. My dick is going to get a treat tonight.

"Fuck, let's get out of here." He turns his head to murmur in my ear.

"Your friends?" I ask.

"Covered. Yours?"

I glance over at the three of them. Sawyer and Logan, my besties from work, and Connor, whose boyfriend, Donnie, also works with us at Mars Fitness. They're all partnered up with the loves of their lives, leaving me the sole bachelor holding down the fort. They wave at me from their spot at the edge of the dance floor and I wave back.

"All good. Let's go." I need to get my dick in some ass before I burst. I take the cutie's hand and we make a beeline for the club's exit.

It's early spring in New York City and the temperature plummets after sunset. Despite growing up in Massachusetts, the few years I spent on the West Coast have turned me into a sunshine and beaches kind of guy. The cold night air cools the sweat on my skin, leaving me shivering, and I cuddle closer to the cutie to stay warm.

"You wanna call a car?" he murmurs between kisses.

"Mmhmm." I reach for my phone in my back pocket. As soon as I have it in my hand, it starts vibrating.

Ugh. Another spam call. Nobody actually calls anybody these days.

Without taking my lips from the cutie's, I bring my phone over his shoulder so I can end the call without answering it.

Except... I stop and blink. That's Eden's phone number. Why the hell is my sister calling me now?

"Uh..." The cutie pulls back when my lips stop moving against his. He glances at the screen displaying my sister's picture and cocks an eyebrow. "Do you need to answer that?"

I stare at the screen for a second, tempted to send her to voicemail. She can shoot me a text and I'll deal with whatever it is in the morning. Except, it's the middle of the night and she wouldn't call unless it was important, right?

"Sorry, hold on." I reluctantly step away from the cutie and swipe to answer the call. If she's just bored and wanting to bust my balls, I'm going to strangle her. Way to cock block her little brother. "Hello?"

"Hi, uh, is this Everest?"

The voice one thousand percent doesn't belong to Eden. It's about twenty years too young. I pull the phone away from my ear to check the screen again. I didn't hallucinate Eden's picture, did I?

Nope. That's Eden, all right. From when she was in high school and came home piss drunk, hair all over the fucking place, and vomit down the front of her shirt. I took the picture as blackmail. She hates that I use it as her profile pic.

But then I notice the actual number on the screen. It's not Eden's cell phone. It's the landline from her house. Some stranger is in her house? What?

"Hello?" The young female voice jolts me out of my stupor.

"Yeah, sorry. This is Everest. Who are you?"

"I'm Adeline. Ivy's babysitter."

That explains the landline thing, but why the hell is my niece's babysitter calling me? "Okaaayyy."

"So, um, Mr. and Mrs. Lambert aren't here yet. They were supposed to get home two hours ago."

"Oh." That's... weird. Eden's not the most on-time person in the world, but Jeremy pretty much operates like clockwork. He's never late. "Have you tried calling them?"

"Yeah, of course I did. They're not picking up." Adeline's eye roll is so loud, I can hear it from here. "You're the first person I'm supposed to call if I can't reach them."

"Oh." That's... super weird. Both that they didn't pick up *and* that they told the babysitter to call me. I can never be trusted to answer the phone, but Eden and Jeremy are annoyingly fond of actually talking to people. They wouldn't ignore a call, especially if they've left Ivy with a babysitter.

"So are you coming or not?" Adeline's teenage annoyance comes through the phone full blast, so strong I wince at the impact. "Because I love Ivy and everything, but I gotta get home."

"Uh…" Fuck. What am I supposed to do? I'm not anywhere near their brownstone in Park Slope, and I was gonna bring this guy home with me, and why am I the first person the babysitter is supposed to call? How the hell would I know what to do?

"Hello?"

"Yeah, yeah, sorry. Um, okay, I'm on my way." I pause a beat before continuing. "You'll stay until I get there, right?"

"Yes, I'll stay," Adeline says like I'm the dumbest person in the world. But I don't know how babysitters fucking work, okay?

"'Kay, I'll be there as fast as I can."

She sighs and her breath blows directly into the phone's mic. "Fine. Bye."

The call disconnects so abruptly, I don't realize it's dead for a moment. Not until the cutie who's been waiting for me speaks.

"You're leaving?" His arms are crossed over his chest, hip thrust out to the side. He's giving me the stinkiest of stink eyes.

"I think so?" I'm still not entirely sure what just happened and a part of me wonders if I can bring him with me. Like, maybe Eden and Jeremy are just running late, and they'll show up by the time I get there, and I can still salvage the evening.

But the cutie rolls his eyes hard enough to out-roll Adeline. "Figures. I always pick the wrong ones." He stalks back toward the club, leaving me standing on the sidewalk, alone and cold.

My buzz is gone, but my head isn't quite on straight just yet. Where the fuck are Eden and Jeremy? And why the fuck aren't they picking up their phones?

I try Eden's cell on the way over to their house. It goes directly to voicemail. I try Jeremy's. Same thing. My thumb hovers above a number labeled "The Asshat" in my phone.

Owen.

He probably knows what's going on. And even if he didn't, he'd know what to do. He's so "responsible" and "reliable" and really goddamn boring.

I can imagine it already. The condescending voice. The irritated expression. He'll barge in and take over, leaving me standing on the sidelines like some kind of loser.

No. I lock my phone. I don't need to give Owen any more ammunition. He already thinks I'm useless, I don't want to prove it to him by calling him for help. I'm an adult. I'm resourceful. I can take care of this myself.

Besides, what's the worst that could happen? Maybe both their phones ran out of battery. Totally weird, but it could happen. Ivy's probably asleep by now. I'll just check in on her and then crash on their couch until they get home. It can't be more than a few hours, right? They'll be back by morning, for sure. Everything's fine.

A teenage girl, who I assume is Adeline, is waiting in the foyer when I get out of the rideshare. She opens the door as I jog up the stoop and starts talking before I can even say hello.

"I tried Eden and Jeremy again, but nothing. I fed Ivy dinner, helped her with her bath, and got her into bed. She woke up once, then fell asleep again without any trouble. Questions?" She already has her coat on and one foot out the door.

She rattled all of that off so fast, I could barely follow her. But I'm pretty sure I caught the important stuff—Ivy's in bed, I just have to stick around until Eden and Jeremy get back. "Uh… I don't think so?"

"Good. Eden can Venmo me when they get home. Bye." She skips down the steps and disappears into the night before I can offer to get her a car to take her home.

I'm left holding the door, blinking at the empty street in front of the house. A gust of cold air rushes in, knocking me out of my daze. Quickly, I close the front door and lock it, then I head upstairs to check on Ivy. Her bedroom is on the second floor, along with Eden and Jeremy's home office.

I crack open her door. The heavy shades are drawn, blocking out the night lights of the city, but a softly glowing lamp sits in the far corner. The pink walls are decorated with rainbows and unicorns. Gauzy fabric hangs from the ceiling above her bed in a canopy.

Ivy is nothing more than a little lump in the middle of the mattress, her blonde hair spread in a halo on the pillow. She's hugging Zuzi, her favorite squishmallow, a pink unicorn with a gold horn. I got it for her a couple years ago and she takes it with her everywhere. Owen's gotten her other plushies since but she always goes back to my unicorn.

Take that, Owen.

My chest warms at seeing my niece sleeping so soundly. She's the reason I decided to give up my nomadic van life out west and settle in New York instead. I hadn't planned to initially, but after a few visits when she was a baby, I realized how much I was missing. Kids grow so fast at her age and FaceTime just doesn't cut it.

So I sold off Betsy, my van, couch-surfed for a few months, then landed at Mars Fitness as a personal trainer. I run their classes, mostly boot camps like the one modeled after the training FBI agents have to take. And recently, a super dope skipping class. I'm working on a drumming class based on traditional Japanese drumming and yoga stability balls. I really want to do goat yoga, but my bosses, Beau and Gavin, won't let me bring goats into the gym. Shame.

Quietly, I close Ivy's door and cross the hall to the home office. Both Eden and Jeremy have desks in here. But there's also a futon against the far wall.

It takes a bit of wrangling, but once the futon's flat, I toe off my shoes and collapse face-first onto the cushions. I'm out before my head hits the throw pillow.

OWEN

I really didn't want to leave the hospital, but I had no choice. I've already called Mom and Dad, and they're on their way down from Westchester. I managed to get a hold of Eden's parents too. They live just outside of Boston, so it'll take them a bit longer to get here.

It's Everest I can't get a hold of. Not that I'm surprised. I've never met anyone who fits the description of man-child so accurately. I had wanted him to go to the brown-stone to relieve the babysitter and check in on Ivy, but now I've got to do it myself instead. It's probably for the best, anyway. Everest is the epitome of unreliable.

The house is dark and quiet when I let myself in with my spare key, and I pause in the foyer as all the worst-case scenarios run through my mind. The babysitter has left Ivy on her own. The babysitter took Ivy somewhere else.

Stop it, Lambert. Check the house. The babysitter is probably just sleeping somewhere since it's so goddamn late. No need to catastrophize.

The living room is right off the front door but there's no one sleeping on the couches. The kitchen is empty too. The basement guest room is unoccupied and so is the media room.

My anxiety ratchets up a few notches as I race upstairs as quickly and quietly as I can. Carefully easing her door open, relief washes over me when I see Ivy exactly where she's supposed to be. Fast asleep in her bed, Zuzi tucked in right next to her. My pulse settles a fraction as I close her door.

Now, the babysitter. Where the hell is the babysitter?

Across the landing, the door to the office stands open and I can see the corner of the unfolded futon. I slip into the office intending to wake them up and send them home but freeze when I recognize the large male body sprawled half on the futon and half hanging off. It isn't the babysitter. It's Everest.

I take an involuntary step backward as my mental armor slots into place. I hate that this happens whenever I see Everest. It's like my subconscious is trying to ready me for battle—except, I'm never sure if the battle is with him or with myself.

Don't get me wrong, I'm definitely battling Everest. The guy drives me up the fucking wall. Yet there's also a small part of myself that can't help but be drawn to him. He's an attractive man and he can be quite charming. But that's all there is to him, I keep reminding myself. All facade, no substance. Unreliable. Man-child.

What the hell is he doing here? Why didn't he answer his phone? Did Eden and Jeremy ask him to babysit? Why didn't he raise the alarm when they didn't come home on time?

I stomp forward to shake him awake but stop again before I reach him. He's dressed all in black, tight jeans, tight t-shirt. There's a dusting of glitter across the wide expanse of his back. His hair isn't squashed under the baseball cap he usually wears. I catch a whiff of alcohol and sweat.

He wasn't babysitting Ivy. He was probably out clubbing before he came here and crashed. The babysitter most likely left when he arrived. Or maybe the babysitter called him when Eden and Jeremy didn't come home.

And he came.

Irrational annoyance spikes in me—at the babysitter for calling Everest instead of me, at Everest for answering their call and not mine, at this whole fucking situation that shouldn't be happening in the first place.

I lift a foot to nudge him on the hip… then set it down again. What's the point in waking him now? He'll be confused and incoherent. I'll be irritated and short-tempered. We'll argue and I throw the fact that his sister is dead in his face. I vehemently dislike Everest, but even I'm not that cruel.

Everest's eyelids flutter, his eyeballs shifting back and forth in REM sleep. His breathing is slow and even, not quite loud enough to be a snore. It could actually be soothing, like comforting white noise. His lips are open and there's a bit of drool leaking out the corner of his mouth.

Fatigue washes over me, my eyelids growing so heavy, I can't keep them open. It's only a few hours until sunrise. I'm too tired to deal with him. Let him sleep in blissful ignorance for a little while longer. Never say I haven't done anything kind for Everest.

I sigh and back out of the room.

Downstairs in the kitchen, I dig through the drawer that holds all the fancy coffee pods Eden's addicted to. I should probably try to sleep, but that feels selfish, irresponsible. We're in the middle of a nightmare, someone needs to stay alert and clear-headed. Someone needs to think ahead and plan and figure out what we're doing next.

With more force than necessary, I slam the coffee pod into the machine and mash the start button. The machine gurgles to life and I watch the dark brown liquid stream into the mug. My eyes sting when I blink, dry from being awake for too long. My limbs feel heavy, like I'm moving through water. I jump when the machine beeps, the sound too loud in the stillness of the night.

With mug in hand, I take a seat at the kitchen table and sip at the dark roast, rich and fragrant, with just a hint of chocolate.

A stray tear escapes my lashes and trails down my cheek. Then another. And another.

The dark roast was Eden's favorite flavor. We were just chatting about it a couple weeks ago when I came over for brunch. I sat in this very chair. Looked out that same window. The view hasn't changed. But everything else has.

A few hours later, the sky is just starting to brighten. I haven't budged from my spot at the kitchen table.

A thud comes from upstairs. Everest—it's too heavy to be Ivy.

The stairs creak under his weight, then the sound of sock-clad feet shuffling toward the kitchen. The light flips on a second before a shriek.

"Jesus Christ! What the fuck are you doing here? Why are you sitting in the dark?"

It takes a few moments for my eyes to adjust to the light and when I finally blink them open, Everest is standing by the light switch, looking way too adorably rumpled than any grown man has the right to be.

His light brown hair is standing up on end. There are several creases on his cheek from the pillow he was using. His socks have slid down his feet, leaving them flopping empty in front of his toes. The tight black t-shirt stretches taut across his muscled chest. It follows the taper of his body down to narrow hips. The jeans cup him like a glove, snug enough that I can see his dick print through the denim.

"Yo, dude, are you sleepwalking or something? Hello?" He snaps his fingers at me and I resist the urge to slap his hand away.

"I'm not sleepwalking." Although, my voice is rough enough it sounds like I'm asleep. My eyes feel swollen and my cheeks are tight with dried tears.

And my mug is empty. I'm going to need way more caffeine if I hope to make it through the day. I stand to go brew myself another cup. While the machine whirs, I flick on the faucet and splash some cold water on my face. It helps. But the nightmare isn't washed away so easily.

I pat my face dry with the handkerchief I carry in my pocket, then turn back to the coffee machine.

"Yo, you didn't answer my question." Everest rubs his eyes with the heels of his hands as he shuffles in my direction. "And where are Eden and Jeremy? Aren't they back yet?"

My throat closes up. I can't speak. I've lost the ability to formulate words and voice them out loud. I keep my gaze trained on the mug as it fills.

Everest leans his hip against the counter and frowns at me. Arms crossed, biceps bulging against the fabric of his shirt. "Hello? Earth to Owen. If it's not too much trouble, we mere mortals would like an answer, please."

He's close enough that I can smell the alcohol and sweat from whatever he was doing last night. But underneath that, the unique scent that is pure Everest. Earthy, warm, like freshly turned soil and newly cut grass.

"You stink. You need a shower." I grab the mug from the machine and stalk back to the kitchen table.

Behind me, Everest sighs loudly. "Fine. Don't tell me. They'll have to come home eventually."

Through the reflection in the window, I can see Everest opening the coffee pod drawer to pick out something for himself.

"They're not coming home." The words come out in a strangled mutter.

"What?" Everest looks over his shoulder at me, his expression in the window is genuinely confused.

"They're not coming home," I manage to say, a little louder.

Everest abandons the coffee pod on the counter and rounds the kitchen island to stand in front of me. His brows are drawn together in a scowl.

"What the hell is that supposed to mean?" All traces of sleepiness are gone. He's wide awake and alarmed.

I swallow, pushing down the grief, the despair, and fill my lungs just enough to speak again. "Eden and Jeremy. They died in a car accident last night."

Everest doesn't react. He doesn't move, doesn't speak,

doesn't even blink. Long seconds tick by in silence before he shakes his head and scowls deeper.

"That's not even a little bit funny, asshat."

"I'm not joking."

"Of course you're joking. Eden and Jeremy can't be dead. I just saw them last week." He grips the back of a chair and pulls it out from under the kitchen table, but he doesn't sit down. "No. You don't know what you're talking about. They just got held up. They'll be back any minute now."

I stare at him. He's in shock. It's understandable. I wouldn't want to believe it either. Hell, I didn't fully believe it until I saw Jeremy's body on that slab in the morgue.

I try to keep my voice gentle when I speak. "They won't. Because they're gone."

Everest takes a step backward and sticks both hands into his hair. His eyes go unfocused and a little wild. "No, that's... No..."

"I've already called your parents. They're on their way in. When Ivy wakes up, we'll bring her to the hospital to say goodbye to Eden."

With every word I say, Everest's expression grows a little more unhinged.

"What? What?! No! What are you talking about? Stop it!" He lunges in toward me and practically spits in my face. "Stop saying shit like that. It's not funny."

I shoot to my feet, grabbing the front of his too-tight shirt and giving him a shake. I feel like I'm an elastic band, stretched to its limit and about to snap. We're nose to nose and I can smell Everest's morning breath, the sour scent of dried sweat. I can see the black spots in his light brown irises.

"I'm not fucking joking," I grit out between my teeth, hating the way my voice catches on the last word. "They're dead. Jeremy's in the fucking morgue and Eden has no brain activity. They're gone. I've seen it with my own eyes."

Everest's face is bright red with anger and he looks like he's about to punch me in the throat. Then out of nowhere, all the fight empties out of him and the blood drains from his face, leaving him limp and pale. Staring vacantly into the distance, he staggers backward until he hits the wall.

"That's—that's why they didn't answer their phones last night." He says under his breath, more to himself than to me. "They always pick up when their phones ring." He lifts his gaze to me, his eyes shining in earnest. "I called them. When I was on my way over, I called them because the babysitter couldn't reach them. I swear I did. But they didn't pick up."

Big, fat tears well up in his eyes and when he blinks, they escape down his cheeks.

I can't help but be a little sympathetic. A few hours ago, I was exactly where he is now. But another part of me bristles at the tears, at the horror and despondency written all over his face.

We don't have time for tears right now. We don't have time for sentimentality. We can't just break down and sob on the floor until we're wrinkly and dehydrated.

I latch onto the feeling, the annoyance and frustration, because those will keep me on track, keep me moving, propel me forward. There are things that need to be done, decisions that need to be made, and I can't let myself get distracted by Everest and his rollercoaster of emotions.

I down the rest of my coffee, ignoring the burn as it travels down my esophagus. Then I march over to the sink to rinse it out. When I turn back to Everest, he's still slumped against the wall.

"Pull yourself together," I spit out. I see him flinch right before I turn away to stalk out of the room, but I ignore it. I don't have the luxury of tending to his delicate feelings right now.

I need to wake up Ivy, feed her breakfast, then take her to the hospital. And somewhere in the midst of that, I need to tell her that her parents are dead.

EVEREST

Owen is wrong. He has to be wrong. There's no way Eden and Jeremy are dead. Shit like that doesn't really happen. That's like, movie-type stuff. That's not real life. There has to be another explanation.

My brain runs wild with crazy possibilities. Maybe they got kidnapped and are being held for ransom. Maybe they got abducted by fucking aliens. I'll take any of those over the bullshit Owen was spouting.

I'm still slumped against the wall when he stalks out of the kitchen and goes upstairs. A few moments later, the water starts running in the bathroom. He's gotten Ivy up.

Oh god. Ivy. I have to stop him. He can't tell her right now. Not until we've figured out what actually went down and where her parents are.

I sprint up the stairs, two at a time. They're in her bedroom and Owen is helping her get dressed. I meet his gaze over her head and the look in his eyes stops me in my tracks.

They're hard as steel. The dark circles under them making them look even more menacing. There's a defeated sense of resignation, a reluctant determination. He won't be moved. There's no changing his mind.

It's not the first time I've seen that look in Owen's eyes. It usually gives me a little thrill, like it's a personal challenge directed only at me. Can I get under his skin? Can I provoke him into an outburst? It's a game I've made for myself, one that I'm damned good at.

Not today, though. Today, I'm frozen to the spot, helpless as I watch Owen destroy a little girl's life.

"Ivy," Owen says, voice soft and somber as he lowers himself to her level.

Despite her young age, Ivy seems to sense that something's wrong. She sits on her bed hugging Zuzi the unicorn to her chest. Her chubby little face is way too serious and her large blue eyes blink innocently at Owen.

No. He can't do this to her. He can't shatter her world like this. She's too young, too small. She won't understand.

A strangled sound escapes my throat and I cling to the doorframe.

Owen's shoulders stiffen, but otherwise, he pretends he doesn't hear me. He's on his knees in front of her. Arms bracketing her on both sides.

"It's about your mommy and daddy," he starts.

I don't hear the rest. The sound of my heartbeat in my ears drowns it all out. My vision blurs and all I can see are blobs of pink and rainbow. It hurts to breathe.

Then a high-pitched wail breaks through my trance and I'm thrust back into reality.

Ivy is thrashing around while Owen's trying to hold

her, screaming at the top of her lungs about wanting her mommy and daddy. Owen's shouting on top of her, as if that will make her calm down.

I push off the wall. "Ives! Ives!"

She squirms her way out of Owen's arms and launches herself at me. Her arms and legs snake around me like a boa constrictor and I hold her just as tightly.

"I want mommy and daddy!" she cries.

"I know, sweetie, I do too." I rub circles across her back as her tears trail down my neck and soak into the collar of my shirt.

"Where are they? Why aren't they here?" She kicks her heels and they land painfully on my lower back.

"I don't know where they are, sweetie. But we're going to find them, 'kay?"

Owen glares at me, lips pressed into a flat line and hands curled into fists at his sides. I glare back. What does he expect me to say? That we're never going to find them because they're in heaven now? No, thank you. I'm not going to be the bad guy here. He can play that role.

"We should go," Owen bites out. He scans the room before grabbing Ivy's pink and rainbow backpack and fills it with a few toys and some books. He snatches Zuzi from the floor where Ivy dropped it and squeezes past me and out of the room.

I carry Ivy downstairs. Owen's banging around in the kitchen, pulling snacks from the pantry and fruit from the fridge. He stuffs it all into Ivy's backpack and fills her little pink water bottle.

In one swift motion, as if he's going into battle, he swings her backpack onto his shoulder as he marches out to the foyer. I hold Ivy in my arms as he struggles to put her shoes on, then he shoves her coat at me with a look that says "you deal with this."

"I'm calling a car." Then he opens the front door and flees out into the early morning air.

Carefully, I bend down and set Ivy on her feet. Her face is wet and blotchy. Her bottom lip is still trembling. My heart breaks to see her like this. I mean, I've seen her cry before, obviously. But this is different. This is fear and confusion and a touch too much understanding that makes it all so much worse.

I wipe her chubby soft cheeks with my thumbs, then hold out her coat. "Come on, Ivy-bear. Let's see if we can find your mommy and daddy."

Her movements are sluggish as she threads her arms through the sleeves, and the moment the jacket is on, she scrambles to be picked up again. I carry her outside. Owen locks the front door. We climb into the backseat of the rideshare that pulls up.

The drive to the hospital is silent save for the radio playing quietly in the background. When the car pulls up in front of the hospital, I awkwardly climb out with Ivy still attached to my front.

"My mom and dad should be here by now. Your parents are on their way down. I tried calling you last night, by the way. You didn't pick up," Owen rattles off as he speed walks through the hospital hallways.

I rush to keep up, trying to pull my phone out of my back pocket without dropping Ivy. The screen is black and no amount of tapping will get it to light up. "It's out of battery," I shoot back. "Do you even know where we're going?"

The elevator doors open and he steps in first, punching

the button for the eighth floor. "More than you do," he mutters.

When the elevator spits us out, Owen leads the way down the hall, slowing as he approaches an open door. He stops in front of it, but he doesn't go in.

When I look inside, I can't really tell what I'm looking at. It takes my brain a second to piece together the scene. But when I finally do, I squeeze Ivy so hard she whimpers.

"Sorry, sorry, sweetie." I'm in a daze as my feet carry me inside.

Eden—my beautiful big sister—is lying on the bed, hooked up to all these machines. They beep and whir and there's a screen showing the steady beating of her heart.

"Mommy?" Ivy lets go of me and reaches for her, straining so far away from me that I almost drop her.

"Careful, Ivy-bear," I say, shifting her weight in my arms and stepping closer to the bed.

"Mommy? Wake up. Mommy, it's me. Wake up!" Ivy squirms, desperate to be let down.

"It's okay, you can put her on the bed." The gentle voice comes from Alyssa, Owen and Jeremy's mom.

I hadn't even noticed her and her husband, Martin, sitting next to the bed.

She puts a hand on my arm, her expression full of grief and sadness.

"Mommy!" Ivy squirms again and I let her crawl onto the bed next to Eden. She shakes Eden's shoulder. "Mommy! Why won't you wake up?"

"Ivy, my dear," Alyssa steps in and I stumble backward, struggling to breathe.

"Grammy, why won't Mommy wake up?"

"I'm afraid she's not going to, sweetie."

A strong hand claps my shoulder and gives it a squeeze. When I glance at Martin, it looks like his hand on my shoulder is as much to hold himself up as it is to give me reassurance.

"Wha—what happened?" I ask, sounding strangled.

Martin's throat works and he shakes his head. Owen answers the question instead.

"Multi-car accident. Jeremy had massive internal bleeding and died en route. Eden made it into surgery, but then her heart stopped. There's no brain activity."

I understand all the words Owen says, but I don't know what they mean all strung together. "But they got her heart going again, right? I can see it on the monitor. It's beating."

"There's no brain activity," Owen repeats like it's obvious what he's trying to say.

"I don't fucking know what that means," I stage whisper to him through gritted teeth.

"It means her brain was deprived of oxygen for too long," Martin explains. "I'm sorry, Everest."

"No, but—" I stab my fingers through my hair. "It has oxygen now, doesn't it? She can still wake up, can't she?"

Owen's arms are folded over his chest, glower firmly in place.

Martin's hand drops from my shoulder. "I'm sorry."

A loud gasp comes from the door. "Oh my god." Then my mom rushes to the bed, followed closely by my dad.

"No, no, Eden, honey. Oh god, no." Tears stream down Mom's face and Dad embraces her from behind.

"Nana!" Ivy says from where's she still sitting on the opposite side of the bed. "Make her wake up, Nana."

"Oh, Ivy." Mom reaches across and brushes her hand over Ivy's shiny blond hair. "Oh, Ivy."

I can't. I can't be here. I can't watch this scene unfolding in front of me. The air is too thick for me to breathe. The walls are closing in. I scramble to get out, to get air, to get as far away from this nightmare as I can.

I find a stairwell at the end of the hallway and rush down the steps before bursting out onto the loading dock at the back of the hospital. I stumble a few steps before bending over and bracing my hands on my knees.

It smells like rotting corpses and dog piss back here. But I'd rather breathe this air than suffocate in that room.

I don't understand. None of it makes sense. They're young. Happy. They have a little girl. How can they be dead? They still have so much life to live. They have to watch Ivy grow up. Maybe have a second kid. They have plans to grow old together and cruise around the world when they retire. They have people who depend on them, people who need them.

They can't be gone.

They can't be.

They can't.

OWEN

The next week is the longest and shortest week of my life. Every second is excruciating to live through. Every minute rushes past in a blur. I barely sleep. I definitely don't eat. I've taken bereavement leave from the animal hospital, but I'm expected back on Monday.

An organ donor card was found among Eden's things, and when the doctor brought up the topic, Everest fucking flipped out. He accused the doctor of killing his sister to harvest her organs, then accused his parents of being complicit when they considered the doctor's proposal. In the end, Nell and Graham overruled him, and Eden managed to save several lives before she gave up her own.

Then it's been a non-stop whirlwind of getting the bodies released from the hospital and transferred to the funeral home. Putting an obituary notice in the newspaper and notifying Eden's and Jeremy's employers. Planning the funeral itself and reaching out to all their friends with an invitation.

I've been spearheading all of it. Because I'm not cruel enough to make my parents or Eden's parents do the work needed to bury their own children.

They've been focused on Ivy instead. Explaining the situation to her, comforting her, answering questions and giving reassurances. All things considered, Ivy's been dealing with everything as well as you can expect a six-year-old to.

It's Everest who hasn't managed to keep his shit together. He's been a nuisance every step of the way, complaining and objecting to every decision I make. But when I threaten to make him do the work, he blanches like a fucking coward and claims he's too distraught.

Fuck him. Man-child.

He couldn't even get through his eulogy, breaking down into sobs behind the lectern in front of the whole damn church. His buddies from Mars Fitness pulled him into the middle of some group bro-hug afterward.

But now it's done. Jeremy and Eden are gone. There's just one more thing to get through, and then I can finally breathe. Finally sleep. Maybe eat. Just one more meeting with the lawyers to sort out Jeremy and Eden's will, then Ivy will go live with my parents, and then… and then, we figure out how to live the rest of our lives without them.

The six of us—the two sets of parents, me, and Everest —are gathered in the conference room of a prestigious law firm in Midtown. Apparently, the will Jeremy and Eden put together was very detailed. I would expect nothing less from Jeremy. The lawyers insisted we all be here when they go through it.

"What's the point of a will anyway?" Everest is slumped in his chair, one elbow on the armrest, legs splayed out, swiveling the chair back and forth like he's a tiger pacing inside a cage. He's wearing jeans today while the rest of us are respectable enough to dress in business casual. I suppose I should be thankful he didn't show up in sweatpants and a backward baseball cap. "Everything's just going to Ivy, right? Why do you need a will for that?"

"You don't know that," Nell jumps in before I can snap at him. "Maybe there are some things they wanted to leave to one of us. Or maybe to a charity. Or they have specific instructions for how they want Ivy to be raised."

Everest huffs and drops his head back to stare up at the ceiling. "Do you know how long this is going to take? I have stuff to do this afternoon."

"Apologies for the delay." A tall woman in a crisp beige pantsuit struts into the conference room. Her sharp eyes land on Everest. "I'll endeavor to keep this short so you can move on with your day."

I stifle a groan and rub my fingers over my brow in an attempt to hide my second-hand embarrassment. Can't take the guy fucking anywhere. At least he isn't *so* oblivious that he misses the lawyer's retort. Quietly, he adjusts his posture, sitting up straight and pulling his chair toward the conference table.

"I'm Harriet Dawson and I helped Eden and Jeremy put their will together. I'm terribly sorry for your loss." She flips open a file folder. "Their will was straightforward and structured around their primary concern—Ivy. And even in that respect, they opted for an elegant solution. Custody of Ivy will be jointly shared by her godparents, Owen Lambert and Everest Wheeler. Together, they will also inherit ownership of the house in Park Slope and the family car. All other liquid assets will be transferred into a trust for Ivy, again to be managed by Mr. Lambert and Mr. Wheeler."

The conference room is silent as Ms. Dawson's words sink in. For several long moments, I'm convinced I misheard her. Did she really say that Jeremy and Eden wanted me and Everest to raise Ivy? There are so many things wrong with that statement I don't even know where to begin.

"I think there's been a misunderstanding," I say, leaning forward in my chair. "We've already discussed this and my parents have agreed to raise Ivy in their home in Westchester."

If Ms. Dawson is surprised by that pronouncement, she doesn't show it. "I'm afraid that's not in line with Eden and Jeremy's wishes."

The strange wording of her sentence catches my attention and I narrow my eyes. "It's not in line, but it's also not prohibited, is it? Exactly how binding is this will of theirs."

Ms. Dawson folds her hands on top of the papers in the file folder and levels her gaze at me. "It's binding."

"Which means what exactly?" I push back.

"It means that your brother and sister-in-law want you and Mr. Wheeler here to raise their daughter. Legally, you have custody. If you wish to transfer custody of Ivy to someone else, the courts will first need to rule that you are incompetent as parents. She will then be given into the care of the Office of Children and Family Services. She will stay in their care until the grandparents have been screened and approved as foster parents. The entire process can take months."

My jaw goes a little slack as Ms. Dawson lays out the harsh reality of our situation. I quickly snap it closed. If it was merely a matter of paperwork, that wouldn't be an issue. But handing Ivy over to the foster care system? For months? That is entirely unacceptable. There has to be another way around the bureaucracy.

"We'll raise her." Everest is half out of his seat, eyes shining with more determination than I've ever seen from him. "If that's what Eden and Jeremy wanted, then that's what we'll do."

I almost burst out laughing. Everest, of all the people in this room—Ms. Dawson, the lawyer included—wants to raise Ivy? This man-child who can barely dress himself wants to be responsible for another human being? The idea is ludicrous. It's even more laughable that he thinks the two of us can raise her together.

"Don't be ridiculous," I say dismissively, not bothering to spare him a glance. "Me and you? We can hardly stand being in the same room together."

Everest glares at me. "Yeah, and whose fault is that?"

My head snaps around and I pin him with a scowl. "What do you mean 'whose fault'? It's yours, obviously!"

"Me? You're the one with the stick up his ass!" Everest shoots to his feet and leans over the table at me.

Nell, sitting next to Everest, grabs his arm and pulls him back into his seat. "Everest, now is not the time nor the place."

"What? He started it!"

I snort. "And you think you're ready to raise Ivy? Please. You're the last person in either family who should be trusted with a child. You're practically one yourself."

Everest slams both hands on the table, ready to leap across the table if it wasn't for Nell's hand gripping his shoulder. His face is beet red. His eyes look like they're going to bulge out of his head. If he could kill me with a look, I'm sure I would already be dead and buried.

"Fuck you, you arrogant prick," he grinds out between his teeth.

"That's enough. Both of you." Mom's voice cuts through the tension filling the room.

Everest is perched on the edge of his seat, ready to lunge at me the second Nell takes her hand off his shoulder. I lean back in my chair, fold my arms across my chest, and smirk at him. Maybe I am an arrogant prick. But at least I'm a responsible arrogant prick.

"I think it's fair to say that we're all skeptical about this arrangement." Mom scans the table, daring anyone to disagree with her. "And who knows why Jeremy and Eden thought this was a good idea. *But*, it is what they wanted. So we owe it to them to give it an honest try."

My stomach sinks and all the smugness I felt from getting Everest riled up turns sour.

Me and Everest? Raising Ivy together? It'll never work. Not in a million years. We'll kill each other before Ivy reaches her seventh birthday.

It's not only that. It's everything. I have my own life. A career. An apartment. I have milestones I'm supposed to hit, goals I'm supposed to achieve. Raising a child is not a part of my five-year plan. Hell, I'm not sure it's even in my ten-year plan. I'll have to turn my entire life upside down to make this happen.

"I won't pretend to know the history between you," Ms. Dawson says. She's been watching our heated exchange with more boredom than curiosity. "But I do know that this wasn't a decision that Eden and Jeremy took lightly. There was a lot of discussion and weighing of considerations before they agreed that it would be the best course forward."

She flips through some pages and comes up with an envelope. I recognize Jeremy's handwriting across the front. It's addressed to both me and Everest.

"I'm supposed to give you this after the documents have been signed. But perhaps it will be more helpful now."

I take the envelope from Ms. Dawson and stare at it for a moment. Jeremy held this, wrote on this. This is his last message to us. Goddamn it, I wish I had my letter opener.

Carefully, I tear the envelope as neatly as I can across the top and pull out the letter. It's handwritten by Jeremy, but signed by both of them. As I scan the letter, a heavy cloak of responsibility settles around my shoulders. I have no choice. There's no other option.

I push the letter across the table to Everest as lines from the letter float through my mind.

WE HOPE YOU WILL NEVER SEE THIS LETTER, BUT WE FELT IT PRUDENT TO PLAN FOR THE WORST.
WE NEVER UNDERSTOOD WHY YOU GUYS DIDN'T LIKE EACH OTHER. YOU ARE SO SIMILAR IN SO MANY WAYS, PERHAPS NOT ON THE SURFACE, BUT DEEP DOWN WHERE IT MATTERS THE MOST.
WE CHOOSE BOTH OF YOU TO BE IVY'S GODPARENTS FOR A REASON. WE WANT HER TO GROW UP LEARNING FROM YOU. WE WANT HER TO HAVE OWEN'S SENSE OF RESPONSIBILITY AND EVEREST'S ENJOYMENT OF LIFE.

WE KNOW YOU CAN BE THE PARENTS WE WON'T BE
ABLE TO BE.

Across from me, tears are pouring down Everest's cheeks. Nell pulls a few tissues from the box in the middle of the table and hands them to him.

I wait until he sets down the letter before I speak. "We'll do it." I sound like a death knell, but I can't help it. I love Ivy. I love Jeremy and Eden. But this is going to change everything.

Everest nods as he cries into the tissues. Around the table, more tears have sprung as our parents each read the letter.

"Excellent." Ms. Dawson shuffles through the papers and passes out stapled copies to both me and Everest. "If I can get your respective signatures in the places indicated." She hands over fancy pens branded with the law firm's logo.

The will is only a couple pages, single-sided. Everest scrawls his name on the last page and pushes it back to Ms. Dawson. I take a moment to scan it quickly, to make sure I know what the hell I'm signing.

Right there, in the middle of the first page, are black words on white paper.

Custody of Ivy Amelia Lambert will go jointly to Owen Lambert and Everest Wheeler.

If there was any doubt that this is what Jeremy and Eden wanted, the will makes it undeniable.

A spike of panic seizes me as I grip the pen in my hand. What the hell were they thinking? What the hell am I thinking? I can't possibly be agreeing to this, can I?

I sneak one last glance around the table. All eyes are on me. I don't have a choice. This is on me. Jeremy and Eden are counting on me to raise their little girl.

Taking a deep breath, I uncap the pen and place the tip on the paper. This is it. This will forever change the course of my life.

I sign my name.

EVEREST

"Everest?" Beau's voice booms through the staff locker room at Mars Fitness.

"Over here." I tug on my work t-shirt and toss my street clothes into the locker.

Beau, one of the owners of Mars and my boss, comes around the row of lockers. "Sawyer said you were here. You know you didn't have to come in today, right? We can cover for you."

"I know." I comb my fingers through my hair once before sliding my cap on backward. "But if I have to spend another second with that jerkwad, I'm gonna do fucking murder."

Beau's eyebrows fly up and his lips quirk into an amused smile. "Which jerkwad? And will I need to bail you out of jail?"

"You might," I mutter.

Owen's been a grade-A asshole this past week, bossing everyone around, issuing orders, railroading anyone who dares to question his decisions. It's like he's determined to get the whole ordeal over and done with so he can go back to his fancy, cushy life. It's like he doesn't even care that two people we love have just fucking died. Or that our baby niece has lost both her parents in one day.

I knew the guy was frigid, but I didn't realize he was so utterly heartless.

Even his reaction at the lawyer's office this morning. The blood had drained from his face when the lawyer read out the will, like she was reading his death sentence or something. Jesus.

He'd been so quick to pawn Ivy off onto his parents earlier this week when we'd all sat down to talk about it. He'd had it all planned out, every single detail. Ship her off so she could be someone else's problem.

I hadn't said anything at the time because, well, it wasn't like I had a better idea. His parents had raised two kids, so they obviously knew what they were doing, and they're retired, so they have plenty of time on their hands. It seemed like the only choice we had.

But then the lawyer said that Eden and Jeremy wanted us to raise Ivy. Honestly, I was stunned, shocked, staggered. Someone wants *me* to raise a kid? What the hell do I know about raising kids?

But as the news sank in, the weight of losing my sister suddenly felt a little lighter. I wasn't really losing her. Not all of her, at least. There was this mini-Eden I'd get to hold on to. I could keep a small part of my sister with me. I could keep the memory of her alive.

Owen didn't see it that way, though. All he saw was the work it would take. And yeah, I'm not a complete idiot. I know raising a kid isn't easy. I know it'll take a lot of time and sacrifice and effort. There will be rough patches, especially at the beginning. But come on. It's *Ivy*. She's an angel. We get each other. We're cool.

Besides, it was Eden's and Jeremy's last wish. That means something, doesn't it? Of all the people in the world, they wanted me—and Owen, I guess—to raise their daughter. It's an honor, a privilege. It's our duty to fulfill their wishes, to do everything in our power to live up to them.

But all Owen cared about was his stupid life with his fancy job and his fancy apartment.

"Seriously, dude, you okay?"

Beau's standing at the end of the row of lockers, arms folded and voice gruff. To a stranger, he might look intimidating, but I've been at Mars long enough to know he's merely concerned.

I couldn't be more grateful. For Beau and his husband, Gavin. For Sawyer, Logan, and other guys at Mars. They've been like a family to me from the first day I started this job. We joke around a lot and they sometimes give me a hard time. But when life gets real and shit hits the fan, when it really counts, they're always there for me.

I collapse onto the bench, suddenly feeling overwhelmed by sadness. It's not the first time it's happened and it's always unexpected. Things will be going fine, I'm getting through the day, then *wham*, a bulldozer full of grief slams into me. "I don't know."

Beau leans against the locker like he's settling in for a drawn-out conversation. "Talk to me."

Where do I even start? I'm just… sad. Just so fucking sad. But Beau knows that. He and the guys were at the memorial service.

"There was some lawyer thing this morning, right?"

I nodded. "They gave me custody of Ivy."

Beau tilts his head. "Please tell me Ivy is the name of a motorcycle. Or maybe a plant?"

I roll my eyes. "Ivy is my niece."

"Your human niece?"

I snort. "Yes, very human. Six years old."

Beau looks pained as he speaks again. "Uh, no offense or anything, but… why would they do that?"

I throw my hands in the air. "Hell if I know!"

"For how long?"

I blink at him. "What do you mean 'for how long'?"

Beau shrugs. "I don't know. Is it for like, a year or two, and then someone else takes over?"

"What? No, that's not how it works. I have custody until she's eighteen."

Beau's lips form a silent O. "Shit."

"Yeah. Shit." I swing one leg over the bench so I can lie down, feet flat on the floor. I stare up at the ceiling, feeling a little bit like I'm in a therapy session with Doctor Beau. "That's not the worst part. Actually, that part's not really bad at all. Ivy's a cool kid. We're gonna have a lot of fun."

I already have plans to take her swimming in the ocean and teach her how to skate, how to rock climb. We'll go to the beach and ride bikes through the park. We'll have movie nights and gorge ourselves on ice cream.

"You know that this isn't an extended babysitting gig, right? Raising a kid is nothing like watching them for a few hours."

I scoff at Beau's unnecessary reminder. "Of course, I know. But how hard can it be? I had parents. I've seen my sister parent. And there's the internet. You can learn anything from the internet."

"Right…"

"*Anyways*, like I was saying, that's not the worst part. The worst part is Owen. Fucking jackass." I mutter the last part under my breath, a ball of anger churning in my chest just at the thought of him.

"I thought he was a jerkwad," Beau says with a chuckle.

My brain supplies an image of his smarmy face, with his high cheekbones and plump lips. Amber eyes flashing under thick brows. All I want to do is punch him right on his perfectly straight nose. "He's both. And more."

"Owen is the co-brother-in-law, right?"

"The…" I lift my head from the bench to look at Beau. "The what?"

"The co-brother-in-law. Your sister's husband's brother," Beau says, as if that's a normal thing that normal people know.

"How did you know that?"

Beau shrugs. "I know things."

"Ugh." I drop my head back down and it bangs a bit too hard on the bench. "Ow."

"So Owen. What's wrong with Owen?"

"What's *not* wrong with Owen?" I cross my arms and huff. "He's an arrogant motherfucker and I have to share custody of Ivy with him."

Beau whistles. "You have to raise your niece with a jerkwad slash jackass slash arrogant motherfucker for the next twelve years?"

Twelve years. Beau's words feel like a ton of bricks deposited on my chest.

Twelve years of Owen. Of being cooped up in that house with him. Seeing him every day. Talking to him every day. There will be no escape, nowhere to hide.

A shudder of horror runs through me. All the constant judgment. Endless nagging. Never being able to live up to his impossible standards. Just the thought of it is suffocating.

But there's also something else. Some small part of me perks up at the thought. Things happen when you're in close quarters with someone like that. Unexpected things. Explosive things.

Like that night.

It's been years and I still don't really understand what happened that night. I can't explain how we went from glaring at each other to kissing each other. It was like a switch was flipped. One moment, we could barely stand to be in the same room together, and the next moment, we couldn't keep our hands off each other.

It's like all that pent-up hatred and anger needed somewhere to go and *boom*, it went into sex.

It was really great sex. Maybe some of the best sex I've ever had. And I've had a lot of sex. The hard press of Owen's body against mine. The way our mouths collided. The roughness of his hands on my body. The sound of his growl. The way he threw commands at me, and the way I jumped to obey.

I still think of that night sometimes when I'm jacking off. When I need something quick to take the edge off. It never fails to take me right to the brink in five seconds flat. It's always a bone-melting climax.

Sometimes I wonder. What if he wasn't a stuck-up snob? What if we didn't annoy the fuck out of each other?

What if we could channel all that volatile energy between us into sex rather than fighting? Could we have had another night like that? Could it have turned into a regular thing?

Can it still?

I shake my head. No. That's crazy talk. A regular thing with Owen? Like a relationship? Enemies with benefits? He'll kill me in my sleep before we ever get that far. Or maybe I'll kill him. It'll be a miracle if we both make it through the next twelve years unmaimed. Hell, I could barely make it through a week of seeing him every day.

"Well, we're here if you need anything. Seriously. If you need to re-work your schedule or cut back on hours. She can come hang out in the staff room if you can't find a babysitter. Whatever it is. Just let me know."

With a groan, I push myself up and flash Beau a grateful smile. The weight of grief and responsibility is still heavy, but it helps to know that I won't have to carry it alone. The guys at Mars have got my back.

"Thank, Beau."

"Always." He opens his arms. "Come here."

I stand and walk into the offered hug. It's comforting, soothing. I'm going to need as much of these as I can get.

OWEN

"Are you sure you don't want us to stay an extra few days?" Mom asks as Dad loads up their car.

"I'm sure, Mom," I lie. In fact, I'm not sure at all. I want them to stay. I want Everest's parents to stay. I want them all to stay and be the buffer between me and Everest.

She studies me for a moment and I put on a brave face. I'm an adult. I own my own apartment. I have a successful career as a veterinary surgeon. I don't need my mom to hold my hand through this, even though I secretly really want her to.

She's caught me with tears in my eyes a few times this week already. We were never a boys-don't-cry type of family, but I've never been very comfortable expressing my emotions. They get too big, too unwieldy. Then people look at you differently, like you're suddenly not the person they thought you were.

"I go back to work tomorrow. Ivy goes back to school,"

I continue when Mom still looks skeptical. "The sooner we can establish a normal routine, the better."

She sighs then pulls me into a hug. "If you're sure."

I hug her back, a little embarrassed at how tightly I'm holding on. I have to stop myself from taking back everything I said and begging her to stay.

"Remember we're just a phone call away. It'll only take us a couple hours to get here. If you need a few days off, we're happy to come down. Or Ivy can come stay with us. Whatever you need, okay?"

"Thanks, Mom." My voice is a little thick with emotion and I force myself to swallow it all down. I've been so good at keeping my composure this week. I can't afford to break down now when Ivy needs me to stay strong.

A few feet away, Everest and Ivy are saying goodbye to his parents. He's holding her and she's got her arms around his neck, clinging to him like she's never going to let go.

She looks miserable. And scared.

I know the feeling.

Not for the first time, I question the wisdom of what we're doing. Everest and I are completely unequipped for a task like this. We're not parents. We don't know the first thing about raising a child. I've loaded up my Kindle with every parenting book ever published, but I'm still terrified I'm going to fuck her up.

I don't trust myself to be a good parent. I trust Everest even less.

Nell leans in to give Ivy a kiss, then gives Everest one too. Graham rubs Ivy's back and claps Everest on the shoulder. We switch parents.

"Thank you for everything you've done this week,"

Nell says, pulling me into a tight hug. "I know we don't live as close as your parents do. But you can always call on us if you need any help, okay? Even if it's just to vent about..." She casts a sideways glance at her son to finish the rest of her sentence.

I let out a strangled chuckle. "Uh, sure, thanks." It's comforting and alarming to know that even Everest's mom questions his capabilities.

"We've spoken to your parents about going to their place for a long weekend sometime," she continues. "It'll be good for us to all get together."

I nod. "That sounds nice."

Dad comes back from loading up the car and we all say our final goodbyes. Then Everest, Ivy, and I stand in the doorway as both sets of grandparents drive off. I have a feeling all three of us want to run down the stoop and stop them.

When the cars finally disappear around the corner, we step back and I close the front door.

The house suddenly feels so big and empty. Time stretches out in front of us, vacant and needing to be filled. The three of us stare at each other, none of us quite certain what we're supposed to do now.

"Hey," Everest says, after several long moments of silence. He gives Ivy a tickle. "How about a movie night with popcorn and ice cream?"

I frown. "Tonight is a school night. Staying up watching movies and eating junk food isn't a good idea. She should have a proper dinner and get an early night. It'll be her first day back at school tomorrow."

Ivy shrinks, clinging even more tightly to Everest. "I don't wanna go to school," she whines.

Shit. I didn't mean to sound so strict. Softening my voice, I try again. "Ivy, sweetie, you've already missed a whole week of school. You need to catch up or you'll fall too far behind. You wouldn't want that, would you?"

She whines even louder and I brace myself. The sound is a precursor to the crying temper tantrums she's been having all week. Her face gets all scrunched up and she throws her limbs around. It doesn't stop until she's tired herself out.

It hurts my heart to see her like this, overwhelmed with emotions but without the skills she needs to regulate them. I can't imagine how frustrating it is, how helpless she must feel. A part of me wants to coddle her and tell her she doesn't have to do anything she doesn't want to.

But according to the books I've been reading, that's not going to serve Ivy in the long term. I can't just be a friend who does whatever she wants. I need to establish myself as a parental figure and putting it off isn't going to do anyone any good.

"Ivy," I say, trying to find that precarious balance of gentle but firm. My stomach churns uncomfortably as I speak. "Crying isn't going to get you out of school tomorrow."

"But I don't wanna!" She turns away from me and buries her face into Everest's neck.

He glowers at me while rubbing circles on her back. "It's okay, Ivy-bear. It's okay. You don't have to go to school tomorrow if you don't want to."

I bite back a curse. *What the fuck?* I mouth silently at him, shaking my head and throwing my hands into the air. Did he seriously just undermine me, not five minutes into this doomed co-parenting arrangement? We're supposed to be a united front. We're supposed to set boundaries for Ivy and then keep them. She needs to learn that there are rules and there are consequences if she breaks them.

Instead, Everest has the audacity to smirk at me and give me the middle finger—the irresponsible bastard. I'm still sputtering, trying to process just how juvenile he is, when he carries Ivy off, cooing at her the whole time.

They go upstairs and I hear Everest suggest they play with her dolls, leaving me standing in the foyer, completely fucking gobsmacked. In one fell swoop, Everest has just made me the bad cop. What the hell?

A part of me wants to march up those stairs and give him a piece of my fucking mind. Ivy is going to school tomorrow and that's the end of the discussion. He doesn't get to have an opinion, especially not if he's going to act like a six-year-old himself.

But I stop myself. What good will it do to confront Everest like that? To get into an argument that will undoubtedly turn into a shouting match. And right in front of Ivy. What kind of example would that set for her? Definitely not a good one.

No, I'll have to find some other time to sit Everest down and impart to him exactly how this parenting thing works. If he can't make responsible decisions, then he doesn't get to make any decisions at all.

I stalk to the kitchen and wrench open the refrigerator door. Taking a calming breath, I let the cold air wash over me and cool my bubbling anger.

I can't let him get to me. I can't let him drag me down to his level. Ivy needs parents, not an overgrown man-child to be her best friend. And if Everest isn't capable of that, then I'll need to be the parent for both of us.

I scan the inside of the fridge, still filled with takeout containers and casserole dishes from neighbors and friends. With so much going on, none of us have had the time or desire to cook. So we've been surviving on the generosity of others and the swiftness of the food delivery guys.

But tonight's not the night for leftovers. It's the first night of our new normal, and even if Everest is determined to sabotage it, the least we can do is eat dinner as a… "family."

I twitch even just thinking the word. Ivy and I are family, there's no question about that. But me and Everest? God, I rue the day.

Before Mom left, she and Nell made a trip to the grocery store for some basics. Fruits and vegetables. Family packs of chicken that I can divvy up and freeze. I'm not a gourmet chef, but I'm pretty decent. I've cooked for myself regularly since college and I have an impressive collection of cookbooks back at my place. I make a mental note to look up more kid-friendly recipes. Maybe even ones that Ivy and I can cook together.

I pull out vegetables and chicken for an Asian stir fry. It's simple. Easy. It's a recipe I got from Eden and I know for a fact that Ivy likes it.

My mind wanders as I cook. Everest and I need to figure out a game plan for getting Ivy ready for school in the mornings. Most days, I should be able to drop her off on my way to work. But Everest will need to pick her up when she's done. I don't know if he's spoken to his bosses at Mars yet, but he'll need to change his work schedule to accommodate.

We'll need to get in touch with that babysitting agency.

I'm loathe to leave Ivy with a babysitter if we can avoid it. Especially considering what happened the last time she was left with a babysitter. But there might be days when it's unavoidable.

And I need to set up an introductory meeting with the child psychologist her school recommended. This will be a difficult few months for Ivy and I'll feel better having a professional who can guide us through the process. Hell, I should probably call up my own therapist and schedule a few sessions myself.

When I'm finished cooking, I venture upstairs and find them in Ivy's room. Everest's built her a blanket fort and they're both huddled up inside it, surrounded by all of her stuffed animals. Zuzi takes center stage under her arm.

Everest whispers something I can't hear from the door and a small, almost reluctant, smile appears on Ivy's face. I think it might be the first time she's smiled all week.

Irritation skitters across my skin. Everest is good with her. He always has been. He can make her smile and laugh when no one else can, not even her parents. I'm not too proud to admit that he's probably better with her than I am. But then, I shouldn't be surprised. Emotionally, he's closer to her age than to mine.

"Knock knock." When they both turn to look at me with matching wide-eyed expressions, my heart thuds hard against my ribs. This is us now. For better or worse, this is who we are. The weight of that reality sits heavily on my chest and it takes a moment for me to draw in a full breath. "Dinner's ready."

To his credit, Everest immediately climbs out of the blanket fort. "Come on, Ivy-bear, let's see what Uncle

Owen's whipped up for dinner, 'kay?" He reaches back to help Ivy out, but she doesn't budge.

"I'm not hungry." She burrows deeper into the mess of blankets and stuffed animals.

Everest glances uneasily in my direction. "I bet it's really yummy, though, right?"

"It's Asian stir fry. The same kind your mommy used to make."

My comment hangs in the air for a split second before Ivy lets out a high-pitched whine and thrashes around, fists pummeling her poor animals. Fucking hell. Why did I have to mention her mommy?

Everest shoots me a glare, as if I purposefully set out to upset Ivy.

"Ives! Ivy-bear! Ivy-poo! Hey, hey, it's okay. It's not exactly the same as your mommy's. No one could make it as good as your mommy did. Uncle Owen just made his own version of it."

"I don't wanna! I don't wanna!"

"That's okay. You don't have to have any if you don't want to."

What? No. Of course she needs to eat. We can't let her skip meals just because she's in a bad mood. I step in closer and crouch down next to Everest.

"Ivy, you have to eat dinner."

Everest elbows me out of the way and the only thing keeping me from pushing him back is the fact that we're right in front of our niece.

"Yeah, but you don't have to eat anything you don't want, 'kay?"

"Everest," I grit out between clenched teeth. We can't

let her dictate her own meals. What if she wants cookies for dinner? Or ice cream for breakfast? She needs a healthy, balanced diet.

"What do you want for dinner, Ives? Listen to your tummy. What does it want?" Everest puts his hand on her rounded stomach and Ivy puts both of her hands on top of his. Together, her two hands are barely the same size as one of his.

She makes a concentrated listening face before announcing. "Chicken nuggets. My tummy wants chicken nuggets."

"Chicken nuggets!" Everest exclaims like it's the best food in the world. "I love chicken nuggets!"

I suppress a groan. Of course Everest loves chicken nuggets. Child. "We're not having chicken nuggets. There aren't any in the house, to begin with. And also, they're not good for you."

In fact, chicken nuggets are gross. There's no telling what kind of shit they put in those things. I know Eden didn't like feeding them to Ivy. But I also know she and Jeremy sometimes gave in because, well, kids.

"But they're not *bad* for you." Everest shoots daggers at me with his eyes. "Better to have chicken nuggets than nothing at all."

Ivy joins him with the full weight of a six-year-old's glare. "Yeah, chicken nuggets or nothing."

I honestly, genuinely sputter, not sure how I'm supposed to respond. "But I've already made Asian stir fry." I want to smack myself in the forehead. What was I hoping to accomplish with that statement? It's not like either of these two are going to listen to me.

Everest rolls his eyes and opens his arms to Ivy. "Let's go find some chicken nuggets."

She quickly launches herself into his arms. "With lots of ketchup."

"We'll drown them in ketchup." Everest picks her up and carries her out of the room.

I hurry after them. "Where are you going?"

"To find chicken nuggets!" Everest points into the distance like they're about to embark on an adventure.

"To find chicken nuggets!" Ivy shouts.

"But…" My protest dies on my lips. *But what about the stir fry I made?*

Everest and Ivy are already at the front door and he's helping her into her shoes and coat. He throws a smirk at me. "We'll pick you up some too."

I don't dignify his comment with a response. Instead, I cross my arms defensively over my chest as my insides twist with jealousy and pain.

The door closes behind them and I stare at it for several long seconds before I head back to the kitchen.

The stir fry is still in the wok, covered to keep it warm. So much for cooking. So much for sharing our first dinner together. Why did I even bother? What was the point of trying?

We're not really a family. I'm not really a parent. Ivy would rather be with fun Uncle Everest than boring Uncle Owen. Everest and I can barely stand each other.

I was delusional, thinking that tonight matters, that it means something, that it's important. It's not. This whole farce is doomed and all I should hope for is to simply get through each day.

I go to the refrigerator and pull open the freezer. The tub of salted caramel ice cream sits in the corner and I send up a silent thank you to Mom. Somehow, she knew I would need this. I rip off the lid, grab a spoon, and dig in.

EVEREST

"Uggghhh." I sprawl awkwardly across the top of the front desk at Mars, head slumped forward, arms hanging off the opposite edge.

From behind the counter, Sawyer pats me on the head. "There. There."

Without moving, I give him the middle finger. "Shut up. You have no idea what it's like raising a kid."

"Nope!" Sawyer agrees with way too much delight. "And I don't plan on finding out. Not for a long while, at least. Preston and I really aren't kids people."

It's been a couple weeks—or maybe three, time is meaningless—since Owen and I were left to raise Ivy on our own. I knew raising a kid wasn't easy. Everyone warned me that it wasn't. But no one told me it would be this fucking hard!

Ivy is an *angel*, a cranky, moody, stubborn angel who goes from dead tired to hyper and back in the time it takes me to do a burpee. She's adorable, but she's *exhausting*. I don't know how the hell Eden and Jeremy managed to both hold down full-time jobs and parent at the same time.

Sawyer shoves a newly laundered towel at me. "Fold." He grabs a second one from the pile he pulled from the dryer and shakes it out. "Is it really that bad? I mean, it could be worse, right? You could be doing it all by yourself?"

With a loud groan, I heave myself upright. Doing it all by myself sounds like both a dream and a nightmare at this point. Splitting the responsibilities with someone else is obviously better, but with Owen, of all people? Ugh. Kill me now.

"I don't know, man. It might be easier that way. Owen's like a fucking drill sergeant trying to get Ivy to grow up and fall in line. Like, dude, she's six years old and she just lost her parents. Chill the fuck out."

Sawyer looks alarmed. "What's he doing?"

I slide my folded towel to the side and gesture for another. "Just like, stuff. Like, get up early, wear these clothes, eat this food, go to school, pick up your toys, go to bed."

Sawyer arches an eyebrow at me. "Isn't that what parents are supposed to do?"

"Yeah, but like, not like that!" I exclaim, throwing my hands into the air. They land with a soft thud on the fluffy towel.

"Then like what?" Sawyer looks at me like I'm delusional.

But I'm not. Sawyer doesn't get it. He doesn't have to go home to Owen and Ivy facing off, with tension crackling in the air. It feels like I'm stepping into a war zone every single time, but the thing is, it doesn't have to be.

Owen just needs to stop being a fucking asshole. But that's never going to happen.

"It's like this. Owen is like, determined to make Ivy's life a living hell. He's an emotional robot, you know what I mean? They're constantly arguing over every little thing, and then she starts crying and throws a temper tantrum, and guess who has to step in to get her to stop?" I point at myself with both hands. "Me. That's who."

Sawyer looks skeptical, like he's not buying what I'm selling. That irritates me even more. He's supposed to be on my side, damn it. He's *my* friend.

"Maybe he's just grieving in his own way. Like, he needs more structure or like, forward momentum, or else he'll fall apart."

"Or maybe he's just an unfeeling asshole," I mutter.

"Who's an unfeeling asshole?" Logan comes bouncing over from the juice bar on the other side of the front lobby. He's the barista and he's always coming up with the weirdest—but oddly tasty—concoctions.

"Owen," Sawyer explains. "They're not getting along."

Logan's eyes go big. "Ooo… you mean that hottie? The one you're living with now?"

I roll my eyes and scoff. "Not even. Did you know that he hasn't given up his apartment yet? I've already moved all my things into the house, but he's still going back to his place all the fucking time."

"Maybe he's got too much stuff to bring over all at once?" Logan offers unhelpfully. "Or maybe he's got a pet tarantula he needs to feed. Or maybe he's got a sex dungeon where he takes unsuspecting victims. Or you know, maybe he's a spy!"

Sawyer and I exchange a guilty look. A few months

ago, Logan's boyfriend was being sketchy AF and we'd made up a bunch of wild theories. It turns out he was actually a spy. Oops.

"I'm like, ninety-nine point nine percent sure Owen's not a spy. He's nowhere near that cool."

"Either way, you should talk to him," Sawyer says. "You know, 'cause you're both adults? And communication is good?"

"Yeah." Logan nods enthusiastically. "Communication is the key to every healthy relationship."

Sawyer lifts a hand and Logan slaps it in a high-five.

I glare at my two best friends. "I hate you both."

They burst into giggles.

With a roll of my eyes, I push away from the counter. "Whatever. I have a class to teach. Later, losers."

The fitness studio I use for my classes is next to Mars's spin studio. Donnie, the spin instructor, is just finishing up his class as I pass by. I give him a wave and he up nods in return. Most of my regulars are already warming up when I step inside the fitness studio, spaced out from each other with skipping ropes ready and waiting at their feet.

"Hey, hey, hey!" I call out, as much for myself as for them. My classes are upbeat and intense and I need to get myself into the right headspace before they start. Owen is a problem for future me. Present me needs to deliver the best fucking class I can. "You guys ready to get your skip on?!"

"Yeah!" They shout back, their enthusiasm helping to get my blood pumping.

"Hell, yeah!" I grab my own rope and pull out my phone to sync it up with the sound system. I take my hat off to loop the mic headset over my ears, then settle my cap on backward again. When it's time to start the class, the room is at capacity.

"We're gonna show the rope who's boss!" I shout as I crank up the music and bop my head to the beat. "Let's gooooo!"

This is one of my favorite classes. It's almost like dancing, but with a skipping rope, which makes me feel like a kid again. I can get fancy with the footwork, do some neat tricks, put it all together into a routine. The music reverberates through my body, almost therapeutic. And it's just so much damn fun. We're all smiling and laughing and the hour flies by.

"Woooo!!!" I holler as we run through the routine I taught them one last time. "Good job, guys! Y'all did amazing!"

They'll all feel it tomorrow—in their calves, thighs, abs, arms. It might not seem like it in the middle of class but skipping is a full-body workout.

I drop my rope to the side and hop over to the sound system to switch to the cooldown playlist. Except, when I wake the screen of my phone, a dozen notifications are waiting for me. What the fuck?

I scan them quickly as my stomach drops. They're from Ivy's school. Missed calls and voicemail messages and text messages—half a dozen of them. From Owen too, same thing. They've all been trying to get a hold of me while I was teaching.

"Everest, you okay?" one of the regulars in the class asks me.

"Uh…" I stare at my phone, paralyzed with indecision. There are only a few minutes left of class and cool down is an important part of any workout. I should stay and finish out the hour.

But Ivy. Something's happened. Probably something bad. I've already missed so many messages, I shouldn't waste any more time, right?

"Hey, you alright?" The regular—Willis, I think his name is—comes up to ask quietly.

"It's my niece." I show him my phone, as if the notifications will mean anything to him. "I think something's happened."

"You want to call them back?"

"I should, shouldn't I?"

Willis nods with a sympathetic smile. "Yeah, you should."

"But what about..." I glance at the other students milling around waiting for me.

"Don't worry about us. I can do the cool down," Willis says, already backing away.

"Are you sure?" I ask with my heart in my throat. Owen may think I'm a kid, but I take my job seriously. I don't want to leave my class before it's finished.

"Yeah." He laughs. "I've done it a million times. We're good. You go."

"Thank you." Gratitude sweeps through me as I rip off the mic and my hat goes tumbling to the floor. Someone swipes it up and hands it to me. "Thank you!"

I hit redial on my phone and hold it to my ear as I sprint to the staff locker room to grab my things. The call rings and rings before someone finally fucking picks up.

"Hello! Hi! I'm Everest Wheeler. Ivy's uncle. You called me? What happened? Is she okay?" I squeeze the phone between my ear and shoulder while throwing all my things into my duffel bag.

"Mr. Wheeler, thank you for returning our call." The woman on the other end of the line sounds way too calm.

I don't need her to be calm. I need her to tell me why the fuck they called me in the middle of the school day. Slamming my locker door shut, I grab my duffel and race back toward the gym's main entrance.

"There was an incident—"

"Incident? What the fu—uh, what does that mean? Is she okay? Is she hurt? Do we need to take her to the hospital?"

"No, Ivy's not injured. But there was an altercation with another student. When we couldn't get a hold of you, we called Mr. Lambert."

I screech to a halt in the middle of the front lobby. My heart is pounding, fueled by the high from my class and worry about Ivy. But at the mention of Owen's name, it stops. My stomach twists into a giant knot. "You called Owen?" That must be why I had all those notifications from him too.

"Yes, she was quite distraught, so we thought it best to send her home."

"He picked her up already?" *Please say no, please say no.*

"Yes. About ten minutes ago."

Fuck. Fuck, fuck, shit, fuck. I was supposed to pick Ivy up from school today because Owen has a shift at that animal hospital of his. If he picked her up, it means he had to leave work, which means he'll lord it over me and I'll never hear the fucking end of it.

"I suggest you get in touch with Mr. Lambert."

I shove down the urge to scream. "Yeah, yeah, right. Okay. Thanks."

"Everything alright?" Logan asks from behind his juice bar.

I shake my head. "No, something happened with Ivy. I need to go."

Logan's expression of concern would be comical if I wasn't so amped up on adrenaline and worry and dread. He makes a shooing motion with his hands. "Go. Go. I'll tell Beau."

I race out onto the street, my stomach threatening to empty its contents. I don't know what I'm going to find when I get home, but it's not going to be anything good.

OWEN

I have to force myself to walk instead of jog through the hallways of Ivy's school. When I got the call from the school's secretary, I nearly had a coronary.

First, because Everest is the primary contact in case of emergencies. His gym is closer to Ivy's school than my hospital, so if anything happens, he can get there faster than I can. But if they're calling me, it means they can't get a hold of him. Why the fuck isn't he answering his goddamn phone? I was finishing up a fucking surgery on a cat when the call came through and I still managed to answer it.

Second because the fucking secretary wouldn't tell me what happened. She just said there was an altercation, that Ivy was physically uninjured, and that the principal wanted to talk to me when I got here. Physically uninjured is a hell of a low bar if she was trying to ease my worry. News flash, it didn't work.

I spot Ivy the second I'm through the office door. "Ivy!"

"Uncle O!" She flies off the chair and across the room. Her face is tear-streaked and her eyes are red and puffy. Her hair, which I'd tied into pigtails this morning, is a disheveled mess.

I bend down just in time for her to launch herself into my arms. Her little body is so small against my chest and she clings to me so tightly my heart breaks. She cries with her face pressed to my neck. My poor girl. What happened? Who do I need to yell at? Who do I need to get fired?

I hoist her up into my arms and carry her over to the secretary's desk. "I'm Owen Lambert, Ivy's uncle. I was told the principal wanted to speak to me?"

"Mr. Lambert?"

I spin around at the soft female voice calling my name. The principal looks to be in her forties, with kind eyes and an apologetic smile.

"I'm Ms. Livingston, the principal. If Ivy can wait out here, we can speak in my office."

"No!" Ivy hugs me even tighter, wrapping her legs around my waist. I don't even need to hold her up at this point. She's hugging me so hard, it's like she's stuck to me with glue. There's no prying her off.

"It's fine," I say, rubbing Ivy's back.

Ms. Livingston hesitates for a second before acquiescing. She gestures to a chair in front of her desk and I perch on the edge of it, holding Ivy in my lap.

"It was a boy in Ivy's class," Ms. Livingston says, sitting down behind her desk. I appreciate her getting to the point without beating around the bush. "He made fun of Ivy for what happened with her parents."

Horror descends upon me. Some kid did *what*?! I knew

that bullying is something we might have to deal with at some point, but none of the parenting books I've read mentioned it would start in grade fucking one.

I'm still trying to process what this all means when Ms. Livingston continues. "I've already spoken with the boy's parents and they will be taking corrective action. He's been sent home with his nanny for the rest of the day and he'll also have to serve detention for a full week during recesses."

I sputter in disbelief. "Detention? That's it? This is bullying. Shouldn't it warrant a harsher punishment? Like suspension or something?"

Ms. Livingston nods sympathetically, but her tone is firm when she speaks. "If the student's behavior continues, that is an option. But there are intermediary measures we can take to teach and promote positive behavior. I want to assure you that we are taking this situation very seriously. As are the boy's parents. They were quite dismayed when I spoke with them on the phone. They asked me to extend their sincerest apologies to you and Ivy."

My jaw is on the floor. Their sincerest apologies? Are they fucking kidding?

What good are apologies when the damage is already done? Ivy's already been hurt. Her self-esteem has already taken a hit. Who knows what kind of long-term impact this will have on her sense of self and mental health. Is an apology going to fix any of that? Can an apology turn back the clock and prevent this all from happening in the first place?

I grit my teeth and draw on the patience I usually reserve for unreasonable pet parents. "What about changing classes? So Ivy doesn't have to sit in the same room with that bully for the rest of the year."

Ms. Livingston's expression tightens just a fraction, but it's enough for me to pick up. "I'm afraid that's not possible. It would be more disruptive than constructive, not just for Ivy or her classmate, but also for the other students in the affected classes."

The desire to bang on the desk and demand that she do more has me nearly vibrating with anger. Ivy's already been through so much and now she has to put up with this bullshit? But I push down the urge to yell. *Keep it professional, Lambert.*

One thing at a time. First, I need to get Ivy out of here and settled at home. Then assess the damage and figure out the appropriate remedies. Any changes that need to happen at her school can only come after everyone's had time to cool off and think things through.

With a game plan in mind, I shift forward, making to stand. "Is there anything else?"

Ms. Livingston looks like she has more to say, but she wisely shakes her head. "Not at the moment. I'll be sure to keep you in the loop should there be more developments with Ivy's classmate."

Ivy and I take our leave of the principal's office, grabbing her coat and pink unicorn backpack on the way out. I carry her all the way to the main entrance of the school before setting her down on the floor.

Her crying has subsided, but she's still sniffling and the collar of my coat is wet with tears and snot.

"Hey, sweetie." I brush her hair back from her face, then pull out my handkerchief to wipe her nose. "That boy was mean, huh?"

She nods, looking so sad and dejected. My heart hurts for her, so much so it's hard to breathe.

"You want to go home?"

"Can—can we get ice cream?" She blinks her big, blue eyes at me. The picture of innocence.

I can't help but chuckle, squeezing my eyes shut as emotion makes them prickle with tears. Of course Ivy would try to negotiate a benefit out of this situation. She wouldn't be Ivy if she didn't. Maybe she'll be alright after all.

"One scoop in a cup." I open with a lowball offer.

"Two scoops in a waffle cone." She counters, completely unfazed.

"One scoop in a plain cone."

She twists her lips to the side as she considers how far she can push her luck.

I sweeten the deal. "And chicken nuggets for dinner?"

She gasps softly, eyes going wide in surprise. "Really?"

I smile because, little does she know, I've researched the healthiest chicken nuggets money can buy in the tri-state area. They're still disgusting, but at least the meat is supposed to be organic. There's a box tucked deep inside the freezer, hidden by the frozen veggies so Everest doesn't find them.

"Really."

"With ketchup?" There's a hopeful spark in her eyes and the worry that had felt so suffocating eases a little.

"With ketchup," I confirm. Especially since the ketchup I've stocked in the kitchen is homemade from a farmstead upstate. I'm going to sneak in as much healthy food into her diet as I possibly can.

"Okay!"

I laugh as Ivy grabs her coat and stuffs her arms into them. Then she pulls on her backpack all by herself. I pick her up again and we set out.

"What flavor of ice cream do you want?" I ask, shifting her weight a little. Everest is usually the one who carries her around, while I'm all about making her walk on her own. But if there's any day to make an exception, it's today.

She makes some thinking sounds before announcing, "Bubblegum."

I throw up a little bit in my mouth, but I infuse as much enthusiasm into my voice as I can. "Yummy!"

She rests her head against mine and her short arms wind around my neck. It never ceases to amaze me how fast time flies. It feels like only yesterday I was holding her in the hospital, all swaddled up in a blanket, but it's been six years. Six years. So long and yet far too short. She still has so much of her life ahead of her. She still has so much to learn and experience. And Jeremy and Eden won't be here to see any of it.

I hold her close. The weight of her pressed against me is bittersweet, filled with sadness, but also the reassurance that we're both still here. Together.

Ivy starts to wriggle the second the ice cream parlor comes into view, and when I set her down just inside the door, she races to the counter.

"One scoop of bubblegum ice cream in a plain cone, please!"

I order myself a single scoop of salted caramel in a cup and we settle into a table by the window. Ivy digs into her ice cream like she's starving, getting the sticky stuff all over her face. I fight back a cringe and sigh internally, wishing I had Ivy's go-bag on me. I keep it stocked with snacks, a couple small toys, and a very essential box of wipes.

Ivy is well on her way to becoming a human ice cream cone when she stops. A pensive expression comes across her face. "Is there ice cream in heaven, Uncle O?"

The question startles me into stillness, with my hand hovering halfway between my ice cream cup and my mouth. There can only be one reason for her to be asking about heaven, and that's not a topic I really want to talk about at the moment. "Um, uh, I… probably?"

Ivy's mouth twists to the side as she thinks. "Daddy doesn't like ice cream, but Mommy loves it, like me. She said that we can't have too much ice cream, because then it won't taste as good anymore. But, it's different in heaven, right? She can have all the ice cream she wants?" Ivy lifts hopeful eyes at me, leaving me completely at a loss for what to say.

I don't know whether there's a heaven. I'm not sure I believe in one. The scientist in me suspects that when we pass, our bodies decompose and our consciousness vanishes. But for this little girl, for Jeremy and Eden, I pray to whatever god or deity or higher power that exists that heaven is real.

"Yeah, I think there's tons of ice cream, with every flavor in the world," I say, voice tight with anguish over the loss of the people we love and the loss of Ivy's innocence at so young an age. "And she can eat as much as she wants without getting a stomachache. Have you ever gotten a stomachache from too much ice cream or candy?"

Ivy shakes her head, surprised and curious at the same

time. Knowing Eden, she probably never let Ivy have enough to get that far.

"Do you know why your daddy doesn't like ice cream?"

Ivy shakes her head, rapt, her melting cone forgotten.

"It was when your daddy and I were kids. I was probably your age and he was a few years older. He found a huge bucket of ice cream in the freezer." I make a circle with my hands, about the size of a pumpkin or watermelon. "We got spoons and ate ice cream straight out of the bucket."

Ivy gasps in shock and wonder. "Grammy and Grandpa didn't stop you?"

I shake my head and shrug. "I don't remember where they were at the time. They didn't find us until later. But by then, we'd eaten so much ice cream that we both had stomachaches."

Ivy gasps again. "Oh no! That's why Daddy doesn't like ice cream?"

I hesitate and cringe. "Well, I ate so much that I threw up. And a lot of the ice cream had melted all over the floor. So when Grammy and Grandpa found us, they made your daddy clean it all up."

"Including the barf?" Ivy looks horrified.

I nod. "Including the barf."

"Ew!" She shrinks back from her abandoned cone, currently melting in a mess on the table.

"Yup, and *that's* why your daddy doesn't like ice cream."

"Ew!" She squirms like there are ice cream spiders crawling all over her skin.

Just then, my phone explodes in my pocket. I fish it out

and find text after text coming in from Everest. Fucking finally.

I bite back a curse. Is he fucking kidding me? I had to scrap my entire afternoon because of this. I called in favors with the other doctors at the hospital, rescheduled appointments with patients who had been waiting months to see me. What the hell was he doing that was so important he couldn't pick up his damn phone?

And now he has the audacity to be indignant about not getting responses? Just the type of juvenile, childish behavior I'd expect from him. I have half a mind to ignore him and give him a taste of his own medicine. If he wants prompt responses, he should be a little more prompt himself.

I smash my thumbs on my phone as I type a message back.

The three little dots pop up immediately.

I almost growl. I don't want Everest to meet us. I want him to sit his ass at home and wait for us to get there. I smash my thumbs on my phone again.

OWEN

I said, we'll be home in 20.

Then I set my phone face down on the table. "All done, sweetie?"

Ivy nods, giving the remnants of her ice cream a disgusted look. If the story I just told doesn't warn her off too much ice cream for a good long while, then nothing will.

If only classroom bullies were as easy to ward off. The anger I felt in the principal's officer wanes as the unfortunate truth dawns on me. That bully won't be the only one. There will be others, no matter what age she is or where she goes. Selfish people who will try to take advantage of her, who will push her aside to get ahead.

I won't be able to protect Ivy from all of them and that realization sits like a rock in my stomach. I want to wrap her up and keep her in the safety of her room, making sure no harm ever comes to her. But that's not how the world works.

Did Jeremy feel this? This gut-deep terror that so many things are outside his control? That Ivy will get hurt and there's nothing he can do about it?

How did he do it? How does any parent do it? Because this might be the most difficult thing I've ever had to do in my life.

EVEREST

The house is empty when I get home. There's no sign of Ivy or Owen. No sign of them having been here since this morning.

Owen said they'd be home in twenty. Well, it's been twenty. So where the hell are they?

This is bullshit. We're supposed to be working together and I've been trying to do my part. I pick Ivy up from school almost every day. I calm her down when *Owen* riles her up into a temper tantrum. I spend every waking moment when I'm not at work taking care of her. He keeps accusing me of being irresponsible, but I've been fucking responsible! What more does he fucking want from me?

I check my phone again. Twenty-five minutes now and still no update from Owen. I jab the call button. It goes to fucking voicemail.

"Hey, asshole, where are you? Call me back."

I drop my phone on the table next to the door and stare at it with my hands on my hips.

Ring, damn it. Ring. It doesn't. I need to steal Owen's phone and link it to mine so I can track his location.

Twenty-eight minutes.

Should I go to Ivy's school to look for them? If they've already left, then maybe I'll find them along the way. But what if they went somewhere else? No, I shake my head at myself. Owen would bring her straight home. He'll probably dump her with me so he can go back to work.

Twenty-nine.

One more minute. I'm giving them *one more minute* and then I'm going to search for them. I count down backward from sixty, eyes glued to my phone, waiting for the number to flip. The second it does, I snatch it from the table and wrench the door open. I step into the vestibule that separates the inner and outer doors and almost collapse with relief.

Owen and Ivy are back.

Holding open the door for them, I bite back the dozens of questions I want to throw at Owen. Where the hell have they been? What the hell happened at school? And most importantly, is Ivy okay?

She looks okay as she scrambles up the steps of the stoop and into the house. "Uncle Ev! We got ice cream!"

"That's… amazing." I crouch down so she can give me a sticky-fingered hug. Over her head, I shoot Owen a glare, but he's busy locking the door behind us and taking off his coat. "What flavor did you get?"

"Bubblegum! And Uncle O said we can have chicken nuggets for dinner!"

"He did?" I say, genuinely surprised. Ice cream *and* chicken nuggets? Two items on Owen's *I Hate Fun* list. What the hell?

"I need to check in with the hospital. Can you help her get washed up?" Owen might've phrased the last part as a question, but since he threw it over his shoulder while walking away, it was definitely more of an order.

I scowl at Owen's back as I help Ivy out of her backpack and coat. "Come on, Ivy-bear, let's get cleaned up, 'kay?"

"Okay!"

Upstairs, I sit her on top of the toilet seat and wet a hand towel. "So, Ives, you wanna tell me what happened at school today?"

She immediately loses the bubbly happy vibe she came home with. "No."

My heart hurts at how dejected she sounds and I don't want to press the issue, but I need to know.

"Did someone hit you?"

She shakes her head slowly. "No."

"Did someone call you names?"

She wriggles on the seat like she's uncomfortable. "Maybe."

"Was it someone in your class?"

She nods. "Chad."

Chad. Sounds like a douchebag name. "What did Chad say?" I ask as anger rises to a simmer inside me. Who is this fucking Chad kid and where do I find him so I can return the favor?

"He..." Ivy takes a deep breath, like having to tell the story is physically draining. "He said that I don't have a mommy or a daddy. He called me a or-fin."

Orphan? Is this fucking kid for real? How the hell does he even know that word at six years old? Anger heats to a boil in my veins, hot and violent, threatening to burst from me.

Does Owen know about this? How can he be so fucking calm about it? *I need to check in with the hospital—* my ass. We need to be raising holy hell over this. That kid needs to be taught a lesson. He needs to pay.

I toss the towel into the sink and spin around to go give Owen a piece of my mind, only to find him standing just outside the bathroom. The fucker moves like a cat sometimes.

"Did you know about this?" I spit out, clenching my teeth to keep my anger in check.

"Not that part," he says, way too cool and collected for my taste. Christ, he gets more animated when talking about the goddamn weather.

"What are we going to do about it?"

He cocks an infuriating eyebrow. "What do you *want* to do about it?"

Outrage and frustration rage inside me, but before I can unleash it on Owen, the doorbell rings. We stare at each other.

"Are you…?" I start.

"No. You?"

I shake my head. We make a beeline for the front door.

On our doorstep is a woman and when we open the outer door, it reveals a child. A boy. About Ivy's age.

"Hi, I'm Scarlett Kimball, Chad's mom. Are you Ivy's uncles?"

I'm stunned by fury and disbelief. *This* is Chad? This scrawny little shrimp of a boy? He's so small, I could drop-kick him across a football field. *He* dared call my Ivy—my perfect angel Ivy—names?

But here he is, standing in front of our door with his mom who looks genuinely embarrassed and ashamed. He's got the hem of his coat fisted in his tiny hands, chin to chest, hunched in on himself like he wants to disappear into the ground. He doesn't look like a bully. He looks kind of pathetic.

"Yes. I'm Owen Lambert. This is Everest Wheeler. Would you like to come in?"

My head snaps around at Owen's request. *Would they like to come in?* Why in the world would we want to invite them inside our house? We should make them stand on the stoop, in the fucking cold.

"That's so kind. We won't take up too much of your time. Chad just needs to say something to Ivy." Scarlett gives her son a nudge and he stomps up the remaining steps.

Owen moves to the side, pushing me out of the way at the same time, and ushers them into the foyer. "Ivy! Can you come down here for a minute?"

Small footsteps make it halfway down the stairs before they stop. When I glance up, Ivy's got Zuzi under one arm, and she's clutching a post on the banister with the other, staring wide-eyed at Chad. Fear is written all across her face.

This is why I didn't want them in our house. Ivy's already traumatized and Owen's just making it worse.

"Hey, Ivy-bear." I go to get her, taking her hand and leaning in close. I whisper softly, only letting my voice carry the few inches between us. "Let's just see what they have to say, 'kay? I'll be right here. I'll protect you."

She hesitates, but when I give her hand a gentle tug, she follows me down the stairs.

"Chad?" Scarlett gives her son another nudge.

He shuffles his feet and *very* reluctantly lifts his head. He glances quickly at Ivy, then away again. "I'm sorry," he says. His voice carries that distinct tone of I-know-I-did-something-bad-and-now-I'm-in-trouble-and-I'm-not-happy-about-it.

"For?" Scarlett's starting to sound threatening.

"For being mean to you and making fun of you and calling you an orphan." Chad rushes through his sort-of apology so quickly all the words blend together.

Behind him, Scarlett looks like she's about to throttle him, and for some reason, seeing that helps to calm my own anger. The kid's such an asshole even his own mom can't stand him.

"What do you say?" Owen puts a hand on Ivy's shoulder.

She peers up at him through long, pale lashes. Her eyes are glassy with unshed tears.

"You should say 'thank you' and 'I accept your apology.'"

I try to kill Owen with my eyes. How dare he? How fucking dare he ask Ivy to accept this little rat's pathetic apology? She shouldn't accept anything! She should demand payback. Maybe call him a couple ugly names herself.

Ivy clings to me, trying to hide behind my leg. I put my hand on her back, dislodging Owen's in the process. She lets out a little whimper.

"She doesn't have to do that," Scarlett jumps in, a pleading look on her face. "Really. Chad knows what he did is wrong and there is no excuse for it. He's getting grounded for two weeks, no playing at friends' houses, no video games. I am so sorry. My husband is too. Not just about this, but also for your loss. I've met Ivy's mom at PTA meetings before and she was so lovely. That's why I wanted to bring him here to apologize again in person. I wanted to let you all know how sorry we are."

The longer Scarlett rambles, the more irritated I get. So she's met Eden before, so what? And two weeks? The kid should be grounded for the rest of the year.

But while I'm seething, Owen's smiling like she's just crowned him uncle of the year.

"Thank you," he says. "We really appreciate it. It means a lot."

I have to physically bite my lip to keep myself from lashing out.

Scarlett pulls Chad toward the door, then hurries him down the steps. "Again, so sorry. This will never happen again. I promise."

"Thank you. I hope we'll see you at PTA meetings soon." Owen sees them out and closes the door behind them.

"Hey, Ivy-bear." I struggle to keep my voice steady and even. "Why don't you go upstairs and play with your plushies until dinner?"

She sniffles but lets go of my sweatpants. "Okay." Slowly, she climbs the stairs one at a time.

Owen and I glare at each other in the foyer, both listening for her steps to fade.

"What the actual fuck?" I spit out, taking two large steps toward Owen.

His chin lifts, eyes blazing with defiance as he meets my gaze.

"Accepting his apology? We really appreciate it? It

means a lot?" Red-hot anger roils in me, desperate to be released. How could Owen turn on Ivy like that? He's supposed to stand up for her. He's supposed to defend her and be on her side.

Except, all he's done in the past few weeks is be Ivy's worst enemy, making her do all the things she doesn't want to do, making her cry all the time. Forget that fucking kid. Owen's the real bully here. *Owen's* the one I need to protect Ivy from.

"What was I supposed to say?" Owen's voice is quiet, steady, calm. Cold. That's what he is. He's so frigid.

"Anything!" I get right up in his face. "Make the kid pay!"

"He's six years old."

"I don't fucking care!"

We're inches apart. Close enough for me to see the ring of gold around his amber-colored irises. Close enough for Owen's exhales to blow across my chin.

This guy. This fucking guy.

I hate him so much. But I hate that my body reacts to him even more. Even now, when I'm seething in fury, my groin tightens and desire pools low in my stomach. I want to kiss that arrogant, dismissive expression off his face. I want to take him apart piece by piece and destroy him. I want him reduced to a trembling mess and I want him to know that I did it to him.

Owen's jaw works and he lets out a short, derisive huff. Then his gaze slides away from me and he moves to the side like he's trying to slip around me.

I don't fucking think so.

I grab him by the arms and slam him back against the wall.

OWEN

I hit the wall with an *oomph* that expels all the air from my lungs. What the— Did he just—

My lips curl into a snarl as I glare up at Everest. No, not glare. What's stronger than glare? Stronger than glower. Stronger than looking daggers. How fucking dare he put his hands on me?

And why is heat racing through me, pooling in my groin?

Everest seems to realize what he's done a second later. His eyes go wide in shock and his jaw goes slack. His hands loosen from my arms and he lifts them away. His weight shifts like he's about to step back.

"I'm—"

I don't let him finish. I grab the front of his hoodie with both fists and spin us around. With my forearm across his upper chest, I pin him against the wall where I was a second ago.

He thinks he can talk to me like that and just walk

away? He thinks he can manhandle me, then toss up an apology like it's nothing? I've had to put up with his bull-shit for weeks and I've had enough of it. I've had enough of his laissez-faire attitude, his juvenile eye rolls, his non-existent approach to parenting. I'm trying to do things right and he's undermining me left, right, and center.

Everest gasps quietly, then lets out a shaky breath. His Adam's apple bobs and a shudder runs through him. His eyes go a little dazed.

I sense more than see or feel his hands move. They float through the air slowly, inching closer and closer until they land feather-light on my hips. A shiver runs up my spine at the touch, hot even through layers of clothing.

They just rest there for a moment that seems to stretch into eternity. Then his fingers flex, tightening his grip.

Heat floods my veins as blood rushes to my dick. Memories of that night in Vegas flash across my mind. The hardness of his body against mine. Our bruising kisses. The thickness of his cock as he stretched me open. How full I felt when he bottomed out. The way his hands branded my skin.

Like they're doing now.

I don't think. I react. My lips slam against Everest's so hard my teeth hurt. But the whimpering sound Everest makes and the way he softens under my assault obliterates any note of pain.

He opens for me like he's hungry for my tongue and slides down the wall an inch to give me better access. When I lick into his mouth he jerks my hips flush against his. He's as hard as I am and I can't help but grind our erections together.

Goddamn, this feels good. So much better than my

memories from that night. So much better than it has any right to.

I bite his bottom lip, then make him suck my tongue. He's so eager for it, chasing me back into my mouth when I withdraw. My head spins. My balls draw up tight.

Everest's hands moved from my hips to my ass, palming my ass cheeks and kneading them with his strong fingers. My hole twitches, keen on joining in on the action, aching to be filled.

Everest's fingers press the seam of my pants into my crease. He doesn't get nearly deep enough to touch my hole, but the effect is the same. I shudder and my cock pulses. My fingers tingle and my toes curl.

I could come like this. From nothing more than kissing Everest, from humping him. Like some teenager who has no control over his body.

What am I doing? This is Everest. I don't like Everest. He's annoying. He's childish. But more than that, we have to live together and work together for the foreseeable future. We can't get involved like this. I need to stop.

Grasping at any remaining threads of rational thought in my mind, I find the strength to fling myself away from him, stumbling over my feet and almost landing on the floor. My head is swimming and I can't seem to suck in oxygen fast enough. My dick is so hard, it feels like it's going to burst through the zipper. I wipe the back of my hand across my lips. They're bruised and swollen and sore.

Everest looks the same way I feel. He's slumped against the wall, legs barely able to hold him up. His gray sweatpants are tented and his chest rises and falls with his rapid breaths. He looks dazed.

Slowly, his eyes blink open and his gaze collides with mine. The heat in them steals my breath away. He wants me. Just as much as my body wants him. It would be too easy to give in to the lust. But that way lies madness. We can't.

I pull myself together, smoothing out my clothes, running my fingers through my hair. I shove my lingering arousal deep, tamping it down and locking it away. I'm a parent now. I have Ivy to think of. I can't indulge in whatever whims come my way. My wants, especially preposterous ones like sleeping with Everest, have to come second.

When I finally have myself under control, I lift my gaze to Everest. "Don't ever do that again," I say with as much poise as I can muster. I'm impressed with how steady my voice is, considering I'm feeling anything but steady inside.

Everest's eyebrows shoot up and his jaw drops. "Me? I didn't fucking do anything. You're the one who kissed me."

I draw myself up to my full height, unwilling to acknowledge that Everest is technically correct. I did kiss him. But only because he shoved me against the wall first. If he hadn't touched me, if he hadn't gotten all up in my face, this would never have happened.

"Don't be ridiculous," I spit out, sounding too derisive, too defensive, too harsh. Even to myself. But I have no other choice. It's this or succumb to the arousal raging inside me.

Before my eyes, Everest transforms. The soft languidness of his body is replaced with tightly coiled tension. The arousal in his soft blue eyes hardens into steel.

He pushes off the wall, advancing toward me. His clothes are still disheveled and his hair is in disarray. His lips are puffy and red. He doesn't bother to straighten himself out.

"What the hell is your problem? Why do you have it out for me? You always have. From the moment we met. I've never done anything to you, but you're constantly on my case about shit that doesn't matter."

He stops an inch away from me, puffing himself up to appear taller, broader, bigger. Anger radiates off him, palpable in the air. It's the perfect fuel for mine.

I stab him with a finger to the chest. "Because you're an immature and irresponsible child. You don't take anything seriously. Everything is a joke to you. All you care about is having fun while the rest of us have to hold down jobs and pay the bills and be adults."

My words land with laser-guided precision. Everest tries to hide it, but I can see the hurt shining through his irritation and disbelief.

For a split second, guilt surges through me. Everything I said is true. Or at least, it used to be true. Even I have to admit that Everest has stepped up in the past few weeks. But a few weeks of good behavior doesn't mean he's a different person now. It doesn't mean he won't change his mind about raising Ivy and decide he's better off joyriding from one beach town to the next.

I shove the guilt aside. I don't have time to baby Everest and his sensitive feelings. If he really wants to be treated like an adult, then he needs to suck it up and prove he deserves it.

We're staring each other down, neither of us budging, the air around us crackling with tension. Then without warning, Everest spins away and snatches his coat off the hanger.

What the fuck is he doing? "You're leaving?"

He doesn't answer me as he pulls on his coat and stuffs his feet into his shoes.

Panic spikes through me and my hands curl into fists, nails digging painfully into my palms. I want to stop him, I realize. I want to grab him and strip that damn coat off him. I want to make him stay and— and— fuck, I don't know. *Don't let him get to you, Lambert.*

Every muscle in my body is tensed. It's the only way to keep myself from physically rushing him. Everest wants to leave? Fine, let him fucking leave. He's just proving my point: he's not cut out for the tough shit. He runs at the first sign of trouble.

He flings open the front door, throwing a parting phrase over his shoulder. "Don't wait up."

And then he's gone.

I stare at the back of the door for long moments before my muscles gradually loosen. I collapse into a heap on the floor.

I want to punch something. I want to rage. I want to tear shit apart and roar while I'm at it. My eyes sting with unshed tears and a sob works its way up my throat. I can't stop it. I can't hold it back. It escapes as I clamp a hand over my mouth.

I'm so tired. I'm just so goddamn tired. I never asked for this. I never wanted any of this.

Sadness and grief crash into me like a tidal wave. They snag me in their current and drag me out to sea, pushing me under thousands of gallons of water. I can't breathe. I can't tell which way is up. Everything is dark and thick and crushing.

God, I miss Jeremy so fucking much. He wasn't just my big brother. He was my best friend. He always watched out for me, always had my back. He let me tag along with him and his friends when we were kids and never made fun of me if I wanted to play with "girl" toys.

As adults, we saw each other all the time. I came over for brunch and dinner at least every other week. He was the first person I went to when I needed to get something off my chest and the first person I called up when I had good news to share.

And now he's gone. He's just fucking gone. For no good reason. Because of a stupid freak accident.

How am I supposed to do this? How am I supposed to live his life and raise his kid? I don't know how to do any of it. I'm not prepared. I'm not equipped. It's too much. It's just too goddamn much.

"Uncle Owen?"

Still sitting on the floor, I spin away from the stairs and the sound of Ivy's small voice, wiping frantically at my face. She doesn't need to see my tears. She doesn't need to see me fall apart. She needs me to be strong.

"Are you crying?" Her voice is closer now.

"What? Oh, uh, no, I mean, um, just a little." I dig my handkerchief out of my pocket. It's still soiled and a little damp from Ivy's tears earlier. I add mine to the mix.

Short arms come around my shoulders and wrap across the front of my neck. Ivy leans her small weight against me, her cheek pressed to my ear.

"It's okay. I'm sad too."

Fuck if that doesn't make fresh tears spring to my eyes.

I nod, patting her clasped arms. "Yeah, I know. It's okay to be sad."

"We can be sad together."

Jesus Christ. How does this six-year-old girl contain so much wisdom in her little body? I take a deep breath, drawing on the comfort she's offering and letting it soothe my hurt like a balm on a wound.

I don't know how to do this. I'm not convinced I can. A part of me wants to give up and quit, but I can't do that. For Ivy, this precious, smart, strong little girl, I have to try. No matter how hard it is or how demanding, I owe it to her and to Jeremy to persevere and give it my all.

I smile, despite the pain still permeating every part of me. This is not easy, but at least I'm not alone.

"Yeah, we can be sad together."

EVEREST

Numb and in shock, I pull my hood over my head and hunch down into the warmth of the puffy coat as I stalk away from the house. There are too many thoughts and emotions all jumbled up inside me that I don't know what to think or feel. There's anger about what happened to Ivy. Insult from that kid showing up on our doorstep. Shock over Owen's response. Arousal still lingering from our against-the-wall kiss. Hurt.

So much hurt. Because of everything. Losing Eden, getting my life turned upside down, and having to deal with Owen being an insufferable asshole every day.

Did I really think I could do this? I was an idiot. Stupid. Dumb. Maybe Owen is right about me being an irresponsible child. Maybe he's right that I should never have been given custody of Ivy.

Nothing he said today is new. He's said it all before. Numerous times. I've always let it slide off my back because Owen doesn't fucking know what he's talking about. He doesn't know me. He's never had anything to do with me. Why the hell should I care what the stuck-up prick thinks anyway?

But it's different this time. Maybe because he kissed me. Or maybe because we've been spending so much time together in the past few weeks. Or maybe because I'm still raw over what happened to Ivy. Who the hell knows? Regardless, his words struck. And they struck hard.

I've been trying so damn hard to be responsible, to pull my weight and do right by Ivy. I've rearranged my work schedule. I haven't gone out for drinks with the guys in weeks. I've basically written off clubbing and hooking up altogether. My entire life now revolves around this little girl and it's still not enough for Owen.

Nothing I do will ever be enough for him. I will never live up to his impossible standards. I shouldn't even bother to try. I never have in the past. But for some reason, the thought of proving him right, of meeting his lower-than-low expectations… it feels wrong and icky and suffocating. It feels like giving up.

I'm not afraid of giving up. I'm a pro at knowing when to call it quits and skip town. I just didn't think I'd *want* to give up on this—on Ivy.

I find myself in front of the bar down the street from Mars. The guys and I end up here a lot to grab drinks after work. Through the window, I can see some of them at a table near the front. Yes, this is exactly what I need.

Inside, Donnie, the spin instructor, is sitting with Gavin, Beau's husband and co-owner of the gym, and Christian, one of our top personal trainers. They're all quite a bit older than me and I don't usually hang out with them, but they've always been nice.

"Hey, guys," I greet them as I approach their table.

Without prompting, Christian silently pulls out the empty chair next to him and offers it to me. He's a quiet, unassuming guy. He never seeks out the spotlight, but he's by far the most popular trainer at the gym.

I slide into it as Gavin shoots me a concerned look.

"I thought you left early today. Logan said there was some emergency with your niece?" he asks.

"I—" The mess of emotions rises up inside me again, choking off my words. I blink rapidly, trying to fight back the tears.

"Is she okay?" Donnie asks.

I nod. "Yeah," I croak. "She's fine. Mostly."

A waiter stops by to take my drink order, and when he leaves, Donnie picks up the thread. "What happened?"

I jump at the chance to unload all the shit that's been taking up too much space in my head. "Some asshole kid made fun of her because her parents died. And then the kid and his mom show up at our house. Like, what the fuck? We don't want you here. Go away. The kid gives some half-assed apology and Owen's all like, 'Thank you so much. You're so amazing. We accept your apology. Let's hang out.'"

Around the table, the guys exchange slightly worried, but mostly confused looks.

"And then!" I cut myself off before continuing. *And then we made out and he called me a baby and now my feelings are hurt.* Yeah, I'm not saying that out loud. "And then I left. I needed some fresh air."

I plant my elbows on the table and bow my head to stab my fingers into my hair. A heavy sigh *whooshes* out of me, almost strong enough to make me drop to the floor.

Christian puts his hand on my shoulder. It's big and beefy, and the weight of it is so comforting, I can't help but lean into it. The waiter comes back with my beer and I take a healthy swig before setting it down heavily on the table. All three guys are watching me warily, like I'm about to fall apart on them. I can't blame them, I feel like I might too.

Even now, I can feel the lingering kiss. The way Owen bit my bottom lip and his tongue invading my mouth. I can still feel the press of his body against mine, the hardness of his erection on my hip. He wanted me. He wanted me, then he pushed me away.

Why did he do that? What does it mean?

Why does he have to be such an asshat all the damn time? No one else in his family is like that. Jeremy was *nice*, goddamn it. He wasn't stuck up or arrogant or any of that shit.

Maybe Owen got picked on when he was a kid and it permanently damaged his personality. He probably got dropped on his head. Or I know, he was switched at birth and he's not actually Jeremy's brother at all. Because I have a hard time believing the two of them share any of the same genes. They couldn't be more different.

God, I miss Jeremy. I miss Eden. I miss having my big sister around to tell me what to do. Especially during times like these when everything feels awful and nothing makes sense. She always knew what to say, always knew how to make me feel better.

"Hey!" The cheerful greeting draws me out of my self-imposed pity party.

Wooden chairs scrape across the floor and I look up to find Sawyer and Logan sitting down at the table.

"I thought you went home," Sawyer says, giving me a friendly punch on the arm.

"Yeah, I did. And then I came back," I mumble mostly into my beer.

Sawyer's eyebrows lift, and across the table, Gavin jumps in with a quick, "Owen."

That's all the explanation my best friends need. Both Sawyer and Logan nod in understanding.

"Hey, why don't we go out dancing tonight?" Logan suggests, bouncing in his seat.

I gaze skeptically at him. "Don't you have a hot FBI agent waiting for you at home?"

He waves away my question. "He's out on a top-secret mission, so I've got nothing else to do."

Sawyer taps on his phone a few times. "Preston's going to be at the lab late tonight, so I'm good."

Logan looks toward the older guys. "You all want to come too?"

The three of them all grimace in distaste.

"Connor would say that I've outgrown my clubbing era," Donnie says.

Christian shakes his head. "Sorry, I only go out when Sebastian makes me."

"I'm…" Gavin gives us a tight smile. "A no. Thanks for the invite though."

"Fine. Then it'll just be the three of us." Logan claps his hands together excitedly. "We're going to have so much fun!"

I glance at my friend. I'm not sure I'm in the mood for fun tonight, but maybe that's exactly what I need. Get out of my own head. Immerse myself in loud music. Get all sweaty on the dance floor. Maybe I'll even pick up a guy and get my dick wet. God knows it's been forever since I got laid. Yeah, drowning my sorrows in some alcohol and dancing is starting to sound better and better by the minute.

We all eat dinner at the bar together, then Logan, Sawyer, and I hop into a rideshare and head for the club. It's too early and on a weeknight, so the club is barely half-full when we arrive. And since none of us are dressed for a night out, the whole vibe feels off.

There's no energy, no hype. The music is loud, but the sound echoes off the walls, making it noisy and annoying. There's no crush of people at the bar, but it still takes forever to get the bartender's attention. By the time we have our drinks and grab one of the empty high-tops, I'm not feeling it anymore. I kind of want to go home.

Sawyer lifts one of the shots he got us. "To forgetting asshole roommates!"

"To forgetting asshole roommates!" Logan parrots, ironic since both of them live with their respective boyfriends.

I don't bother to point that out, though, since it'll only remind me just how bad my own situation is. I throw back my shot and the vodka burns on the way down.

"So." Logan slings an arm around my shoulders. "Let's get you laid!"

I glance around the club—the pickings are slim. "I don't know…"

"What about that guy?" Sawyer nods to the left and I follow his gaze to a man standing a few feet away.

He's tall, but slim, wearing a too-tight crop and booty shorts. He's also young. Like, really young. Like, definitely not legal and shouldn't be drinking young.

"Dude, I'm not getting arrested for molesting a kid."

Logan pats my shoulder excitedly. "Ooo, that guy's hot!" He points to a bear with a bald head, a full beard, and a rounded belly. Some people love that kind of thing, but not me. At least he's age-appropriate, though.

"Naw, not my type."

"Over there." Sawyer eyes one of the VIP booths. "The silver fox."

The older man is wearing a dress shirt with the collar undone and the sleeves rolled up to his elbows. He's cradling a glass of liquor in one hand, giving off major daddy vibes.

Huh. Not a bad option, checks a lot of boxes, but as I stare at him from across the club, I'm not really feeling it. No curiosity, no interest, no arousal. I can appreciate that he's a good-looking man, but that's about it.

"No, not tonight."

"That guy's watching you." Logan's eyes dart to the right and there's a dude about our age being really obvious about checking me out.

His shirt is tight. His pants are tight. His hair is artfully messy and his jaw has just enough scruff on it to be deliberate. He's not too young or too old. Not too big or too small. On any other night, he would be a no-brainer, an automatic yes. Tonight, though… nothing. I'm entirely uninterested. Not even a hint of a spark. My dick is fully asleep, not even a stir.

"What's wrong with him?" Sawyer asks when I don't jump on the opportunity.

I shrug. "Nothing? I don't know. He's just… not right."

Logan and Sawyer exchange a look.

"Dude, what's wrong?" Sawyer asks. "You're never this picky."

I sigh. "I'm not trying to be picky!"

"Or maybe… you're more interested in someone else?" Logan suggests in a sing-song voice. "Someone whose name starts with an 'O' and ends with a 'wen'?"

Sawyer snickers and I glare at both of them. "Shut up. I hate you both."

But that's when I see him.

A blur of dark hair, neatly combed, a couple inches shorter than me. The shoulders are just wide enough, the waist just narrow enough. He's wearing a dress shirt, buttoned all the way up, cuffs still secured around his wrists.

My dick stirs and heat pools in my groin. That familiar surge of arousal courses through me. The lights in the club flash, casting shadows across his face.

Recognition sparks and my pulse shoots through the roof. Holy shit. Is that Owen? What the fuck is he doing here? Did he come after me? To find me? To bring me home? How did he even know I where I was?

I take a few steps away from our table then stop, caught between outrage that he thinks he has any claim over me and a strange warmth at the possibility that he cares enough to come looking for me. That maybe he's sorry about what happened and wants to apologize. That maybe he's actually a human being who feels shit.

It shocks me—scares me—how much I want that, how much it matters to me.

Then the lights flash again and the man moves out of the shadow. I catch a glimpse of his face and this imaginary scenario I've conjured up in my mind—one where

Owen isn't a robotic asshole—shatters into a million pieces.

It's not Owen. It's just someone who looks kind of like him.

But that's almost worse. What does it mean that out of all the men in this club, the only one I have any interest in is an Owen look-alike? Whatever it means, it's not good.

OWEN

On the TV, Elsa's singing about letting shit go and a part of me wishes I could do the same. Just drop everything and walk out the door like Everest did. Leave behind every responsibility, every burden, every person who wants something from me. I could go somewhere sunny and sit on the beach and read while drinking piña coladas. I wouldn't have a care in the world.

Except I'd probably spend the whole time worrying about how everyone was doing back home. Would Ivy be okay living with my parents? Would my parents be overwhelmed with raising a little girl? Would my animal patients and human clients get the care they need? Would my colleagues be able to manage the additional workload?

I can't shut my brain off the way Everest can. I can't detach myself from the important people in my life. And honestly, I'd miss them too much.

I gaze down at Ivy. She's fast asleep with her head on my thigh.

After I picked myself up from the floor, we made dinner together—chicken nuggets like I promised. With plenty of homemade ketchup. Then she wanted to watch *Frozen*, but she didn't just watch it. No, she acted out *Frozen*, every single line, every single song lyric, dancing across the room while she was at it. After the first run-through, she wanted to do it again, so... we did it again.

She zonked out about twenty minutes ago and I've been sitting here re-watching Frozen *again* by myself. I should carry her up to her room, but I can't quite bring myself to move. My limbs feel heavy with fatigue. I barely have enough energy to keep my eyes open.

The movie ends. The credits roll. It's past ten o'clock. Everest's not home yet.

I'm still pissed at him. For not picking up Ivy this afternoon. For storming out on us. For making me do things and say things I would never normally do or say. For making me feel things I don't want to feel.

It's always been this way with him. Every time he steps into the room. Every time I hear his voice. Something inside me rears up and takes over. I turn into a different person whom I don't have control over, a person who just reacts without thinking, without any sense.

No one provokes me the way he does. No one gets so under my skin that I have no choice but to lash out. What is it about him that my self-control vanishes whenever I'm around him? Why does he have such an outsized effect on me? How does he turn me into a mindless, vacuous fool?

Like today. I kissed him. Groped him. Ground myself against him. I would've done more. I wanted to do more. Strip him down, lick him from head to toe, and have him pound my ass until I'm nothing more than a quivering mass of flesh and bone.

I *still* want that.

I've *always* wanted that.

Everest is wrong. I didn't hate him the first time we met. In fact, I was hoping we would get along, that we could become friends. We were going to be brothers-in-law after all.

He had so many stories about his time on the West Coast, and whenever he spun his tales, everyone within his vicinity would hang off his every word. We laughed at all the right times, gasped in shock at all the right times, praised him at all the right times. He was the brightest person in the room, vibrating with an energy that was impossible to ignore. We were enthralled.

I'm not sure when or how that changed. I don't remember any specific incidents that altered my perspective of him. All I know is by the time we went to Vegas for Jeremy's bachelor party, the shine had worn off.

His voice was so loud, so in-your-face, it drowned out every other sound. He could be heard from across the house, from down the block. It grated on me so much, I could feel my nerves actually beginning to fray. And he didn't have a mute button. Or a pause button. Or any volume control. Just yap, yap, yap, all the goddamn time, like he wasn't able to breathe if he wasn't talking.

He was so charismatic, so magnetic. Always the center of attention. Always commanded the room. Everyone was utterly charmed by him: my parents, relatives, neighbors, family friends. Even Jeremy thought he was the coolest guy ever and kept introducing him to people like they were best friends.

Did you know that Everest blah, blah blah. Everest is so funny and blah, blah blah. We're so lucky that Everest could make it blah, blah blah.

One would've thought he cured cancer or solved climate change or invented flying cars. But he was just an unemployed hipster who couch surfed up and down the California coast. I seemed to be the only one who saw through his bullshit.

He wasn't so impressive. What had he done with his life? What accolades did he have to his name? He didn't contribute to society, didn't think about anyone other than himself. He was nothing more than a pretty shell that was empty inside.

But I had to give him that. He was pretty. Like he'd somehow harnessed a piece of that West Coast sun and carried it around with him wherever he went. He shone. His hair was so sun-bleached back then, it was more blond than brown. His skin was tanned golden. He had that long swimmer's body with wide shoulders and narrow hips. His hands were so big. And he had a way of smiling at a person that made them feel like they were the only one in the entire room.

Not that he ever looked at me that way. I wasn't good enough for that, wasn't cool enough to warrant his time. I was too nerdy, too serious, too much of a rule-follower. He'd walk right past me as if I was invisible. He'd speak right over me as if my voice was inaudible. I didn't exist to him.

Well, good fucking riddance. If he was going to treat me like shit, then I would treat him the same—even if he was the most attractive man I'd ever laid eyes on.

Things are different now, though. Yes, Everest is still as

pretty as he was the first time we met. But perhaps he isn't as empty-headed as I've always believed him to be. He's a person. Who has feelings. Who can get hurt. And he doesn't deserve to be my emotional punching bag, no matter how little I might think of him. I owe him an apology.

If he ever decides to come home.

He's probably out with his gym bro friends. At a club. Drinking. Dancing. Losing himself to the music as his body undulates and rolls. His hair will be damp with sweat. His shirt will outline the contours of his muscles. Someone will be watching him from across the busy club. Their gazes lock. Intentions communicated with nothing but a look. They meet in the shadows of the club, in corners just dark enough to release their inhibitions. Nerves and anticipation ratchet up while en route to the hotel room. Then the inevitable explosion of lust the second the door clicks shut behind them.

I know it well. I was that someone all those years ago. I still remember it.

Every single second.

My gut clenches with an emotion I don't want to examine too closely. Technically, I can't blame Everest for finding someone to hook up with. We didn't vow to become celibate when we took custody of Ivy. He's still his own man. He can sleep with whomever he wishes.

But he has responsibilities now, damn it. Someone who depends upon him, who needs him to be here, to do his part. He shouldn't be gallivanting around with strangers when I'm—when *Ivy's* waiting for him at home.

I eventually fall asleep with Ivy curled up next to me

on the couch. I don't know how long I've been out for or what time it is when I feel a hand settle gently on my knee.

The room is dark and my vision is bleary when I open my eyes. But I don't need light to recognize the shape of Everest's shoulders and the tilt of his head as he crouches down in front of me.

He removes his hand when he sees that I'm awake and my knee feels cold without his touch.

"I'll take her to bed," he murmurs.

I don't object as he gathers Ivy in his arms and lifts her from the couch. I rub my eyes and run my hands down my face. My stubble is getting a little too long to mistake for a five o'clock shadow. It's been several days since I've found the time to shave, and at this point, I might just give up and let it grow out.

Everest carries Ivy up the stairs. I shut off the TV and carry the empty popcorn bowls to the kitchen. I'm clearing up the dishes from dinner when he comes back down.

"I said you didn't have to wait up for me."

I stiffen at the implication. That I was waiting for him, worried he wasn't home yet. That I care.

"I didn't." That wasn't why I was still downstairs in the middle of the night. I was tired. I fell asleep. It had nothing to do with Everest. So I tell myself.

He doesn't respond, just leans his hip against the kitchen island, his crossed arms making his biceps look way bigger than they have any right to be. He watches as I load up the dishwasher and wet a rag to wipe down the counter.

Silence weighs heavily in the air between us, thick and suffocating. I can hear my heart beating. I can hear the rush of air in and out of my lungs.

"Where were you?" The question pops out in my desperate attempt to cut through the unease.

"Why do you care?"

"I don't," I answer too quickly for it to be true. My back is to Everest, but I hear his eye roll all the same.

"I went out with the guys."

I knew it. My hackles rise. "Got yourself some hot ass?" I cringe and grind my teeth together. I sound like a jealous lover. I shouldn't care what he did or who he did it with. He could fuck half the city and it shouldn't matter. So why is there a red, hot, churning mass in my stomach? Why do I feel the urge to punch some nameless faceless person on the jaw?

Everest huffs and mutters something under his breath.

Anger has me spinning around and I growl at him. "What was that?"

His gaze bores into me, eyes shadowed not only by the late hour but also by weeks of non-stop go-go-go. Fatigue wafts off him. It's in the slump of his shoulders, the dark smudges under his eyes, the heaviness in his body he never used to have before we moved into the house together.

The sight of him is a bucket of cold water on my rage.

He's just as tired as I am. He's just as sad as I am. I might not like it, but we're the only two people in the entire world who know what it's like to be here right now. He also lost a sibling he was close to. His life was also upended. He also became a parent to a little girl overnight and was forced to share a house with someone he hates.

The fight drains out of me. Does it matter where he was or who he was with? Does it matter what he did tonight?

He still came home. He's still here. It's still just me and him in this together.

"I said, 'I wish.'"

I frown, my brain sluggishly trying to make sense of his statement. My confusion must be written on my face because Everest shakes his head, drags a hand over his face like I did earlier, and sighs.

"Never mind. I'm going to bed."

He pushes away from the kitchen island and turns for the stairs. The thought of him leaving me again propels a single word from my lips. "Wait!"

He pauses, casting a questioning look in my direction.

I need to apologize, but the words get stuck in my throat. I don't know how to apologize to Everest. I've never had to do it before. The sentiment is so foreign to me, so unfamiliar, it almost feels wrong. Me? Apologize to Everest? How preposterous.

A beat passes and I'm still standing there with my jaw hanging open. Everest shakes his head. "Whatever, dude. I'm too tired to deal with your bullshit."

No, wait, don't go. He's halfway to the stairs before I manage to force it out.

"I'm sorry."

He stops, but he doesn't turn around again.

"I'm sorry," I say again, feeling like the floor is about to give way under my feet. I grip the edge of the counter as my heart ricochets around in my chest. It can't figure out how fast it should be beating or where it should be sending blood. My head is woozy and my stomach is unsettled. Words tumble out of my mouth.

"For earlier, I mean. I shouldn't have said what I said. You've done a lot for Ivy."

Slowly, Everest turns to face me, wearing an incredulous expression. "Is that all?"

No, that's not all. There's so much more I should say, so much more I don't know how to say. "Um, yeah."

He advances on me, like a predator stalking his prey. On instinct, I back away until I'm trapped against the kitchen counter. He doesn't stop until there's only an inch of air separating us.

"What are you going to do to make it up to me?"

Indignation flares, hot and bright. Make it up to him? What the hell does he expect me to do? Clean his toilet? Do his laundry? I already do all that shit because he's not adult enough to clean up after his own goddamn self. I've apologized already. Isn't that enough?

Everest studies me and a smirk gradually appears on his face. "You kinda left me hanging earlier. Maybe you should finish the job."

His voice is low and it reverberates through the gap between us, hitting me low in the stomach. My breath hitches and my dick stirs.

"Fuck you," I spit out at him, though there's not nearly as much disgust in those words as there should be.

Everest's smirk breaks into a smile, a devious, unscrupulous smile. "That can be arranged."

My hands come up to his chest and stop. I mean to push him away, but my arms won't cooperate. Instead, my fingers curl around the fabric of his shirt like I'm trying to pull him closer.

Everest peers down at my hands, then up to my face. He cocks an eyebrow in question.

"Fuck you," I say again because apparently my brain can't access the part where my vocabulary is stored. But I don't let go of his shirt. My fingers have taken on a life of their own and no matter how hard I want to shove Everest away from me, they won't do it.

Everest moves, head bending down like he's about to kiss me. I freeze, breath caught in my lungs, the rest of my body paralyzed as I wait for his lips to make contact with mine. But instead, they ghost along my jaw toward my ear.

I shiver and tilt my head back to give him room. Why am I doing this? Why am I letting him get the upper hand? I should be fighting back. I should be putting him in his place.

His lips graze my ear. His breath is hot against my skin. My dick is straining against the front of my pants and it's all I can do to not plaster myself against him like we did earlier.

"You want me," Everest whispers in my ear. "Don't try to deny it. I know you do. I'm the best sex you've ever had in your life, aren't I? You've never stopped thinking about that night in Vegas, have you? It was so hot. You on top of me, bouncing on my cock. You want that again, don't you? I know you do. So why not give in? Just give in, Owen."

The image he paints flashes vividly in my mind and the sound of my name rolling off Everest's tongue makes me shudder with something primal and raw. Desire coils inside me, tight and primed and ready to explode at the smallest trigger.

Then suddenly, he's gone.

I gasp, eyes flying open to find Everest backing away from me. His expression is flat, closed off and guarded. I search his face for any sign of the arousal coursing through my veins, but all I find is a touch of sadness in his eyes.

Without another word, he turns toward the stairs that lead down to his bedroom in the basement. He shuffles toward them, shoulders slumped with an air of defeat.

I watch as he disappears down the stairs and listen for his door to click shut. Only then do I let out the breath I didn't realize I was holding. The tension inside me unravels.

What the hell just happened? I feel unmoored, untethered, adrift and lost at sea. My life has spiraled out of control and I don't know what to do. I don't know how to rein it all back in and regain some semblance of order. I don't know how to stop everything from careening even further into chaos.

Everest has worn down my defenses. Since the first day we moved into this house together, he's been steadily chipping away at them. An inch here, another inch there. And now my carefully constructed walls are about to crumble. I'm exposed. I'm vulnerable. And I'm afraid that there's nothing I can do to stop him.

CHAPTER
FIFTEEN

EVEREST

Something's changed. I don't know what exactly. But after that day with the Chad kid, the *incident* in the foyer, and the lust-fueled standoff in the middle of the night... something's changed.

Owen is still Owen, but a little less Owen than normal? Like, he and Ivy haven't been arguing as much. He hasn't been nagging her about picking up her toys or being a drill sergeant about eating healthy meals. I found tubs of ice cream in the freezer the other day. Bubblegum and salted caramel. Like, wtf?

And he hasn't been back to his apartment at all, I don't think. I overheard him on the phone one day talking about signing a lease or something. So maybe he found someone to rent the place?

I don't know how I feel about all this, to be honest. I mean, I'm glad he's all-in on raising Ivy with me and I'm ecstatic that I'm not coming home to war zones every goddamn day. But he's also not leaving me with many reasons to keep hating him.

Ugh. Who the hell am I kidding? I don't hate him very much anymore. Don't get me wrong, he is still annoying as shit sometimes, but I think I gave up actively hating him a while ago. Now, I'm more like... tolerant with a dash of intrigued. And horny. Definitely horny for Owen.

And he's horny for me too. I keep catching him staring at me when he thinks I'm not paying attention. Especially my hands, which, not to brag or anything, but I've got pretty sexy hands. And I might be imagining it, but I'm pretty sure his eyes light up just a tiny bit whenever I walk into the room. He tries to hide it, I'm sure, but I know Owen better than he thinks I do. He definitely has the hots for me. It's just a matter of time.

I was really close to kissing him that night in the kitchen. I'm still not entirely sure why I didn't. I was tired, obviously. But like, not just physically tired, I think. After my reaction to the Owen look-alike at the club, it felt weird to come home and make out with the real deal.

He was all messed up too. From the touch of crazy in his eyes to the way he swung from hot to cold and back again, he clearly wasn't thinking straight. It wouldn't have been right of me to take advantage of his moment of weakness. And I can't imagine how much worse it would make things between us.

Neither of us has mentioned what happened since. But whenever we're in the same room, there's a noticeable amount of unresolved sexual tension filling the air. We're just lucky Ivy's a bit too young to pick up on it. Because whew, it's thick. The boys at Mars have a bet going for when we'll finally fuck.

A part of me wants us to just do it already, but there's another part of me that kinda likes the suspense. It's like we're two MMA fighters circling the cage, each waiting for the other to make the first move. The longer we drag this out, the more explosive it'll be when it happens.

Today is Saturday and I've taught a full day of classes. I'm amped and exhausted at the same time. It's the best feeling, like I'm high on some top shelf drugs.

I jog up the steps of our stoop and let myself in the front door. Owen and Ivy aren't in the kitchen or the living room. "Hello?"

"Up here!"

I drop my duffel on the floor and take the stairs two at a time. They aren't on the second floor either, but I hear voices on the third—Eden and Jeremy's bedroom. What the hell are they doing up there?

"Ives? Owen?"

I climb the last flight a little more slowly as a sense of dread comes over me. There's only one reason why they would be up here.

When I reach the landing and peek into Eden's and Jeremy's bedroom, I freeze. It feels like all the oxygen's been sucked out of the house. I'm trying to drag in a breath, but I can't.

There are piles of stuff scattered all over the place. Piles of Eden's and Jeremy's stuff. And in the middle of the room are Ivy and Owen, sitting on the floor. She's hugging one of Jeremy's dress shirts to her chest. He's holding a blow-dryer.

"Mommy used to wear Daddy's shirts a lot. They were too big for her. She looked so funny in them." Ivy giggles, but the sound is muffled by the rush of blood past my ears.

"I bet she did." Owen lifts the blow-dryer. "What about this? You want to keep it?"

Ivy studies for a second, head tilted in thought. "I don't know how to use it."

"I can teach you. You might not want to use it right now, but in a few years you'll be able to do fancy hairdos with it."

A strangled noise escapes my throat and they both turn to look at me, innocently, like this is the most normal thing in the world. It's not. It's absolutely fucking not.

"What are you doing?" I ask, the words barely understandable as my throat closes up.

Owen's expression grows wary and concerned. When he speaks, his voice is level, like he senses danger and is trying to keep everyone calm. "We're sorting through their things."

Yeah, I fucking got that part. But *why*? He's tearing apart their bedroom, rifling through all their things. They don't belong to him. He has no right. He shouldn't even be up here. All the thoughts race through my head, but all that comes out is another strangled sound.

Owen slowly rises to his feet, keeping his eyes trained on me as he speaks to Ivy. "Hey Ivy, why don't we take a break? How about you go watch something on the iPad?"

Ivy glances from him to me and back to him, her curious six-year-old mind picking up on the tension rippling through the air between us. Does she get it? Does she understand? Owen is erasing her parents right now. He is literally tossing them out and scrubbing them from their own house, their home.

Ivy stands, leaving Jeremy's dress shirt on the floor. For a moment, it looks like she might insist on staying, but then she steps over all the shit scattered everywhere, heading for the door. When she gets to me, she gives my legs a quick hug, then she disappears down the stairs.

I grip the doorframe, practically trembling with rage. "How dare you?"

"Everest." Owen's tone is gentle with a hint of resignation.

"How fucking dare you?" I launch myself forward, snatching the blow-dryer he's still holding and tossing it onto the bed.

I grab the front of his shirt and his hands come up to latch onto my wrists. My momentum sends us careening across the room.

"We have to do this sooner or later." His voice cracks with emotion. "They're not coming back, Everest. We can't keep this place as a mausoleum."

"Shut up. Just shut the fuck up." I try to push him toward the door, but Owen's a slippery motherfucker and stronger than he looks. He pushes right back.

"Stop it. Everest. Stop," he implores.

I don't. I push and shove, trying to use my bigger body to my advantage. We stumble over the stuff on the floor—clothes, shoes, toiletries, books. Owen's got one hand wrapped around my wrist when my foot lands on the corner of something hard. I lose my balance and Owen tries to keep me upright. He hauls me to him, throwing his arm around me, but it's not enough.

We go down, landing in a pile of tangled limbs. My face is pressed to Owen's chest and he's holding me tight. I struggle against him for a moment, but he doesn't budge.

"It's okay, Ev. Shh, it's going to be okay," he murmurs in the same tone he uses when he's trying to comfort Ivy.

A sob rips through the room and it takes me a moment to realize it's coming from me. My cheeks are wet and my throat is raw. My lungs burn and it feels like I'm being physically torn apart.

I don't know when I started crying, but now that I'm in the midst of it, it all comes pouring out. Again. I've already cried so much in the weeks since the accident. I've sobbed while lying in bed, hugging a pillow. Stray tears have slipped down my cheeks while I'm working out my shit on the punching bag at the gym. I've stood in the shower, letting the water wash the grief away.

Why am I still crying? How do I still have tears left to shed? When does it stop?

I cling to Owen as my emotions sweep me up and carry me away. He doesn't let me go. He doesn't try to distance himself. If anything, his arms squeeze me tighter, his body curls protectively around me.

I take the comfort he offers, ignoring all the messy history between us, ignoring how out of character this is for him. I soak in the warmth of his body, the solid muscles under my palms, the grounding weight of him.

He smells so good. I want to breathe in that rich leather scent and hold it in my lungs. It makes me feel safe and protected and small.

His lips touch the shell of my ear and his breath tickles whenever he exhales. His stubble catches on my hair. He hasn't shaved in a while and it's really messing with the clean-cut look I'm used to.

Gradually, these little things filter in through the debilitating grief that's consumed me. My tears dry up, my pulse settles, and my breathing slows. Still, Owen doesn't let me go.

We lie there. Holding each other. On the floor. Neither of us speaks. Neither of us moves. It's like we're in a little bubble where time stands still. Nothing from our past can make it into the bubble and neither can anything from our future. Our beef with each other is irrelevant. All that matters is the comfort of being with someone who understands.

At some point, Owen's hand starts rubbing up and down my back. Nothing huge, just a slide back and forth. It feels almost absent-minded and I don't even know if he knows he's doing it. It's nice, though. Soothing. I don't stop him.

I drift, floating in that place between awake and asleep, between dreams and reality. I want to stay here and pretend the rest of the world doesn't exist. I want to forget about all the responsibilities weighing me down and all the work that's waiting for me. I want to be in this bubble forever.

Owen shifts suddenly and I think he's trying to pull away. But he's just adjusting his hips so he's not pressed quite so tightly against me. Under my ear, his heart rate seems to increase and his breathing grows more rapid.

Gently, so I don't headbutt his chin, I lift my face from where it's been cradled against his chest. I only go far enough to be able to look him in the eye. The amber irises are swirling with emotion. Sadness and grief. Exhaustion. Fear and longing. I feel all those same things.

"Owen?"

He swallows and his Adam's apple works in his throat. His tongue sneaks out to wet his lips and my gaze drops to watch. It would only take a tilt of my chin to bring my mouth to his. Then I could taste his tongue again. I could suck on it again. My dick roars to life at the thought.

"We shouldn't do this," Owen whispers, though he doesn't sound very confident.

I huff in disagreement. "Why not?"

"Ivy needs to come first," he says.

"She still does."

A few beats pass in silence.

"It's complicated enough."

"So a little more complication won't hurt."

"We don't even like each other."

My lips curl into a smirk. "That's what makes it even better."

He growls and I'm ready for him when he fits his lips against mine. It's hungry. Our teeth bang together, tongues fighting for dominance. He bites on my lower lip and I can't help the whimper that escapes me. The pain shoots straight to my dick and my hips thrust forward, looking for friction.

I roll Owen onto his back and wedge my thigh between his. His hands go to my ass, gripping hard as we grind our cocks together. Fuck, that's good. Like, unreasonably good. It's just humping, and yet my entire body tingles, my nipples ache, and my balls are drawn up tight.

Owen hikes up a knee and uses his foot to push off the floor, rolling us over again so he's on top. My fingers thread through his thick hair. The strands are shorter on the sides and back, but the top is just long enough for me to get a good grip. He moans when I tug and shoves his tongue deeper into my mouth.

I welcome it, suck on it, pet it with my own. When he

pulls back, I chase his tongue into his mouth and we do it all over again. The kiss is messy, desperate, driven by all the shit we've said and done to each other in the past, fueled by the emotional rollercoaster of the last month.

I want to strip back every layer of protection he's wrapped around himself. I want to lay him bare and see the real man underneath the shield he's hiding behind.

I want to bury my cock deep into his body and fuck him until we're both coming apart at the seams.

His hands slip under the hem of my shirt and his palms are hot irons on my waist. I suck in a gasp and arch up into him. My head falls back and he trails his lips across my jaw, down my neck. His stubble scrapes against my skin, making me shiver and squirm under him.

He drags his hands up my stomach to my chest. His fingers find my nipples, and when he pinches them, I swear I almost come in my pants.

"Fuck, Owen," I breathe, and he reacts by sinking his teeth into the tendons of my neck. Jesus Christ, that's hot. I have to fight back my orgasm with every ounce of self-control I have left. Which, honest to god, isn't much. I'm *this close* to ripping our clothes off and reacquainting my dick with his.

"Uncle Oooweeen! I'm huungrryy!"

We fly apart faster than a speeding bullet, both spinning toward the doorway. But Ivy isn't there. She hasn't seen us—thank fucking god. She was only yelling up the stairs.

I glance at Owen who looks like he's about to die of mortification.

"Coming, Ivy-poo! Give us a minute!" I shout back at her.

Owen shifts, moving farther away from me. He won't meet my gaze. "O—"

"Don't." He cuts me off.

"But—"

"I said, don't." His hands curl into fists like he might swing out and punch me—or like he's stopping himself from reaching for me. He's still panting like he can't catch his breath. His lips are red and swollen. His hair looks like someone's been pulling on it. His clothes are wrinkled and out of place.

I've never seen him this disheveled before and something shifts inside me. He looks so vulnerable, so fragile—so human.

I push to my feet. "I'll go find something in the kitchen." I pause at the door and glance back at him.

He's watching me with an expression I'm not used to seeing from him. He's watching me with fear.

OWEN

I hang my head as a deep well of despair overflows inside me. Why? Why me? Why now? Why with Everest of all people?

Anybody else would be better. Literally, any other person on the entire fucking planet.

But no, it has to be *Everest* I'm stuck in this house with. It has to be *Everest* I share custody of Ivy with. It's Everest everywhere, all the time. In my space, in my face, and I have no way of escaping him.

I can't take it anymore. I'm at my wits' end. I'm losing my ever-loving mind.

Whatever this was just now feels like it's been building for days, weeks. Ever since our confrontation in the kitchen in the middle of the night, I haven't been able to stop thinking about how much I want him. So fucking much. More than is reasonable. More than is healthy.

To the point where I zone out during meetings at work, daydreaming about him. I'm constantly checking my phone to see if he's messaged me. I've turned down extra work shifts so I can be home at the same time as him.

I'm hyper-aware of where he is in the house at all times. My heart skips a beat when he walks into the room. I can't stop staring at his fucking hands.

My ears strain to hear the sound of his voice, the sound of his laughter. I used to find it so fucking annoying. It used to grate on my nerves. Now I could sit and listen to him playing with Ivy, giggling and laughing all day long.

I feel unhinged, obsessed. I need professional psychiatric help.

I should be freaking out right now about Ivy almost finding us in a compromising position. Instead, my lips still tingle from our kisses. My body is still warm from his touch. My blood thrums from the arousal he's awakened in me.

Try as I might, I can't get the taste of Everest out of my mouth, the scent of him out of my nose. Those baggy gray sweatpants hang unseemly low on his hips. That backward ball cap taunts and teases me. His goddamn smirk is seared onto the backs of my eyelids.

I rub the heels of my hands into my eyes, trying to erase the image of him from my mind. I need him out of there to save my sanity. I need to regain control before I do something I really regret, something I won't be able to recover from.

"Owen?"

A hand touches my shoulder and I jump, startled. I didn't hear him come back upstairs. My heart skips a beat at the sight of him crouching in front of me, concern written all over his face.

"Whoa." He lifts both hands, palms out. "Easy. It's just me."

There's no "just" about it. He is the opposite of just. He is the antithesis of just. He's as far away from just as one person could get.

"What do you want?" With my hackles raised, the words come out sharper than I intend.

I expect him to say something snarky or make fun of me somehow, but I don't sense a single ounce of attitude coming from him. He seems genuine, sincere, entirely unlike the Everest I know.

"Ivy wants pizza for dinner. I tried telling her that you probably have something planned already, but she won't let it go. What do you want to do?"

It takes me a moment to understand what he's talking about. Dinner. Ivy. Pizza. Wait, is he…? Is he asking me what I want to do? Like he actually cares what I think? Like he actually wants to parent with me? I'm so surprised, I don't know how to respond.

"So?" Everest prompts when I do nothing but stare at him, dumbfounded. "I know you don't like eating out, but…" He shrugs as he trails off and the implication is clear. *But do we really want to cook right now?* "If you want, I can put my foot down."

I— He— What— This is so far outside our norm I don't know what to say. He's never consulted with me like this before. He usually does whatever the hell he wants—whatever Ivy wants. He's never been so… adult.

Everest's lips twitch. "Hello? Earth to Owen? You still with me?"

Snap out of it, Lambert. I give myself a quick shake. "Um, pizza. Right. We, uh, we can make our own pizza?"

Everest tilts his head like he's some adorable puppy and lets out a soft chuckle. "Are you asking me?"

I huff at his teasing. "No, I mean, we can make our own. I've got a good pizza dough recipe."

Everest snorts and rolls his eyes, but it feels more playful than derisive. "Of course you do." He stands and holds out his hand to me.

I stare at it for several seconds. His fingers are long and strong. His palm is calloused. There's a dusting of hair on the back, lighter than the hair on his head, and it almost shimmers when the light catches it. It's an attractive hand. Hands like that should come with warning labels. Hands like that should be downright illegal.

Slowly, I lift mine and fit it inside his. When his fingers close around me, heat shoots straight up my arm and down to my dick. It's ridiculous. It's only a hand. He's only helping me up. There's no reason for my dick to get hard. And yet, it's straining against the front of my slacks.

Everest hauls me to my feet as if I weigh nothing and I end up standing a little too close. My breath catches in my chest as I gaze up into his shining brown eyes. I can feel the heat of his body, smell the scent of the soap they stock at his gym.

I sway toward him as my stomach tightens with desire again. My skin tingles at his proximity. That hunger I've been trying to suppress roars to the surface, clawing at me to kiss him, undress him, taste him.

Everest steps back first and I have to stop myself from following him. He casts his gaze around the room, taking in all the things scattered on the floor. "Sorry about my meltdown earlier. I know we have to do this. It just took me by surprise, that's all."

I swallow thickly, tamping down the arousal that's threatening to take over. "I should've mentioned it to you before we started."

His eyes light up like I complimented his weightlifting skills.

"Uncle Eeevvv!" Ivy shouts from downstairs, dragging the single syllable of Everest's name out until it's as long as the whole freaking alphabet.

Everest cracks a smile and it feels like the sun shining warm on my face. "Come on. Our little terror is getting impatient. She might start scavenging in the pantry if we keep her waiting any longer."

He turns and leaves, and I follow behind him, caught up in that one word. *Our* little terror, Everest said. As in me and him. Together. The single word winds its way through me. It's never sounded so right and yet so ominous at the same time.

By the time I get down to the kitchen, I'm caught in this off-kilter feeling, like the high of an adrenaline rush without the requisite closure. Like I'm stalled out at the top of a rollercoaster. Like I'm falling from the sky, but the ground never gets any closer.

"Guess what, Ivy-bear?" Everest exclaims when we reach the kitchen.

She looks up from the picture she's drawing. There's a sun and a house, and in front of the house are three stick figures. One is smaller with a triangular skirt and pigtails. The two taller ones are on either side of the little girl, one with stubble on his face and the other with a cap on its head. Me and Everest. With Ivy. In front of our house. All holding hands.

My heart stops and my lungs seize up when I realize

what she's drawn. A part of me revolts at the idea. No, it shouldn't be me and Everest standing on either side of Ivy, it should be Jeremy and Eden. They're her true parents. Everest and I are just poor substitutes.

But another part of me rejoices. Me and Everest and Ivy. We mean something to her beyond the adults she's been saddled with. She sees us as a unit. She sees us as a family.

"Pizza?" Ivy shouts.

"Pizza!" Everest throws his arms into the air. "But it's not just any old pizza! We're gonna make our own."

Ivy gasps audibly. "We are? But how?"

Everest picks her up from the chair at the kitchen table and brings her to one of the stools by the island. "Well, that's where Uncle Owen's magic comes in. He's gonna teach us how."

"Really?" Ivy looks at me with her eyes wide with adoration.

Everest's smile is equally wide and open, unassuming and honest. Standing on the opposite side of the island from them, a warmth spreads through my chest. They're so comfortable with each other, so close and familiar. The connection between them is undeniably vibrant and genuine.

And then it hits me, the connection isn't just between them. It's between all three of us. That's why Ivy drew the picture. That's why they're smiling at me all goofy and uninhibited.

We're a family, or at the very least, we're on our way to becoming one. This hasn't all been in vain. Something good can come out of this. And that scares me to my very core.

I have to clear my voice before I speak. "That's right. We'll make the pizza dough from scratch and then you can put whatever you want on yours."

"*Whatever* I want?" Ivy leans forward so half of her body is on top of the island.

I try to school my face into a stern expression, but a smile tugs on my lips. "Within reason."

She pouts, then heaves a sigh. "Okay, fine," she says, reluctantly giving her stamp of approval.

Under their watchful eyes, I grab the big canister of flour from the pantry and the container of yeast I keep in the freezer.

"Step one is mixing the yeast with some warm water." I fill up a glass and set it in front of Ivy, explaining how the yeast will activate and bubble up.

She stares unblinkingly at the glass, waiting for the chemical reaction. She claps in delight when the first bubbles start to form. I let her help me mix the yeasty water into the flour and she squeals when the wet dough sticks to her fingers. When we set the dough aside to rise, I pull out ingredients for toppings: mushrooms, green peppers, leftover grilled chicken, tomato sauce, and mozzarella cheese.

Ivy's giggles blend with Everest's booming laughter as we each make our own personal-sized pizzas. The sound echoes off the kitchen walls, filling the space with something magical and I catch myself laughing just as hard as they are.

There's a smear of flour on Everest's cheek. I have no idea how it got there. Ivy's hair is falling out of her pigtails and she keeps brushing it back with her dough-covered hands. The counter is covered with bits of mushroom and green peppers, spilled tomato sauce and crumbs of cheese. It looks like a hurricane blew through the kitchen. It looks lived in.

It looks loved.

The air tastes like champagne on my tongue, bubbly and intoxicating. It's the joy that we've created together, the three of us. It's overwhelming and powerful and I feel swept up in its current.

I don't want this evening to end. I want every evening to be like this. I want to smile until my cheeks hurt, laugh until tears spring to my eyes. I want this to continue forever.

My life was good before the accident. I had no complaints. If I could turn back time, I would do everything in my power to make sure Jeremy and Eden stayed safe and Ivy didn't lose her parents.

But this… this is nice. Nicer than anything I've experienced in a long, long time. Nicer than anything I could've dreamed up or imagined.

EVEREST

Ivy's curled up in bed, head resting on Owen's shoulder. I'm pretty sure she fell asleep about fifteen minutes ago, but Owen hasn't noticed and I don't bother telling him. His voice is deep and rich as he continues to read from one of Ivy's favorite books and I let his soothing baritone roll over me.

Sitting on the floor, back against the wall, my eyes drift shut as I listen to Owen. Today was a good day. A very good day. Even my little meltdown when I got home was good.

I know I overreacted. It was just so shocking seeing them upstairs in Eden and Jeremy's room and my emotions got the better of me. Of course we have to clear out their things at some point. Of course we can't seal off an entire floor of the house forever. I just wish Owen had told me he was going to do it beforehand. I want to be a part of the process. I want the chance to say goodbye to them one more time.

I open my eyes and take in the vision of Owen, the softness in his eyes, the delicate curve of his lips, the looseness in the way he holds himself. The scruff on his cheeks is too long and his clothes are more than a little wrinkled. It's so different from his usual tightly wound and highly strung appearance. He looks relaxed and at ease. He looks happy.

For the first time in all the years I've known him, he finally looks happy.

I'm a little surprised at myself for asking him what he wanted to do about dinner. I should've just ordered something, to hell with him. But after that moment we had on the floor of Eden and Jeremy's room, it kind of felt wrong. I want him to tell me about stuff, so maybe I should tell him about stuff too—even if it is whether we should order pizza for dinner.

Owen's reading trails off as he peeks down at a sleeping Ivy. He glances at me and I smile.

"How long has she been asleep?" he asks quietly.

"A while."

"And you just let me keep reading?"

I lift a shoulder and let it drop. "I was enjoying the story."

He huffs, then gently eases Ivy down onto the bed. He pulls the covers tight around her, tucks Zuzi in next to her, and slides the book back into its spot on her bookshelf. I climb to my feet and click on the nightlight in the corner of the room. We slip out.

On the landing outside Ivy's room, I stand at the top of the stairs, waiting for Owen to make the next move. Since we moved in, he's been sleeping in what used to be the office across the hall from Ivy. It's smaller than the guest bedroom I've been using in the basement, but he wanted to be closer to Ivy in case she needed someone in the middle of the night.

"So…" I say.

He clears his throat and stuffs his hands into his pockets. The action pulls the front of his slacks taut across the bulge of his dick. His chest rises and falls a little too fast for a resting heart rate, and his shoulders are an inch higher than they were when he was reading a moment ago.

He's tense. Nervous. He's fighting with himself, it's written on his face, plain as day.

Maybe I should take it easy on him. Make the first move so he doesn't have to step too far outside his comfort zone. I'm nice like that, considerate. But I'm also a tease and a troublemaker, and I kinda like watching Owen squirm.

"How about a drink?" Owen's gaze is downcast as he asks the question.

I chuckle under my breath. Sure, if he needs the liquid courage, we can have a drink. Wordlessly, I turn and lead the way downstairs.

In the living room, there's a mini-bar hidden in a cabinet. I open the door and reach for a random bottle. I'm more of a beer guy, but Jeremy was all about his liquors, so the cabinet is stocked.

"Not that one. The Lagavulin is better for a nightcap."

I cock an eyebrow at Owen and he has the decency to blush.

"What? It's true."

"Okay, Mr. Bougie," I say, rolling my eyes.

His brow furrows and the corners of his mouth turn down into a frown.

"Easy! I'm just kidding!" I grab his arm and give him a light shake.

His frown smooths out a fraction, but he still looks unhappy. I pull him toward me, looping my arms around his shoulders. He resists me for a moment before relaxing into me. His hands come to rest lightly on my hips.

"You know I like to tease," I murmur.

"I wish you wouldn't," he grumbles.

"But where would be the fun in that?"

He harrumphs, but there's a tiny smile on his lips. He looks so adorably grumpy, a little grumpy gremlin. I can't resist. I lean in and give him a quick peck on the corner of his mouth. He takes in a sharp breath, then melts against me.

We stand there for a moment, foreheads touching, savoring each other. The weight of another person, the warmth of their body, the gentle movements of their breathing.

Never in my wildest dreams could I have imagined standing here like this with Owen. We've always been so hostile toward each other. We could never be in the same room without an argument breaking out. But when I put aside my need to poke and prod at him, everything changed.

I never realized it before, but there's something about being with Owen that feels effortless. I don't have to crack jokes or be silly. I don't have to goof off or be the life of the party. I don't have a reputation to live up to. I can just *be*.

So maybe I've been the problem all along.

Slowly, I ease myself away from Owen and turn back to the mini-bar. I reach for the Lagavulin—*because it's better for a nightcap*—and pour two glasses. When I hand one to

Owen, he takes it and immediately throws the whole thing back before setting the glass down with a *thud*.

I stare at him in surprise. I don't know much about scotch, but I'm pretty sure this stuff is pricy. Like, way too pricy to pour down your throat without tasting it.

Also, I never took Owen for a down-it-like-a-shot type person.

"Well? What are you waiting for?" Owen asks, wiping the back of his hand across his mouth.

I glance at his empty glass, then back at my full one. I guess there isn't really anything to wait for. Or rather, I think we've waited long enough.

I toss back the scotch and it goes down nice and smooth, heating me from the inside out. The second my glass is on the counter, Owen grabs my face and yanks me in to slam his mouth across mine.

I stumble forward, catching myself with an arm around his waist. Owen isn't messing around. He shoves his tongue between my lips like he's trying to lick my tonsils and the invasion sends all the blood in my body rushing to my cock.

He pushes me against the wall and plasters himself against me. When the bulge of his erection meets mine, we both shudder and moan. I grab his hips, holding him still as I grind our cocks together. I slide my hands back to fill my palms with his rounded ass.

God, I want to get in there. I want to bury myself deep and touch Owen where no other man has ever touched him before. I want to watch him go wild with pleasure, drive him crazy with lust, and make him crave my cock. I want him with a primal need that I haven't felt in a very long time.

Owen clamps his teeth on my bottom lip and tugs. The pain makes my cock throb and my balls ache. I whimper when he releases his bite and soothes my bruised lip with his tongue.

"I want you to fuck me," Owen whispers and I shiver at the thought. "Hard and fast. Can you do that, Everest? Can you fuck me like you mean it?"

Pleasure ricochets through me at his words. My skin tingles and my stomach tightens. I nod, frantically, digging my fingers into his ass.

"Good." Owen steps back and I whine in protest. But he takes my hand and marches toward the basement stairs.

I scramble to keep up, even as a little bubble of laughter rises in my chest. Even when it comes to sex, Owen is as no-nonsense as always. Cut the bullshit and get right to the point. We both know what we're here to do, so why waste time.

He drops my hand when we get to my room and immediately starts unbuttoning his shirt. "Condoms. Lube."

I have to drag my gaze away from the inches of skin he's revealing as he pulls his shirt apart. Condoms. Lube. I have both. I have plenty of both. I find my stash and toss them onto the bed, then swing back to Owen.

He has his back to me as he shakes out his shirt and folds it. Wide shoulders and a tapered waist. The muscles on his back flex as he moves. I've never known Owen to work out, but he must find time for it because he's a lot more ripped than he lets on.

He unbuckles his belt, then rolls it up into a coil before setting it next to his shirt. Then he unbuttons his slacks and pushes them down his legs. Plain black boxer briefs stretch over his bubble butt. His thighs are thick and his calves are shapely. When the guy finds time to do leg day, I have absolutely no freaking clue.

He turns toward me wearing only his underwear. There's a smattering of dark hair across his chest and a tantalizing treasure trail down the center of his stomach. His dick is clearly outlined in the black cotton and a wet spot has formed at the tip.

He looks exactly the way I remember him from Vegas, right down to how he undresses—but better. The years have given him a little more bulk, making him a little more solid. He was a man before, but now he's a *man* and my dick is here for it.

When I manage to lift my gaze to his face again, I find him giving me the same perusal. Except I'm still fully clothed in an old t-shirt and gray sweatpants.

"Take your shirt off," Owen says in that tone of his that brokers no arguments.

My lips curl into a smirk at his bossiness. He just can't help himself, can he?

I reach up and grab the back of my t-shirt, pulling it over my head and down my arms in some swift motion.

"And put that on."

I follow his gaze to find one of my ball caps hanging on the wall. "This thing?" I point to it.

He nods. "Backward."

Oookay. That's weird, but maybe he's got a hat fetish I don't know about? I grab the cap and slide it on, adjusting it so the bill is angled just right down my neck.

Owen's breath hitches and his gaze trails down my body, lingering on the dips and curves of my chest, my shoulders, my stomach. He takes two steps to close the distance between us, then traces the same path with his fingertips.

My nipples tighten as he grazes them with the lightest touch. I flex my abs when he flattens his hand over them. I forget to breathe when his hand travels lower and cups my cock and balls through my sweatpants.

"You're annoyingly attractive," he growls. "Why the hell are you so fucking hot?"

I can't think when he's massaging my junk in his hand and I can't figure out if he's trying to insult me or compliment me.

He drags his lips along my jaw and up to my ear. His stubble scrapes deliciously across my skin. He catches my earlobe between his teeth. My knees go weak and I grab ahold of him, clinging to him. My head drops back as Owen rakes his teeth down my neck. He latches onto my collarbone, then twirls his tongue in that dip at the base of my throat.

"Fuck, Owen." I sound desperate. Because I am. Desperate for this man who is supposed to hate me and yet can't keep his hands off me. Desperate to see him come apart, to see him give in to the pleasure I can give him.

Owen growls again and directs me toward the bed. When the backs of my legs hit the frame, he gives me a shove and I fall backward onto the mattress. He sets one knee on the bed beside me and reaches for the waistband of my sweats. He yanks them down, along with my underwear, leaving them hanging around my ankles.

Then he stands back and takes in the view. I tuck one arm behind my head and bring my other hand to my chest. Owen watches, lips parted, eyes heavy-lidded. His breaths are fast and shallow and his hands are curled into fists like he's trying to stop himself from reaching for me.

I pinch a nipple, letting myself gasp out loud at the pleasurable pain. I work the one nipple between my fingers, and then the other one, until I'm practically vibrating with need. Slowly, I drag my hand down my body and Owen tracks its progress with laser focus.

I grip myself at the base and slap my cock against my stomach a few times. The sound is loud and wet from the pre-cum I've been leaking. The impact makes me throb harder and more pre-cum spills from my cock.

Owen grabs my wrist and shoves my hand out of the way, then leans down and licks up the puddle of pre-cum. I gasp at the feel of his tongue, wet and dexterous, drawing circles across my skin. He laps up every drop before taking the head of my cock into his mouth.

"Holy fuck." His mouth is a furnace and he's sucking like he wants to drink the pre-cum from my balls. My hips come off the bed, but Owen pushes me down with far more strength than I thought he had.

He works the tip of my cock with his mouth. His tongue swirls around the sensitive head, wiggles against that spot on the underside, dips into the slit. It feels like every single nerve ending in my body is concentrated in just that bit he's got between his lips and they're all firing at the same time. It's so good, it's almost too much.

Owen gradually takes in more of my cock, sliding down my length an inch then pulling back. The slow descent is delightful and torturous at the same time. His mouth is so hot and he's got the perfect amount of suction, and when my dick hits the back of his throat, he swallows around the head.

"Jesus Christ!" I don't blink. I don't want to miss a second of this blowjob. Owen's got his nose flush against my pelvis and my entire cock is engulfed in his delicious mouth. He has my balls in the palm of his hand and the way he's squeezing them gently, I swear to fucking god he's trying to milk me.

My hand goes to his hair, fingers dragging through the thick locks. Owen groans and the vibrations travel right to that spot deep inside that makes me quiver and shake.

"Fuck, Owen." I grip his hair and tug. He groans again and my balls draw up as I approach the brink. "I'm going to come!"

He pulls off and I let out a cry of distress. I was so close. I was almost there.

He lets my cock drop to my stomach, the head an angry red, the veins bulging along the shaft. I can't move. If I do, I'm pretty sure I'll explode all over myself.

Owen steps out of his boxer briefs, then *folds them* and sets them down with his other clothes. If I wasn't fighting so hard to keep from coming, I might've tried to make fun of him. But all I can do is curl my fingers into the sheets under me and hold the fuck on.

OWEN

Everest is debauchery personified. His zero-percent body fat physique laid out on the bed for me. Gray sweats hanging off his ankles. Ball cap askew on his head. His cock glistens with my spit, as hard as a steel rod on his stomach. It's perfectly framed by the V just above his hip bones. He's got every muscle contracted, hands fisting the sheets on his bed.

But it's his face that's the real piece of art. His eyes are glazed over and dazed with lust. His lips are parted, rosy and swollen. He looks like he's drowning in desire, barely able to gasp for breath.

My hole twitches in anticipation. I want that thick cock inside me, filling me up. I want him to pound into me so hard and so fast that I can't think anymore. I want to lose myself to pleasure and banish all the confusion and contradiction that's been plaguing me. I want Everest to fuck it all out of me.

I grab the lube that Everest threw onto the bed. I almost

expected him to have a jumbo-sized bottle, but it's actually a respectfully normal size. Squeezing out a good amount onto my fingers, I set one foot on the mattress, stance wide. It's been a while since I've had sex, what with work and Ivy and everything. It's going to take some work to get me loosened up.

Everest watches with heavy-lidded eyes as I smooth the pad of my finger around my hole. I press at my opening, and though I don't push all the way in, that tiny bit of stimulation has my cock leaking generous amounts of pre-come. I grip myself with my free hand, stroking gently.

Everest's tongue slips out and he licks his lips. He swallows and his Adam's apple bobs.

"Come here." My cock twitches when Everest immediately jumps at my instructions.

He crawls to me, propped up on his elbows, legs stretched out behind him, ankles still bound together by his sweats. For some reason, it thrills me that he hasn't kicked them off yet. There's nothing stopping him except the fact that I didn't say he could.

When he gets close enough, I swipe the tip of my dripping cock over his lips. The clear, sticky pre-cum smears across them and he licks it up like it's the juice of the most succulent fruit.

"Open up."

He drops his jaw, tongue sticking out a bit, waiting for me to feed him. I slap my cock against his outstretched tongue and he whimpers so prettily. Everest doesn't move as I slide a little deeper into his mouth. He doesn't try to take control, doesn't try to hurry things up. He just lays there, mouth open, letting me ease my way inside.

"That's it. Such a good boy."

His lashes flutter at the compliment and he whimpers again.

He's still wearing his ball cap and I hold the back of his head as I carefully fuck his mouth. My hips push forward until I'm met with resistance at the back of his throat. Then I pull back, using the movement to press my fingers into my hole. The dual stimulation is exquisite.

Gratification, deep and fulfilling, settles into my bones. I have Everest exactly where I want him. Laid out in front of me, back rippling with muscle, two rounded globes of his ass, thick thighs, and muscled calves. He's so quiet, so compliant, taking what I'm giving him without a hint of hesitation or complaint.

His whimpers grow louder and louder until they're more like moans. He's writhing around on the bed, most likely rubbing himself against the mattress. Spit drips down his chin.

I've worked two fingers into my hole and quickly I shove a third one in. It's tight and I hiss at the sting. Everest's eyes blink open and he peers up at me through his long lashes. Our gazes collide and it takes my breath away.

I can't identify what it is I see in his eyes. It's not just arousal or even pleasure. There's something deeper, something more profound. It's almost adoring, but that would be ridiculous. We might not hate each other the way we used to, but adoration? We're at least several steps removed from that.

But I can't tear my eyes away from this visual connection we've made. He draws me in and wraps me up in a tangled web. I might be the one issuing directions tonight, but he's got more control over me than either of us realized. I'm at his mercy, at his beck and call. My life now revolves around Everest as much as it revolves around Ivy.

The implications of that have me stumbling away from Everest. It's too much. Too soon. I can't be thinking beyond anything but the physical right now. Anything else and my brain will short-circuit and die.

"Get back." My voice is gravelly and a little unsteady.

Everest keeps his gaze on me as he complies, scooting backward to give me space on the bed. I climb on, arranging myself on my hands and knees, facing away from Everest. I don't want to see his face while we fuck. I want to be able to pretend that it's an anonymous cock in my ass. I want to escape this thing brewing between us, even if it's just temporary.

The mattress dips as Everest shifts behind me. Then a rough, hot hand settles on my hip. "O?"

I stiffen at the shortened form of my name. I've never had a nickname before. None of my friends, not Jeremy or my parents, no one has ever thought to call me anything other than Owen. Ivy is the only one who calls me O, but mostly because she couldn't pronounce Owen when she was little.

Everest's use of the nickname now invokes such contradictory reactions in me that I'm paralyzed. It's so intimate—*too* intimate. It suggests that he knows me, that he's in my inner circle, that we have a mutual understanding. All things I've never wanted with Everest. Things I would have actively fought against not that long ago.

And yet, a warmth spreads through me at the simple nickname. It makes my cock pulse and my hole clench. It makes me yearn for more, for deeper, for closer. The incongruity of my two reactions rips a cry from my throat.

I need him to fuck me. Now. I need him to drive away every thought until I'm nothing more than a mass of flesh and bones.

"Fuck me." There's no movement behind me, so I turn to glare over my shoulder. Everest looks like he's caught between two competing demands and he doesn't know what he should do. I grab the condom and throw it at him. "I said, fuck me."

He hesitates for a moment before ripping open the condom packet and rolling it on. I grab a pillow and bury my face in it, realizing my mistake too late. It smells like Everest, all dark and musky, yet fresh and clean. It smells comforting and safe. It smells like home.

I cling to the pillow even though I should be shoving it away. I hug it tighter as the tip of Everest's blunt cock brushes against my hole.

"Hurry up already," I bark, but Everest ignores me.

He takes his time running his cock up and down my crack. Every time the tip catches on the rim of my hole, my lungs seize.

Fuck. I hate this. It's too much. He needs to get on with it. "Please." The plea slips out unintentionally, so quiet that a part of me hopes that Everest doesn't hear.

He does, though, because the next time his cock catches on my hole, he presses forward.

"Yesss," I hiss as my body gives way to his invasion.

"Is this what you want?" Everest asks when the head of his dick pops inside.

"Yesss."

"You want my cock filling you up?" He grips my hips and pulls back while he pushes forward.

"Yesss."

"Are you hungry for my cock?"

A denial is at the tip of my tongue. No, I'm not hungry for it. I'm not a heathen. I don't need his cock. I can pick up a hot guy just as well as the next person.

It's all lies. I am hungry for him. It's *his* cock I want inside me. It's Everest I want destroying me from the inside out.

"Yes." The word comes out in a sobbing cry, muffled by his pillow, but still plenty audible.

Everest's hips snap forward, bottoming out in one swift motion. The force of the thrust and the spike of pain expel all the air from my lungs. Everest doesn't give me time to recover, though. He immediately pulls out and slams back in.

I struggle to breathe as he does his damnedest to destroy my hole. It's marvelous. It's spectacular. It's exactly what I need, what I want.

I brace myself as Everest pistons in and out of my ass, showing absolutely no mercy. His hips slap against my ass cheeks, the sound echoing in my ears. It blends with the harshness of his breathing and the grunting sound he makes whenever he bottoms out.

My elbows slide along the mattress, nudged forward by the ferocity of Everest's fucking. I try to keep myself on my knees, but I'm no match for the pounding Everest's giving me. With one particularly hard drive of his hips, I land flat on my stomach.

Everest doesn't miss a beat. He adjusts his angle, pushing my legs wide and balancing himself with hands on either side of me. His cock hammers against my prostate, lighting up every nerve ending like a fucking firework show.

I scream into the pillow.

My cock rubs against the mattress underneath me. I'm so sensitive that the friction is almost painful. I squirm. I can't stay still, but my body can't decide whether it wants to escape the sensory overload or if it wants more.

Everest doesn't give me a choice. He lays himself down on top of me, trapping me under his larger body. His thrusting has slowed a touch, but he's now so much deeper inside me. He's touching me where no one else has ever touched me before. He's gone farther into me than anyone I've ever been intimate with.

Suddenly, I wish he wasn't wearing a condom. I want him to shoot his cum into me. I want him to paint my insides with his seed. I want to be marked by him. I want to feel him drip out of me.

The thought of his cum, his essence, drives me right to the edge and tips me over. My scream is muffled by the pillow as my orgasm erupts through me. Lightning flashes behind my closed eyes. Thunder roars in my ears. My entire body is ripped apart by pleasure beyond anything I've felt in a long, long time.

Sharp teeth sink into the fleshy part of my shoulder and Everest lets out a growl. His hips stutter to a halt and his cock pulses, thick and hot, inside me.

Next time. Next time, no condoms. The unbidden thought races through my orgasm-addled mind. I'm so thoroughly spent that I don't even have the mental capacity to argue back. Next time? Who says there will be a next time?

Slowly, as my orgasm recedes, I note the weight of Everest's body squishing me into the mattress. I try to dislodge him but I'm too weak and he's about two hundred pounds of deadweight.

"Ev." I shove uselessly against him.

"Mmm, sorry." He carefully extracts himself and rolls off me.

I roll in the opposite direction so I'm not lying in the wet spot. Gradually, I push myself up and onto my feet. I step into my underwear and reach for my pants.

"You're leaving?" Everest asks.

I glance back at him with a questioning look. What else would I be doing? That's what happens after two people have sex.

He still looks delectable, spread out on the bed, skin glistening with sweat, hair all mussed up. His cap fell off at some point and is lying on the floor. He extricated one foot from his sweatpants, so it's just hanging off one ankle.

But I'm not nineteen anymore. I'm not going for round two tonight. So shouldn't we just go to bed?

He reaches a hand out to me. "Can we cuddle for a bit?"

My eyebrows shoot up. "Cuddle?" The word comes out strangled, like he's asking me to jump off a bridge.

A look of vulnerability flashes across his face. "Yeah, I like a little cuddling after sex. It makes me feel less, you know, cold."

From the hint of insecurity I hear in his voice, I don't think he's talking about the temperature.

I hesitate. Cuddling with Everest should not sound the least bit appealing. I should put my clothes on, go take a shower, and climb into the bed in my own room upstairs. But the softness in his voice and his damn puppy dog eyes tug at my heart so insistently that I find myself giving in.

"Fine. But we need to cover this up." I point to the wet

spot like it's personally offended me, never mind it's my own cum I've left on Everest's sheets.

He pops up and races to the bathroom across the hall. When he comes back, the condom's gone and he's holding a big towel that he lays across the bed. He also has a smaller, damp hand towel.

"Here. Let me…" He trails off when he sees my furrowed brow. "Or, you could…" He holds out the towel to me.

I sigh. He's being so earnest, so sweet. I really am an unbearable asshole, aren't I? Wordlessly, I climb back onto the bed, lying face down so Everest can clean me up. He does so with such incredible gentleness that my throat starts closing up from the sudden tenderness rushing through me. Then he tosses the towel aside and lays down next to me.

I'm not really a cuddler. I've never done it with any of my former lovers. I've never felt the need for it. So I'm a little lost on how it works. Everest seems to have no issues with that. He blissfully arranges me where he wants me and fits himself into my side. His head is on my shoulder, arm thrown across my stomach, legs tangled between mine.

He sighs contentedly, his breath cool over my heated skin. "Thanks," he murmurs quietly.

"Uh, you're welcome."

It takes a while before I can actually relax into the embrace. It's odd, unfamiliar, but also comforting in a way I've never experienced before.

Everest was right, damn the man. It makes me feel less cold.

EVEREST

It turns out that Owen isn't so bad when he doesn't have a stick up his ass. In fact, I credit myself for removing it. And replacing it with my own little rod. Heh heh.

After that first night when he bossed me around in my own bedroom, he's become fucking insatiable. Every night after we put Ivy to bed, he's shooing me down to the basement and ordering me to strip. I gladly comply. I haven't had such regular sex or such good sex ever in my life, and that's saying something.

I always demand cuddles after we've both come our brains out. Owen always puts up a fuss, but then gives in. I think he secretly likes it but is too much of a grumpy gremlin to admit it to me. Although, he always disappears at some point before the morning, which kind of sucks.

It's weird. I've woken up alone in bed for most of my life and it's never bothered me before. But waking up alone these days, knowing that I didn't fall asleep alone... it leaves a grimy feeling on my skin that I don't like.

I mean, I know why Owen leaves early and I have no reason to ask him to stay. But even so, there's a part of me that wishes he would just give in to the inevitable. That he would give in to us.

This weekend will be interesting. We've been careful to act normal around Ivy, whatever the heck normal is. She's too young to pick up on the changes between me and Owen, but our parents definitely won't be. An entire long weekend with both sets of parents—I can already see Owen reverting back to his natural state of assholery.

That is, if we ever get to Owen's parents' house up in Westchester. Right now, it's twenty minutes after five on Friday and he was supposed to be home an hour ago. I took the day off work so I could pack all our things, pick Ivy up from school, and be ready to go the second Owen got home. Could Owen be bothered to do the same? Nope. Of course not.

So now I'm fucking pacing the foyer like some worried house husband, switching between checking my phone and peering out the window for any sign of him.

I'm doing my best not to jump to the worst-case scenario because I know Owen would tsk and say I'm overreacting. But hey, guess what, the last time someone was late getting home without a single text or call, they wound up dead. Forgive me for not wanting to live through that horror again.

Ivy's sitting on the couch, Zuzi hugged to her chest, watching me like a hawk. I'm trying to play it cool, but smart girl that she is, she seems to sense my low-key panic.

Fuck. Jesus. Where the hell is he?

Fifteen minutes later, Owen finally jogs up the front steps to our house. I wrench open the door.

"Seriously?"

He doesn't even glance at me as he sets his briefcase down on the bench next to the door and yanks at his tie.

"Where the hell have you been?" I hiss at him. "We were supposed to be on the road over an hour ago."

Owen shoots me an unimpressed glare. "I had a patient. He needed emergency surgery."

"A patient?" I scoff. "What, like a dog? Couldn't someone else do it?"

Owen's at the foot of the stairs and he spins around on me. "Yes, he's a dog, and no, no one else could do it. It's called my job. Which saves lives. Which, by the way, also pays for the bills of this house."

Both of my eyebrows shoot up at what he's implying. The fucking audacity. "And what do you think my job does? The job that I took a day off of so we can go to *your* parents' house for Memorial Day weekend."

Owen huffs dismissively. "Your job, sure. I'd love to see how far your measly paycheck would stretch with the expenses of a house like this."

My jaw drops. No, he didn't. My job at Mars Fitness might not pay as well as his veterinarian job at some animal hospital, but it's honest work and I earn an honest paycheck. I contribute to the household expenses just as much as he does.

"You—" My blood is boiling, but I cut myself off when I catch sight of Ivy lingering in the doorway to the living room. She doesn't need to see us fighting over... god, I don't even know what. But I'm pissed and Owen's in a bad-ass mood and we're going to be stuck in a very enclosed space for the next several hours.

I swallow down my anger and irritation. This latest spat can wait until we're at his parents' house and Ivy has been safely pawned off onto her grandparents.

"Just go get your sh—stuff." I grab one of the bags I've piled next to the front door. "I'll load the car."

"Should've loaded it while you were waiting," Owen mutters on his way upstairs to his room.

Motherfucker. If Ivy wasn't standing right there…

I stomp out to the car parked on the curb a couple doors down. It takes me a few trips to get everything loaded. By the time I'm done, Owen's changed into his weekend clothes—slacks and a polo shirt—and is bringing the last of the bags out.

"Come on, Ivy-bear." I strap her into her car seat and make sure she's got Zuzi, a juice box, and a bag of crackers within easy reach.

When Owen approaches the car, he holds out his hand.

I stare at it. I know what he wants, but there's no fucking way I'm giving it to him.

"Give me the keys," he says, sticking his hand out a little farther.

"No." I shut Ivy's door and start walking around to the driver's side.

"Everest." Owen grabs my arm. "I'm driving."

"The hell you are. Knowing you, we won't get there till next week." I try to shrug him off, but his grip is strong.

"You don't even know where you're going."

I hold up my phone. "That's what Google Maps is for, smartass."

Owen steps in close, his chest presses against my arm,

and he glares daggers up into my face. "I said, give me the keys," he grits out between his teeth.

Fuck, but I want to say no. I want to shake him off, dive into the driver's seat, and lock the door behind me. He can get in the passenger side if he wants. Or he can stay in Brooklyn for the weekend for all I care. That would show him.

But there's something dark and dangerous in Owen's eyes. Something that slithers right into me and makes my dick plump. Jesus Christ, what is wrong with me? I'm fucking angry at him and he's being a jackass and my dick is like "hot, awesome, yes, let's go."

This thing between us is beyond fucked up.

Because I give him the damn keys.

We climb into the car and despite Owen's claim that he knows where he's going, I punch his parents' address into my phone anyway.

We settle in for the long crawl out of the city, inching along with every other family trying to get away for the long weekend. Ivy's merrily singing along to the kid's road trip playlist I found, and Owen and I are doing a fantastic job of ignoring each other.

As I expected, it takes us *hours*, and by the time we're pulling up to the big suburban house where Owen grew up, we're all cranky as fuck. Ivy hasn't stopped whining for the past forty minutes. Owen's been huffing and grumbling under his breath. I am about to scream.

The second the car rolls to a stop, I shove open the door and scramble out. Fresh evening air hits me in the face and I take in the crisp scent of spring. I stretch, lifting my arms over my head and bending side to side to work out all the kinks and tightness in my muscles.

The front door opens behind me and both sets of grandparents rush out—I'd texted them earlier to let them know we'd be arriving late. I open Ivy's door and help her with the straps of her car seat. The instant I set her down on the driveway, she's racing toward the grandmothers.

"Nana! Grammy!"

I watch as the two older women envelop her with hugs and kisses, and the irritation that's been plaguing me all afternoon and evening finally melts away.

We made it. A few hours later than planned, but we made it in one piece. No one starved to death and no one got strangled, we're going to have a relaxing weekend, and everything is going to be fine.

The two grandfathers and Owen unload the bags, and with everyone helping, we get all our things into the house in one trip. Owen heads towards the stairs when his mom, Alyssa, calls out.

"Oh wait, Ivy's upstairs in your old bedroom, but you and Everest are downstairs on the sofa bed."

Owen's grumpy scowl deepens. "What? Why?"

"The fourth bedroom is a painting studio now," Owen's dad, Martin, says.

"Painting studio?" Owen echoes.

Martin shrugs with a "don't ask me" expression.

"I took up painting recently and that room has the perfect lighting," Alyssa explains.

"Since when do you paint?" Owen sounds incredulous.

"Since *recently*," Alyssa shoots back at him with a pointed look.

The rest of us watch the exchange like it's a three-way tennis match, and I have to say, it's kind of fun seeing Owen get put in his place by his mom. Go, Alyssa.

"Fine, whatever," Owen grumbles before shoving Ivy's bags toward his dad. "You take these. Give me those."

Martin hands over the bags and Owen stomps his way toward the basement stairs.

"Come on, Ivy, sweetie. Let's go to your room." Alyssa holds Ivy's hand and leads her up to the second floor. "It used to be your Uncle Owen's room, remember? Isn't that cool?"

I'm left standing in the hall with Mom and Dad.

"How are things, dear?" Mom asks, pulling me into a belated hug.

I hug her back, sinking into the comfort of her embrace. Dad wraps his arms around the both of us and we all just stand there, enjoying the moment.

A part of me wants to complain, to spew out all the sharp-edged and shadowy worries eating away at my insides and blame it all on Owen. But that's not fair. Today was a bad day. But otherwise… "Actually, things are okay. Better than okay."

Mom and Dad both look surprised.

"Really?" Mom asks skeptically.

"Yeah. Really." A sense of peaceful contentment settles over me, smothering the last remnants of my irritation.

"What about Owen?" Dad asks.

Owen. It always comes back to him, doesn't it? If I'm having a good day, it's usually because Owen and I are getting along. If I'm having a crappy day, it's because Owen's being an asshat. More than Ivy, Owen's become this measure of how things are going in my life. When did that happen? When did everything start revolving around him?

"Owen's… good." I'm not sure what else to say. I'm

certainly not going to tell my parents that we've been fucking each other on the DL. But he brings up so many feelings inside me, many that I've never experienced before, that I don't understand or have a name for. He makes me feel things that I didn't know were possible to feel.

He pushes me and pulls me. Living with him has been so much harder than I thought it would be. But I can tell that I'm changing. I'm growing. I'm becoming a version of myself that I don't quite recognize, but I like.

Owen's making me a better person.

"Really?" Mom exclaims under her breath. "Because we thought you two were going to murder each other the second we left you alone."

I chuckle, remembering the early days when I thought we were going to murder each other too. "You know, maybe I didn't give him a fair chance before. He's not that bad. He's…"

I search for the words to describe his unique mix of surly and strict and vulnerable. I don't know if there's a word that would do him justice in the English language. "He's more than I gave him credit for."

Mom and Dad exchange a look. They don't believe me, but that's okay. It doesn't matter what they believe. All that matters is I'm beginning to know the real Owen underneath all his bluster. And I'm finding that I like what I see.

OWEN

The basement is split in two with a large games room housing a pool table and dartboard. Sliding glass doors lead out to the backyard pool. The other half is a media room with a giant wall-mounted TV and a large modular sectional.

The sectional is normally set up in a U-shape with an ottoman in the middle as a coffee table. But Mom's already rearranged it so it can be slept on like a bed. It's plenty big enough for two grown men, but the only way to climb in or out of the thing is to scramble on and off the narrow end.

I drop onto the couch and hold my head in my hands.

I'm a little embarrassed, to be honest. I had a bad day at work and took it out on Everest. There were complications with my morning surgery and we lost the kitten we were operating on. Then I had to recommend euthanasia to a pet parent who lost it in my office. Then I got pulled into an emergency surgery on the dog who we ended up losing too.

It's just been a completely shit day and I'd actually been looking forward to seeing Everest and Ivy at home. I'd wanted the comfort and reassurance of their presence, something good after so much bad. But then he opened the door, throwing attitude in my face, and I couldn't stop myself from lashing out.

I was an asshole. He didn't deserve it. And now I'll need to apologize. Ugh. I hate apologizing. *Especially* to Everest. But I seem to be doing it a whole hell of a lot.

Heaving a sigh, I push myself to my feet and trudge back toward the stairs. I'm halfway up when I hear my name.

"What about Owen?" Everest's dad, Graham, asks.

I freeze in between steps, hand gripping the banister as my ears strain to pick up the conversation. They're talking about me. Why are they talking about me?

"Owen's… good," Everest says.

I put a hand to my chest and my heart skips a beat. Good. What the hell is good supposed to mean? Good at what?

"Really?" Nell sounds surprised. "Because we honestly thought you two were going to murder each other the second we left you alone."

Everest chuckles softly and I latch onto that familiar sound. It winds its way through me, spreading warmth everywhere it goes. It soothes my fatigue, washes away the grit scraping against my nerves. I close my eyes as it wraps itself around me and sinks into the deepest parts of me. I need that sound. I need to bury myself in it until it drowns out absolutely everything else.

"Yeah, I did too. But, you know what, I don't think I gave him a fair chance before. He's not that bad. He's…"

I lean forward, eager to hear what he's going to say next. For a split second, I'm convinced he's going to say something snarky and rude. He's going to say I'm stuck up, that I'm an asshole, and he wouldn't be wrong.

I am stuck up. I am an asshole. That truth is plainly obvious. I like my life structured in a very particular way and I'm not great at compromise. But if I've learned anything since moving in with Everest, it's that life doesn't work that way. It's unpredictable. It's unruly. It doesn't follow a straight line or any logical rules. Trying to force life into my neat little boxes is always going to end in disaster.

Everest taught me that.

I gulp.

Everest has taught me a lot.

"He's more than I gave him credit for." Everest speaks so softly I almost can't hear him.

"Really?" Nell asks again, practically incredulous.

I hate to admit it, but I kind of agree with her.

"Yeah, he's… I don't know, he's cool."

I can hear the smile in Everest's voice, the sentimentality, the fondness. It breaks something inside me and sends me staggering. Because I feel the same way.

I drag in a shaky breath and sink down onto a step.

God, what's happening? What are we doing? How did we get here? We definitely still hated each other when we first moved into the house, but in the blur of the past several months, we went from enemies to tolerating each other to… whatever this thing is called. Friends with benefits? Co-parents with benefits?

I cringe at myself. Both of those descriptions are awful.

I drag my hands down my face and scratch my fingers through the beard I've unexpectedly grown. After a few weeks of not shaving, I gave up on the clean-cut look and just embraced the damn thing.

Isn't that the perfect metaphor for this year? Wave after wave of life buffeting me from all sides until I have no choice but to give up and sink beneath the water. The metaphorical water that is Everest. And the unsettling thing is, I like it here. I don't want to leave. If anything, I think I want to dive deeper.

"Owen?"

I stir, looking up just as Everest descends the stairs, stopping a few steps below me so we're level with each other.

"What are you doing? You okay?"

I regard him for a moment, taking in his mess of light brown hair, his eyes that always seem to be laughing, that little scar by his ear from a surfing accident years ago. The jaw that I love dragging my lips over. The mouth that makes a perfect O when we're in bed.

Everest smiles at me and it feels like the sun is filling the stairwell, like there's no one else on earth but us.

I hold out my hand, he doesn't hesitate to take it, and I pull him down onto the step next to me.

"I'm sorry," I say, holding his big hand between both of my own. My fingers run over his knuckles, smooth down the hair on the back, trace his callouses. "For being a jerk earlier."

Everest sighs and curls his fingers so they're inter-twined with mine. "You didn't text, didn't call. I couldn't reach you. A part of me thought that maybe…" He clears his throat. "I was worried."

Guilt hits me hard. I'm *such* an asshole. It didn't even occur to me that he would be worried about me, that not being able to reach me might trigger some painful memories. "Fuck, I'm *so* sorry. Everything was going wrong at work today, and I just got so caught up in it all, I didn't even think to—" I cut myself off and take a calming breath. "I'm sorry."

"I'm sorry too. I shouldn't have snapped at you. Just… don't do that to us again, 'kay?" His voice trembles, adding fuel to my guilt.

"I won't. I promise." I lift our clasped hands and press a kiss to the back of his.

After a moment of silence, Everest speaks. "Did you have time to eat today?"

I shake my head.

He scoffs. "And you're always harping on us to eat healthy." He stands and tugs me to my feet. "Come on. They kept dinner warm for us."

Just outside the kitchen, we drop each other's hands. I have to stop myself from snatching his back into mine. We didn't talk about it, but I think it's fair to say that we're not telling our parents about us. What would we even say? I don't even know what we are.

Everest heads to the kitchen table and slides into an empty chair next to Dad and Graham. They immediately draw him into their conversation about some sports team. Nell is chatting with Ivy while Ivy munches on green beans drenched in ketchup. Mom's at the counter, making a few mugs of tea.

I stand at the doorway, watching.

They're smiling and laughing. They're comfortable and familiar with each other. There's no question that they belong here, together, like this is the way their lives were always meant to be.

A wave of grief crashes into me and I grab the edge of the counter to keep from collapsing. My heart hammers in my chest and my lungs struggle to draw in breath.

Thoughts, dark and heavy, pile into my mind. This picture of a beautiful family is only possible because we lost Jeremy and Eden. This life that I've found myself in is the result of an incredible, heartbreaking tragedy. This thing between me and Everest—for better or worse—would never have happened if Jeremy and Eden were still with us.

They should be here. Jeremy and Eden should be sitting around the kitchen table with their daughter and both sets of grandparents. They should get to talk about sports and drink tea and have silly conversations with Ivy. They should get to watch Ivy grow up.

But they're not here. And they're not coming back. The life I knew—the lives we all had—is over. Forever. We'll never be able to turn back the clock. We can only move forward.

A strangled cry tries to escape my throat. I manage to stifle it, but Mom hears. One glance is all she needs to know what I'm thinking.

"Oh, sweetie." She comes to me, drawing me into her arms. "I know."

I don't trust myself to speak. I'm exhausted and my defenses are weak, leaving me an emotional mess. If I open my mouth now, I'll completely fall apart.

"We all wish they were here," Mom says, her own

voice a little unsteady. "It's not fair, is it? Why them? Why not me? They still had their whole lives ahead of them. I've already lived mine."

Her words are a dagger straight through my heart. "Mom." I draw away to look at her, grief and guilt filling me. God knows I've had similar thoughts but hearing them from my mother drives home how horrifying they are. "Don't say that. You still have a lot of life to live."

There are tears in her eyes. She swipes at them, but a couple trail down her cheeks. Her lips curl into a sad smile. "I know. But sometimes…"

I pull her back into a hug. "I know."

"It's so hard."

"Yeah, it is."

The quiet chatter dies away and suddenly the silence sounds so loud. Everyone at the kitchen table is watching me and Mom. Ivy's curled against Nell's side, hugging Zuzi to her chest. There are tears in her eyes and in Nell's too.

Everest blinks and sniffles. Graham and Dad are stoic and grave.

Keeping one arm around Mom, I lead her toward the family—my family. It's incomplete, but it's still whole. For Jeremy and Eden's sake, we have to live the lives they'll never be able to live. We have to carry on in their stead.

When I step up to the table, Ivy slips out from under Nell's arm and reaches for me. I gather her to me, taking the empty chair next to Everest, and settle her into my lap. Mom brings the steaming mugs of tea to the table—one for Nell and one for her. She takes the seat Ivy vacated.

A beat passes in silence.

Under the table, Everest places his hand on my knee.

For a moment, I consider ignoring it or even shaking him off, but then, as with everything, I give in. There's no use resisting it anymore, is there? We're past the point of denial and we can only move forward. I cover Everest's hand with mine.

After another minute, I finally manage to string words into a sentence. My voice is rough when I speak. "They would be happy to see us all gathered here."

"They're here too," Everest adds. "In spirit. In our memories."

I give his hand a squeeze. He flips his over so we're palm to palm and squeezes back.

We all cast sorrowful smiles at each other before Graham breaks the silence. "So, what about those Yankees, huh?"

EVEREST

It's late when I finish brushing my teeth and return to my and Owen's bedroom for the weekend. Ivy's fast asleep upstairs and both sets of parents have retreated to their own rooms.

Owen's tucked into our makeshift bed. Actually, he's not only tucked in, he's cordoned himself off with a wall of couch cushions.

"Seriously?" I ask, nudging the cushion closest to me.

He glares at me from under the blankets, pulled up so high that only his face is showing. "What?"

"I'm not going to attack you in the middle of the night, you know."

The corners of his lips turn down into a little pout. "You're a notorious cuddler. What if one of our parents barges in here in the morning and finds you wrapped around me like a damn octopus?"

I shoot him a heated look. "What makes you think I'll

be wrapped around you? Maybe you'll be wrapped around me."

Owen rolls his eyes. "Not possible. I don't cuddle."

"Mmhmm, sure you don't." I flick the overhead light off and the room is plunged into darkness. Using the light on my phone, I carefully shuffle my way to the couch.

"I don't!" Owen protests.

"Whatever you say." I crawl up the length of the bed and slide in under the covers.

There should be more than enough room for both of us to spread out on the bed, but with the chastity barrier Owen's erected, I feel like I'm sleeping in a coffin.

I roll onto my side and throw an arm and a leg over the cushions like they're one long body pillow. As my eyes adjust to the darkness, I can just make out Owen's scowl.

"That's not what that's for."

"I don't know. It's pretty comfy, if you ask me."

"Well, I didn't," he grumbles.

"Oh, come on." I poke him with my foot. "You know you like cuddling with me."

"I most certainly do not." He rolls away from me like a sulking child. It's so freaking adorable.

I inch my foot in his direction, then trail my toes up his leg.

"What are you doing?" He tries to kick me away. "Our parents are upstairs."

"They're two floors away. And the door is closed." I slide my hand toward him, finding the hem of his shirt and slipping underneath to tease the skin at the small of his back.

Owen gasps and reaches back to grab my wrist. "Everest," he hisses.

"Hmm?"

A beat passes in silence and when he doesn't reply, I try moving my hand, flattening my palm against his waist. He doesn't stop me. He doesn't push me away. I hook my foot around his knee and tug him toward me. Not only does he not resist me, he lets me roll him onto his back.

"We shouldn't," Owen breathes.

"Shouldn't what?" I slither over the cushions separating us and directly into his space. My knee slides in between his. My hand sneaks up his stomach to his chest.

"Shouldn't..." He gasps when I grind my erection into his hip.

"Shouldn't what?" I ask again, whispering it against his ear this time.

"Stop."

I freeze, holding myself stock still. Half of my body is covering Owen's and I can feel him trembling beneath me. His breaths come in fast and shallow. His heart is hammering against my palm.

"Do you really want me to stop?" I pull back far enough to see his face.

There's a longing shining in his eyes that takes my breath away. A longing not just for sex, but for something more, something *real*. I want that too.

Feelings from this afternoon flood back into me. The worry and fear when I couldn't get a hold of him, the worst-case scenarios I tried not to dwell on. If I'd lost him... I don't know what I would do if I lost Owen.

Suddenly, with a growl, Owen flips us over and smashes his lips against mine. The kiss is aggressive. Our tongues battle for dominance, chasing each other back and forth between his mouth and mine.

God, I love kissing Owen. How it's like a fight each and every time. But it's more this time, it's primal, raw, and stripped bare, fueled by our deepest fears, unspoken but ringing loud in the darkness.

We need this, the closeness, the intimacy. We need the reassurance that we're both still here. That nothing bad happened. That we've averted disaster.

Owen rolls his body against mine, chest to chest, stomach to stomach, erection to erection. It's so good. It's so perfect. My nipples ache and my cock pulses and fucking hell, I *need* him.

I shove my hands down the back of his pajama pants, sliding my fingers into the crease of his ass and pulling the two cheeks apart. He grunts and arches his back like he trying to impale himself on my fingers.

I tap a single finger against Owen's hole and he whines directly into my mouth. I drink down the sound, such beautiful music to my ears. I tap my finger a few more times, a little harder, and Owen wrenches his mouth away from mine. He glares at me while reaching back to push my hand more firmly against his ass. "Fuck you."

I smile as the curse winds through me like an endearment.

"You're hungry for my hole, aren't you? You're such a slut for it. Can't go a single day without getting your dick wet, can you?"

The filthy words go straight to my cock, making me throb.

"Fuck, O."

"Tell me how much you want me." He growls the demand directly into my ear. "How much do you want my hole?"

I squirm and my finger presses more firmly against the wrinkled entrance to his body. "A lot. I want it. I want you."

"What are you willing to do to get it?"

I whine, pressing my face into the crook of Owen's neck. I breathe in the rich, leathery scent on his skin, wanting to cover myself in it, to drown in it. I want to lose myself in Owen and all his gruff abrasiveness. I want to crawl inside him where I know there's a sweet, soft center. "Anything. Everything."

A shudder runs through Owen and his hips buck to grind his cock against mine. "Give me your hand."

He doesn't wait for me to draw my hand out of his pants but grabs my wrist and yanks it out for me. He opens his mouth, looking like he's going to bite my fingers off. But when his lips close around them, there are no teeth. Just hot wet suction and a slippery sliding tongue.

"Oh fuck."

Owen's gaze drills into me as he sucks on my fingers. My breath catches when his tongue slides in between the digits to coat them in his spit. It feels like his mouth is on my cock, like his tongue is twirling around the head. And when he releases my fingers, I moan in protest as if he's pulling his mouth off my dick.

He pushes my hand back down toward his ass. "Fuck me, Ev. Fuck me like you mean it."

Jesus Christ. Owen being a control freak in real life is annoying as hell. But Owen being controlling in bed is the sexiest thing I've ever experienced.

I shove my hand down his shorts and made a beeline for his hole. I push one finger inside, moaning when the muscle immediately gives way. Owen moans and drops his head onto my shoulder.

"That's it. All the way in. The second one too. That's a good boy."

I gasp at the praise and I cram my fingers into his ass as far as they will go. He clamps down around me when I pull out, like he's trying to keep me inside, like he's trying to milk cum from my fingertips.

My cock is in agony, trapped in my boxers. I tighten my arms around Owen, holding him close as I tilt my hips up, seeking any bit of friction I can find. "Please, O. Please."

Owen slides a hand between us and pushes our shirts up so the bare skin of our chests and stomachs slides against one another. The heat of his skin is searing. My nipples burn at the contact.

Then he dips his hand into my boxers and draws me out. It's pure relief and pure torture at the same time. His fingers are a brand on my cock, searing me through. I'm on fire, every inch of me smoldering and sizzling because of Owen's touch.

It's always like this with us. Hot. Scorching. Almost too much to bear. It's like I'm dry kindling and he's a lit match, and the second we touch, it's a fucking inferno.

He pushes his pajama pants down, releasing himself, then takes both of us in his steady, dexterous hand. He wields the damn thing like a fucking scalpel, with precision and control. Always the exact amount of pressure at the exact right angle to drive me out of my mind with pleasure.

He rubs us together, our pre-cum mixing and easing the way. He thrusts his hips and the head of his cock bumps against the underside of my mine. My whole body tenses from the rush of electricity that races through me.

I scissor my fingers inside Owen's body. I curl them and tug on the ring of muscle as it pulses.

"Motherfucker," he mutters as a gush of pre-cum lands hot on my stomach. "Put in another."

I pull my hand free so I can line up three fingers. It's a tight fit and Owen bites on my shoulder as he bears down on the intrusion. When I'm in as far as I can go, we still, breathing hard, hovering on the brink.

"What are you waiting for, asshole? Fuck me already." He twists his hand around the tips of both our cocks.

I bite on his ear to stifle my moan.

He bites my neck.

I finger-fuck his hole.

He grinds our dicks together so good, I see fucking stars.

We go at each other, frantic with need, racing toward the finish line, except I don't know who the winner is supposed to be: the one who comes first or the one who hangs on for longer.

It doesn't matter in the end, because I come a microsecond after Owen does. He slams his lips against mine and we groan into each other's mouths as we come all over my stomach.

My fingers pump in and out of his ass while his hand flies up and down our cocks. We ride out our orgasms until we're both sensitive and tender and totally wrung out.

Carefully, I extract my fingers from Owen's ass and he slides to one side, head on my shoulder, one leg still hooked over mine. When we've caught our breath, Owen pulls his shirt off and uses it to wipe up our cum. I take mine off too and throw the extra cushions off the couch.

Then we come back together, wrapping our arms around each other, legs fitting together like puzzle pieces. Our heads are on the same pillow. Noses an inch apart.

Owen's eyes are shut and I take the moment to soak him in. Dark lashes fan across his high cheekbones. His beard is short, but it's enough to soften the stern vibe he gives off. His lips are pink and puffy.

My heart skips a beat. I need him. Not just to help cover the bills or to raise Ivy together. I *need* him. *I* need him. He's gone from a fucking pain in my ass to an absolutely essential part of my every day life.

I draw Owen closer, wrapping my body around his. He stirs but doesn't struggle to pull away. I close my eyes, taking comfort in his solid mass, his weight, his scent.

He's my safety net, my life preserver in this scary, terrifying world. He gives me strength and courage, even when I didn't realize I needed it. He fixes my mistakes and makes sure everything is done right.

I don't know what these feelings mean. I've never felt this way about anyone before, like I wouldn't be able to live without his steady presence, so grounding and unwavering. Like a piece of me would die if I lost him.

OWEN

The sky is just brightening when I awake, and for a second, I panic when I can't remember where I am. This isn't my bed. This isn't my bedroom. There's someone in the bed with me.

Then I remember. I'm at Mom and Dad's house. In the basement. With Everest. The panic doesn't fade. It just transforms. Wide awake, I stare up at the ceiling.

Something is happening between us that I never foresaw, that I couldn't have predicted, that I don't fully understand. It's not just the physical aspect of our relationship. In fact, that part is probably the most straightforward. I've always been physically attracted to Everest and him to me. We've always known we were compatible in bed.

It's all the rest of it. The way he occupies every nook and cranny of my mind. How I crave his presence, his touch, the sound of his voice. How my first instinct is always to turn to him. I've never depended upon anyone like this before. I've never needed anyone so fundamentally. I've never felt like I'm only one half of a whole.

That's terrifying.

I've already given up so much of the life I knew. And still, this thing with Everest is demanding more of me. It's overshadowed every other desire, obliterated every other aspiration. It's consuming me until there's nothing left, until everything I am and have is his.

And yet, I want more. I want to go deeper into this thing and get closer to Everest.

I want to wake up like this every day.

Everest is wrapped around me like a goddamn octopus. Like I said he would be. His face is pressed against my cheek. His body is half on top of mine. Our legs are tangled together like knotted ropes.

I want to turn into him and burrow into his warmth. I want to find shelter and safety in his arms. I want to drown in him. So much so that I don't recognize myself anymore.

Is it possible to feel scared shitless and exhilarated at the same time? Is it possible to want something with my entire being and yet be petrified of it?

From the first floor come sounds of shuffling feet. Someone's awake.

With more reluctance than I want to admit, I ease myself out from under Everest's tentacles. Arms empty, Everest grabs the pillow and curls himself around it, burying his face into the spot where my head rested. My heart somersaults in my chest at the sight, at how much Everest doesn't want to let me go.

I don't want to let you go either, asshole. And that is precisely the problem.

A quick trip to the bathroom and a change of clothes later, I quietly ascend the stairs. Mom's in the kitchen and the coffee is already brewing.

She turns and smiles when she sees me. "Sleep well?"

I clear my throat before answering. "Yeah, fine."

"The sectional wasn't too small?"

I choke on my damn saliva. With Everest sprawled across me the entire night, we definitely had more than enough space. "No, nope, it was fine."

Mom lifts an eyebrow at me. "Everything okay?"

"Everything's fine." My voice is several tones higher than normal.

"You're saying 'fine' a lot, which makes me think that perhaps everything is not fine."

Arms crossed, I stare into the distance, not really seeing anything. I don't know how to respond, what I'm supposed to say. I'm not entirely certain how I feel, never mind finding the words to voice it out loud.

A steaming mug of coffee appears on the counter in front of me. "Come on, let's go outside."

Picking up the mug, I follow Mom out to the patio just off the kitchen. It overlooks the backyard, with a full set of furniture and Dad's big fancy barbecue.

This early in the morning, it feels like we are the only two people on the planet. The sun is still low in the sky and the air has a sharp crispness to it. The freshly cut grass is covered in dew—reminding me of Everest's unique scent—and the only sound to be heard is the chirping of birds in the distance.

Mom and I sit side by side, soaking in the peacefulness. Neither of us speak for several long moments. Mom eventually breaks the silence.

"You'll feel better once you get it off your chest."

I turn away from the scene in front of us to find Mom regarding me with a knowing look. Does she know? Did Everest tell her? Has she just picked it up from the way we've been interacting with each other?

She lifts a questioning eyebrow.

"Everest and I are sleeping together."

I hold my breath, waiting for I don't know what. For a sinkhole to open up under the house. For a meteor to fall from the sky. For the furniture we're sitting on to spontaneously combust.

None of that happens, though. The world doesn't end.

Mom doesn't react either. She just lifts her mug to take another sip of coffee, then lowers it into her lap. "Oh."

"Did you know?"

She lets out a soft chuckle. "No, I definitely did not."

"Are you..." I search for the right word, not certain what it is I'm trying to ask. "Surprised? Disappointed?"

Her gaze goes soft. "Surprised, yes. You two have never gotten along. But disappointed? No. Why would you think that?"

Hell if I know. The question just formed on my tongue.

"Are *you* disappointed?" she asks and my reply comes hurtling out of me.

"No! I'm... terrified and... not excited necessarily, but... anticipatory." I have to drag each word out from the depths of my soul, and even then, the vocabulary doesn't seem sufficient to describe the full scope of my feelings.

Mom gives me a small smile. "It sounds like you're in love."

My gaze snaps to her as shockwaves roll through me. "What?" I spit out.

She holds up innocent hands. "I'm not saying you are. I'm just saying it *sounds* like it."

Love. Am I in love with Everest? No. I can't be. Can I?

Less than six months ago, I couldn't stand to be in the same room as him and now I supposedly love the guy? Is that possible? Can it happen this quickly?

I don't know. I don't know anything anymore. Nothing makes sense, and unfortunately, I don't think there's a book that can explain it to me.

"How long have you been sleeping together?"

"For a few weeks now."

"Does Ivy know?"

"No," I say vehemently. "We've been careful, I swear." That would be a nightmare we definitely don't need. How the hell would we explain it? What if things don't work out? What if we end up hating each other more than we did before? How would we continue co-parenting? Jesus. I don't even want to contemplate that.

Mom nods like she doesn't quite believe me, but she doesn't press the issue. Patting my knee, she continues. "You know, now that I think about it, I can see how you and Everest work together."

Is she messing with me? "Really?"

Mom shakes her head. "It's not obvious, I'll grant you that. But you're like two sides of the same coin. You both want the same things. You care about the same things. You just have different ways of going about it."

I can't tell if she actually believes that or if she's just saying it to appease me, but the idea is... intriguing. I never would have agreed six months ago, but after all this time living with Everest and working with him, I can't rule it out entirely.

We both love Ivy. We both want what's best for her. We're both still grieving. We're both trying to build a life around this new normal. We definitely have different parenting styles and different ways of dealing with grief, but maybe our visions of what a fulfilling and meaningful life looks like aren't as disparate as I once believed.

"I'm scared, Mom."

She wraps her arm around me and I slouch down a little so she can reach. "It's perfectly reasonable to be scared, Owen. Love is scary, especially when you have so much at stake."

Is love supposed to feel like this? The need to be around Everest all the time, to touch him whenever I can. The lightness I feel when we're in the same room. The soul-deep satisfaction I have when we're all tangled up together in bed. This bubbly feeling in my stomach that makes me more than a little giddy.

If it is, then I might be in love with Everest. And he might love me back.

Footsteps, then voices, filter through the patio's screen door. Mom gives me a sideways hug and plants a quick kiss on my head like she did when I was a little boy.

"I should go get breakfast started."

I follow her inside to find Ivy sitting at the kitchen table with Nell and Graham. She's still in her PJs, but her hair has been pulled back into an elaborate braid.

"Look, Uncle O! Nana did it for me!" She turns around to present me with the back of her head.

I run my fingers lightly over the complex pattern. "Wow! That looks so cool! Maybe Nana Nell can teach me how to do that. Then I can braid your hair when we go home."

Ivy gasps in excitement. "Can she?"

I nod toward Nell. "You'll have to ask her."

"Can you, Nana? Please, please, please?!"

Nell smiles and nods. "Of course, sweetie. We can do it tonight when we get back from the zoo."

Ivy squeals and claps her hands in glee.

"The zoo?" I ask. My mind immediately runs through an inventory of Ivy's go-bag. There's usually a bottle of sunscreen in there, but the last I checked, it was running low.

"I mentioned it to them yesterday before you guys arrived," Mom explains from the kitchen counter where she's making the fixings for omelets. "Remember when we used to take you and Jeremy? You two ran off on us once. Nearly gave us heart attacks."

I chuckle at the memory. "We wanted to see the giraffes."

"I wanna see giraffes!" Ivy exclaims.

I pat Ivy on the head. "Sure, sweetie. We can go see the giraffes."

Dad comes lumbering down the stairs then, leaving only Everest still in bed. I grab an empty mug and fill it with coffee. Plenty of milk and sugar. Just the way he likes it.

In the basement, Everest is still curled around the pillow. I stand and watch him for a moment. His light brown hair is a messy halo around his head. The hairs on his forearms are so light and fine they look like golden dust. The blanket has fallen halfway down his torso, leaving his upper back exposed. His shoulders are so damn wide. The muscles on his arms and his back are defined even when he's relaxed and unconscious.

I wonder what he looks like when he's at Mars. Sweaty and panting. Muscles all pumped up from working out. Giant grin on his face and his playful brown eyes sparkling with mirth and adrenaline. I bet he'd be a sight to behold.

I grab Everest's ankle and give it a hard shake. "Hey, wake up."

"Mmm." Everest rolls over and slaps the pillow over his head.

I shake his foot again. "Wake up, Ev. Everyone's waiting for you."

He pulls the pillow down just enough to peek out at me and immediately zeros in on the mug. "Is that mine?"

I hold it up and pretend to drink from it. "Maybe."

Everest shoots out of bed, flying at me. "Gimme." He grabs the mug from me with both hands and brings it to his nose. "Mmm, perfect."

His voice is gravelly from sleep and warmth fills my stomach expanding up to my chest. I fight the smile that tugs on my lips. I fight the need to comb my fingers through his hair, the urge to take the mug from his lips and replace it with my lips instead.

I take several steps away from the bed, not trusting myself not to dive back in—to hell with the rest of the family upstairs.

I don't think I like this love thing. This staggering compulsion that overrides every logical cell in my brain.

"O?"

My head snaps up and I realize I've been scowling at the floor.

"You okay?"

I nod, the movement jerky. "Yeah, I'm fine."

Everest throws me a lopsided smile. "Thanks for the coffee."

I clear my throat to push down the tenderness rising inside me. "You're welcome. Um, we're taking Ivy to the zoo. We'll need to stop and pick up more sunscreen for her."

Everest shakes his head. "Nope, I got a new bottle yesterday. It's in her go-bag, along with her hat and sunglasses."

I curl my hands into fists as my heart threatens to burst from my chest. Fuck. Mom's right. I'm in love with Everest.

EVEREST

Owen's being weird.

I mean, that's not saying much. He's weird all the time. But he's been especially weird today.

He won't say more than a single word to me at a time. He won't look at me. He's got his nose buried in the map of the zoo, as if there aren't arrows on the ground directing us where to go. He moves away whenever I get close.

He seemed okay this morning when he brought me my coffee, doctored exactly the way I like it. He was definitely more than okay last night when we fucked each other's brains out. So what happened? What is my grumpy little gremlin overthinking now?

We've been at the zoo for a couple hours already, six adults trailing behind a tiny little girl like she's our tour guide. The grandparents have been non-stop feeding Ivy sweets, so she's all hyped up on adrenaline and sugar and excitement. I'm not looking forward to her crashing when we get home, but right now she's ecstatic and it's a delight to watch.

Ivy insisted on getting her face painted as soon as we arrived—with a unicorn, of course. A glittery one. Then the grandparents bought her a hairband with a unicorn horn and a pink wand with streamers on the end. We went to the children's zoo where she squealed while petting the goats. In the butterfly garden, she walked around with her eyes wide and her jaw on the ground. I got a couple great photos of her hugging a goat and several more with a butterfly on her head.

And through it all, Owen's been avoiding me like I'm the fucking plague. It's just me, as far as I can tell. He hasn't been grumpy or short-tempered with anyone else. He chats with his parents and my parents perfectly normally. He gives Ivy all the attention she wants. But it's like I don't even exist to him. Like I'm a ghost.

I'm not gonna lie. It hurts. It's how we treated each other in the before times. When we weren't at one another's throats, we stayed as far away from each other as we could. But that was before. Before Ivy, the house, *us*.

I thought we were past that. I thought we… well, I wouldn't call us friends necessarily and "couple" sounds way too serious. But we're something, something more than two people who happen to live in the same house, raising a kid together.

Have I been reading our whole situation wrong? Does he still hate me? Am I just a convenient fuck?

My stomach churns as unease eats away at me. By the time lunch rolls around, I've lost my appetite. In fact, my stomach is so twisted up in knots that I kind of feel like vomiting.

The Zoomobile arrives to take us from the butterfly garden to the restaurant on the other side of the zoo. For a moment, I almost want to maneuver myself in next to Owen so I can confront him on being an asshole. But I chicken out at the last second.

He's just going to say that everything's fine, but I'll know he's lying. The ride will be too short for us to really hash it out. Then I'll be second-guessing myself even more than I already am for the rest of the afternoon. I'd rather not know. I'd rather be not-so-blissfully ignorant than have confirmation that something is actually wrong.

I end up several rows behind Owen, sitting with Mom. I have the perfect view of the back of his immaculately styled head. He's got his arm laid across the back of the bench seat where Ivy is sitting next to him. The sweater he's wearing molds to his shoulders, his biceps. When he turns to talk to Ivy, I can see the corner of his smile and the way his cheeks bunch. When he chuckles at something she says, his shoulders shake and his head tilts back a few degrees.

My chest feels both hollow and too full at the same time. Like I'm desperately hungry for something and that hunger is clawing at my insides. I've never felt anything like this before. I've never felt like I was going to die just because someone was ignoring me.

"Everest?"

I jump, snapping my head around to find Mom regarding me with a concerned expression.

"Are you alright?"

Out of the blue, my eyes start to sting. That gnawing feeling rips through me like a physical thing, trying to crawl out of my skin. I hiccup and slap a hand over my mouth to swallow down the unexpected sob.

"Everest?" Mom grows alarmed. "What is it? What's wrong? Are you hurt?"

I shake my head. I am hurt, but not that kind of hurt.

I slump down instead, making myself as small as I can so Mom can wrap her arms around me and I can rest my head on her shoulder.

"Is it Eden and Jeremy?" Mom asks in a whisper, rocking me back and forth like I'm a child again. "I miss them too. I don't know if they ever got the chance to bring Ivy to a zoo."

I'm too slow to stop the sob this time. It escapes my throat as I realize I haven't thought about Eden and Jeremy all day. I've been so wrapped up in Owen that I totally forgot about them. Jesus, I'm a selfish bastard, aren't I? Obsessing over a boy when I should be remembering my sister and brother-in-law, Ivy's mommy and daddy.

Mom rubs my head and I kind of wish I wasn't wearing a cap so she could run her fingers through my hair like she used to when I was a kid. The Zoomobile drives past the penguins, the puffins, and the sea lions. We're passing the polar bears when my neck starts protesting the cramped position I'm sitting in.

Reluctantly, I straighten, but Mom keeps her hand on my shoulder.

"It's not actually Eden and Jeremy," I admit sheepishly.

Mom looks a little surprised but mostly curious. "It's not?"

"No, it's..." I glance up at Owen again, who is pointing out something in the distance to Ivy. "It's Owen."

Mom glances toward the front of the shuttle too. "I thought you said you guys were getting along."

"I thought we were, but..." I sigh heavily. "I dunno. He's been weird all day."

Mom furrows her brow a bit. "He seems fine to me."

"Yeah, I know." I roll my eyes. "He's fine with everyone else. He's just being weird with me."

Mom eyes me silently for a few long seconds. "I get the sense there's more to it than that."

I pout and shift uncomfortably on the hard bench seat. "Maybe."

"Mmhmm?" She knows not to rush me, that I'll end up spitting it out when I figure out how to put what I'm feeling into words.

"Owen... I..." I peek over at Mom who is still wearing her patient, non-judgmental expression. "I think I might feel some kind of way. About Owen."

"Some kind of way?" Mom gives me a "really?" look.

I throw my hands into the air and then land heavily on my thighs with a slap. "I don't know. I just... feel something."

"As in romantic feelings?" she prompts gently, walking me through my own emotions.

"I don't know. Maybe." I cross my arms and lower my chin toward my chest. "Kinda."

"Is this a sudden thing? Or has it been developing for some time?"

"It's..." My cheeks heat as I realize what I'm about to say. "We've, uh, kinda been, you know."

"Kinda been, you know?" Mom echoes me, her voice flat with a hint of amusement.

I give her a meaningful look. "*You know.*"

She gives me a meaningful look in return. "We're adults, Everest. We can use the appropriate words."

"Fine! We've been fucking!" I hiss quietly at her.

Mom's lips twitch like she's fighting back a burst of laughter.

"It's not funny!" I whine, a little louder.

She snickers. "It's a little funny."

"Mom!"

"Okay, okay, I'm sorry. This is serious. I get it. Your feelings are on the line." She pats me on the shoulder.

I stick out my bottom lip in a pout so she knows I don't appreciate her teasing.

"So, you two have been… intimate. And now you have kind of romantic feelings for him." She pauses for a second, considering. "That seems perfectly normal given your circumstances. Actually, now that I think about it, it was probably inevitable."

I stare at her. "What was?"

"You and Owen."

"We were?"

Mom's expression turns sympathetic. "You said Owen's been weird with you all day?"

"Yeah."

"And that's why you're in a bad mood?"

"I'm not in a bad mood," I protest as an uncomfortable mass twists in my stomach. "I'm just… Ugh, fine. Maybe I'm a little upset."

"Because you care about him and you think he might be angry with you."

I squirm at how precisely she's able to describe the aching, almost painful feeling inside me. "Yeah, something like that."

Mom sighs, but her lips curl into a sappy smile. "Oh sweetie, you really like him, don't you?"

I scowl at how she makes me sound like a lovesick teenager. "Maybe. I don't know."

She bumps me with her shoulders. "You've changed—I've noticed. So has Owen. You guys aren't the same people you were when you moved into that house. You didn't like the old Owen, because he was more…"

"Uptight, arrogant, and snobby?" I provide.

She laughs. "Yeah, something like that. But this new Owen, what's he like?"

I think about it for a moment as the truth reveals itself to me. "He wants people to think he's tough, but on the inside, he's not. He's… softer."

"And he's let you see that side of himself. That means something."

I hesitate as doubts creep in, wrapping their tentacles around me. "But it might just be because we're spending so much time together. We never liked anything about each other before. So this might just be a proximity thing." Even as I say the words, the deepest part of my soul rejects that explanation.

Mom gives this some consideration before she speaks. "So what? Even if it is just proximity, who cares? That doesn't make your feelings any less real, does it?"

I blink, genuinely unsure of how to answer the question. "I don't know?"

"Don't you?" Mom puts her hand in the middle of my chest, right above the spot where my heart is hammering against the inside of my ribs. "What do you feel here? Tell me if that's real."

I feel hunger, yearning. Eager and impatient and

greedy. I want Owen to come to me, to smile at me and laugh at my silly jokes. I want him to boss me around, talk dirty to me in bed, then come apart in my arms. I want us to take Ivy on bike rides and to swimming lessons and to visit museums. I want this life I've gotten just a small taste of. I want all of it and more.

I gasp as the full weight of this realization descends upon me. I'm not a single dude anymore who likes going out partying and hooking up. I'm not a floater anymore, going wherever and whenever I want. That life is behind me. Ahead of me is this world of possibilities and in the center of it all are Owen and Ivy.

I grip the back of the seat in front of me as I struggle to calm my racing heart.

"Everest?" Concern flashes in Mom's eyes. "Are you okay?"

I shake my head, not able to speak. Memories of pizza nights and movie nights flash through my mind. The small touches we exchange in the kitchen every morning. The palpable relief when we both come home from work in the evenings.

Our nightly routine, each taking turns getting Ivy ready for bed, reading her a bedtime story and tucking her in. Slipping away to my room in the basement when she falls asleep.

Christ, we're living together. We're raising a little girl together. We're sleeping together. We're partners. We're a family. He feels essential to me because he *is* essential to me. This life doesn't exist if he's not a part of it.

My heart is ricocheting around in my chest so fast I think it's going to shoot right out of my body. My lungs can't keep up.

"Everest?" Mom sounds alarmed, her voice filtering through the sound of blood rushing past my ears

"Ev?"

The deep baritone comes from my other side and I spin around to find Owen standing next to the shuttle. We've stopped and everyone's climbed out. And now, they're all staring at me.

Owen steps in close, brows drawn together, lips set in a firm line. In the before times, I would've assumed that he was angry, pissed that I was making a scene in public. But I know better now. He's concerned, worried. His mind is probably whirring at a hundred miles per hour, trying to triage the problem and create an action plan to address it.

His strong, steady hand wraps around my wrist. "What's wrong? What happened?" His gaze flicks to Mom, then back to me. "Ev?"

I shake my head again and push past him. I can't deal with him right now. I can't deal with him being all take charge and solve the problem and fix all the things. I can't handle him being so goddamn Owen.

I need space, air. I need time to feel my feelings without him hovering above me. I need to come to terms with being in love.

OWEN

Everest is full-on sprinting away like he's being chased by a goddamn ghost. My heart is in my throat, racing a mile a minute, and my brain kicks into crisis management mode. What happened? Is he okay? What should I do?

I'm about to go after Everest when Nell grabs my arm.

"Give him a minute. He just needs to feel his feelings." She gestures for everyone to head toward the restaurant where we were planning to grab lunch.

He needs to feel his feelings? What the hell kind of feelings does he need to feel in the middle of the day? In the middle of the zoo? What in the world were he and Nell talking about in the shuttle?

I stare in the direction Everest ran off in, guilt and worry eating away at me as I try to will him to reappear.

This is my fault. I've been avoiding him for the better part of the day and I know Everest doesn't like to be ignored. I just...

The conversation with Mom this morning really threw

me. Realizing that I love Everest is… it would have been a big deal with anyone, but with Everest, it's like a freaking bomb went off in my head and I've just been trying to keep my shit together.

Because if I looked at him for too long, if I listened to his voice too closely, if he touched me, I might crumble into a blubbering mess. The only way I can make it through the day is to keep everything locked down until we're back in the safety of our home.

That's not the way Everest operates, though. Everything is immediate for him, amplified and extreme. There's no regulation, no measured control. He'll keep spinning until he crashes and then who has to pick him up and put him back together? Me.

I can't do that if he's disappeared on me. I can't fix things when I don't know what happened or what's wrong or what he's feeling. I need to know where he is, damn it. I need to know that he's going to be okay, that he's safe—that he's coming home.

My every instinct is screaming at me to go in search of him, to find him and demand he talk to me. But as much as I'm loath to admit it, Nell is right. When Everest gets overwhelmed, he needs time and space to "feel his feelings."

Ugh. I hate that phrase. What does that even mean? Feelings are inherently felt. The whole sentiment is redundant.

"Come on." Nell tugs lightly on my arm.

With gritted teeth, I reluctantly follow her and the rest of the family toward the restaurant. Even so, I can't help glancing backward every few steps. Sitting still and doing nothing is not my style. Especially not when someone I care about is out there, hurting. Especially not when I was probably the cause of the hurt.

At the restaurant, we grab one of the large picnic tables outside and Dad and I go to place the family's orders at the counter.

"Where did Everest go?" Dad asks.

I stop myself from making an annoyed sound. "I'm not sure. To cool off or something."

"To cool off?" Dad echoes in confusion.

"He gets like this sometimes. He'll come back." He better. And quickly. Or else I'm going to scour every inch of the damn zoo until I find him.

While Dad gives the pimply teenager behind the counter our order, I pull out my phone to tap out a message, thumbs punching the screen.

OWEN

What happened? Message me.

I stare at my phone, willing those three little dots to appear, but they stay stubbornly hidden.

OWEN

At least tell me where you are.

Are you coming back for lunch?

Should we order something for you?

Nothing. Fucking nothing. Worry gnaws away at me, mixing with anger. Anger at him for running away instead of communicating like a goddamn adult. Anger at myself for making him want to run away in the first place.

If I'd just dealt with my shit faster. If I'd just given him the attention he needed.

The food arrives and Dad and I bring it back to our table. Everyone else immediately digs into the burgers and fries, and chicken nuggets for Ivy. I barely touch my food. The few fries I manage to choke down sit like rocks in my stomach. I keep tapping my phone to keep the screen awake, as if I might miss a message or a notification if I let the screen go dark.

Across the table from me, Dad catches my eye. "No word?" he asks quietly.

I give him a small shake of the head.

"He'll be back. I'm sure everything's fine."

Still, my stomach threatens to eject the minuscule amount of food I've fed it. I have to clamp my hands over my knees to keep them from bouncing up and down.

Fifteen minutes. Twenty.

The table is littered with the remnants of lunch—balled-up burger wrappers, half-empty cartons of fries—but Everest still hasn't shown his face.

Fuck it. I'm going to go look for him. I'll fucking call security if I have to.

I stuff my phone into my pocket and extract myself from the picnic bench. But when I turn around, I practically collide with the man himself.

My initial shock of relief quickly gives way to outrage. "Where the fuck have you been?" I only just manage to keep myself from shouting.

Everest flinches like I hit him, but I don't let myself get distracted by my guilt. I grab his arm and drag him away from the restaurant's patio area.

Everest doesn't fight me, but he doesn't cooperate either. He stumbles lackadaisically wherever I direct him.

"Nowhere. Just made a couple loops. Needed to clear my head."

I push him behind a shrub. "What happened?"

He crosses his arms and sighs like he's exhausted. He drops his chin to his chest, gaze glued to the ground between us.

My heart twinges at how defeated he looks. Where is the overconfident, über-cocky Everest I know and apparently love? Where are the eye rolls and the snarky jabs and the taunting smile? Worry makes my words come out too harsh.

"What the fuck happened?" I hiss at him.

"Nothing." His bottom lip sticks out in a pout.

Seriously? He's going to be like this? Reverting to the same old teenage bullshit? "What the hell is that supposed to mean?"

"It means, I don't want to talk about it." He tries to step around me, but I shift sideways to block him.

"Why not?" I demand, hands curling into fists so hard my nails bite into my palms. "Why can't you just talk to me like a goddamn adult?"

His gaze snaps up to mine, flashing with anger and irritation. We're both running high on emotions and the air crackles around us.

Rage bubbles up inside me. No, not rage, something stronger, more primal and unvarnished. It's raw and potent and visceral. I want to grab Everest and devour him. I want to tie him up and shove him into a hidden, secret place where no one else can find him and nothing else can hurt him. I want to shake him until he understands. I want to pull him inside me so he can feel what I feel—the debilitating intensity of it, how it knocks me off my feet and sends me reeling.

Doesn't he know? Doesn't he get it? I fucking love him and it's fucking killing me.

I can't breathe. I can't move. My head is spinning and the ground tilts under my feet.

"O." Everest's breath brushes across my lips a split second before his mouth fits over mine. His arms come around me and I circle mine around his waist. We plaster ourselves to each other from knee to chest, like two magnets, inextricably drawn together.

My body melts into his. My lungs gradually expand. All the disorderly thoughts ricocheting through my brain settle into one single idea.

Everest—I need him, with all my heart and soul, with my whole mind and body. Because I love him—deeper, stronger, more thoroughly than I've ever loved anything else in my life.

"Boys?"

We jump apart, startled, and Everest lets out a little squeal of surprise. Spinning around, we find both of our moms standing there, grinning at us.

"Jesus Christ," Everest mutters, holding his chest.

"A little warning next time, please?" I shoot our moms an unimpressed look.

"Uh no, no next time at all, please," Everest objects.

"Sorry about that." Nell winces sympathetically.

My mom, however, just smirks at us. "We just wanted to tell you that we're all done with lunch."

"Ivy's getting restless," Nell adds. "So we're going to take her to watch the penguin feeding."

"You guys take your time with..." Mom waves her

hand vaguely at us. "Just catch up with us when you're done."

"Byeee!" Nell waves her fingers and the two of them dissolve into giggles as they retreat.

I drag a hand over my face. This weekend could not be any more disastrous. I have an emotional breakdown and realize I'm in love with the one guy I'm supposed to hate more than anything in the world. We can't keep our hands off each other, even when we're supposed to be fighting. And now Mom and Nell know all about it.

Roughened fingers wrap around my wrist and pull my hand away from my face. Everest slides his palm against mine and intertwines our fingers.

A shiver runs up my arm. It's so intimate, so vulnerable, holding hands with him like this. Who knew such a simple thing could have such an outsized impact?

He takes my other hand and holds it the same way.

"Sorry I ran off," Everest murmurs.

A hint of grumpiness trickles back through me. "I was worried."

"I know you were, but..."

"You needed time to sort through your feelings."

"Yeah."

I peer up at him as my chest tightens. "And have you? Sorted through your feelings?"

Everest nods, a wry smile on his lips. "We should probably talk."

I harrumph. "Probably not behind a shrub in the middle of a public zoo, though."

Everest laughs, warm and low. The sound is a balm to my soul.

"Come on," Everest tugs me out from behind the bush. "I'm starving."

"Serves you right for missing lunch."

Everest gives me some playful side-eye. "You could've saved something for me."

I snort. "And it would be cold and gross by now if I did."

Everest's expression turns saccharine. "Aw, you do care about me."

I roll my eyes and bite my tongue because even though I do love him, I'm not about to admit it for the first time in the middle of the goddamn zoo.

Everest spots a hot dog stand and drags me toward it. Standing in line, I'm about to make a comment about mystery meat when Everest beats me to the punch.

"Not a single word," he says, putting his hand over my mouth. "It's delicious and I don't care what's in it."

I stick my tongue out and lick his palm.

"Ew!" he cries, snatching his hand away. He glares at me and I smirk back at him.

The worry and anger from earlier melt away, leaving me feeling strangely light. Like I've dropped a heavy weight from my shoulders and now I'm floating through the air.

Everest orders two Italian sausages on hot dog buns, even when I tell him I don't want one. He shoots me a mischievous look. "Good, because they're both for me."

But when the hot dog guy hands over the buns, Everest gives me the second one. I think about protesting, but my stomach grumbles, reminding me that I was too preoccupied to eat before.

I opt for some mustard and sauerkraut, while Everest

loads up on every single condiment available. He holds my gaze as he lifts the sausage and bun to his mouth and takes a giant bite. He moans as meat juices and runny condiments cover his lips and drip down his chin, but he doesn't bother to wipe any of it away.

"Mmm, so good," he mutters, mouth still half-full of food.

"You're gross." I shudder in disgust and turn to grab a handful of napkins from the hot dog stand. We're going to need them all. Good thing I have wipes in Ivy's go-bag too.

Everest laughs and takes a couple napkins from me. His eyes sparkle brightly with amusement and joy and I realize he did that on purpose, just to get a reaction out of me. Ugh. Heathen.

"Come on, you can walk and eat at the same time, right?" I don't wait for his answer before turning toward the penguin exhibit.

We arrive just as the feeding demonstration is ending and by then, Ivy's energy levels are running on fumes. Everest carries her to the parking lot and we make our way to my parent's house.

Later that night, after dinner and endless games of UNO—most of which I won—I find Everest in the backyard.

He's gazing up at the moon. The water in the pool dances, illuminated by the lights below. The neighborhood has fallen quiet, leaving only the soft chirping of crickets in the background.

I hand him one of the tumblers I brought with me and he lifts the blanket he's got spread across his lap. I settle in next to him, squeezing in close so we can tuck the blanket around both of us.

"Is this a Laga-whatever-it's-called?" Everest asks, lifting his glass.

"Lagavulin," I supply.

"Yeah, right, good for a nightcap."

"See? You're learning."

He shakes his head with a soft laugh. "You're such a snob," he mutters.

"A snob who brings you top shelf scotch, so who are you to complain?"

Everest shifts, sliding lower to lean his head on my shoulder. I lift my arm so it's resting across the back of the patio sofa.

"I would've been fine with a beer."

"Shut up and drink the scotch."

We fall into a comfortable silence and I tilt my head to bury my nose in his hair. He smells earthy and warm, like freshly cut grass. It's familiar and comforting and soothing.

Never in my wildest dreams would I have ever thought...

The probability that Everest and I, out of all the people in the world...

If someone had told me a year ago that I would be sitting here, holding Everest in my arms, smelling his hair, I would've laughed them out of the city.

But this thing inside me, the thing that wants Everest, that loves Everest, that I've fought for so long. It's grown and grown and grown until it's filled up every inch of my existence. Until it's overwhelmed me and overpowered me.

Everest has permeated every corner of my life. He's saturated me, through and through. He's a part of me now, so intertwined that I wouldn't be able to extricate myself from his clutches. I can't imagine my life without him anymore. When I try, it's just hollow, empty, nothingness.

"O?" Everest whispers into the night.

"Hmm?"

"We should talk."

I sigh. My breath stirs Everest's hair, which in turn tickles my nose. We do need to talk. There's a lot we both need to say. But there's also a part of me that's terrified of what will happen when we pull wide that door.

It's only open a crack at the moment. We can still slam it shut and pretend none of this ever happened. We can still sleep together and raise Ivy together—why risk everything by putting a label on it?

With my eyes squeezed tight, I murmur almost silently into Everest's hair. "I'm scared."

He squeezes my knee and turns to press his cheek against mine. "I know, babe. I am too."

EVEREST

I'm like ninety-five percent sure Owen feels the same way I do. He wouldn't have reacted the way he did at the zoo today if he didn't. He wouldn't be scared right now either.

I'm scared too. I mean, it's not like we can really turn back the clock or put the genie back in the bottle or anything. But like, saying the things out loud and putting labels on our feelings, that's fucking terrifying. That's serious stuff. And I've never been a very serious person.

I turn to gaze into Owen's eyes. Light from the pool reflects off their amber color, making his eyes dance and shimmer. They're mesmerizing.

"I love you." The words kind of slip out without me thinking about them too much. They hang in the air between us while my heart lodges itself in my throat.

Owen's response is a short, aborted inhale that I notice only because I'm pressed right up against his chest. We stare at each other, not breathing, not moving, just waiting. Waiting. Waiting.

Pressure builds in me, pressing against my insides, my ribs, my skin. I know he wants to say it back to me. I can see it in his eyes, the longing battling against the fear. Disbelief that we—of all the people in the world—could find ourselves here.

Silence stretches on, interrupted only by the sound of chirping crickets and the occasional car driving past in the distance. Owen's throat works as he swallows and his tongue slips out to wet his lips.

Still, he doesn't say the words. He doesn't say anything.

Motherfucker. I can't take the waiting anymore. Frustration bursts from me and I fling off the blanket we've been sharing. "Just say it back to me, goddamn it! I know you want to."

Owen blinks once and a thin, hard barrier slams into place. He narrows his eyes and clenches his jaw. "Who says I want to say anything?"

You've got to be kidding me. Of all the fucking times for him to shove that stick back up his ass. He's being difficult and stubborn for the hell of it. He doesn't like being told what to do—especially by me. But news flash, buddy, I know him better than he knows himself.

"You are such a fucking asshole, you know that?" I say right before grabbing his face with both hands and hauling him toward me. I smash my lips onto his hard enough that our teeth bang together.

He makes a sound of protest, trying to push me off. But he doesn't try very hard, and after a couple seconds, he's pulling me toward him instead.

I slide my hands down his back and drag him into my lap, his knees going to either side of my hips. He stabs his fingers into my hair and tugs hard enough that I gasp at the spike of pain. Owen shoves his tongue between my parted lips and the invasion goes straight to my cock.

He fucks my mouth with his tongue, angling me exactly how he wants me with sharp tugs on my hair. He's attacking me, devouring me, and my head spins from the onslaught.

Fuck, I love it when he gets like this. Aggressive. Controlling. Taking exactly what he wants and bossing me around while he's at it. I never used to be submissive in bed, and Owen's habit of power-tripping always drives me up the fucking wall. But there's just something about that combo when he's got his tongue down my throat that triggers every single pleasure switch in my brain.

I'm helpless in the face of his demands. I'm defenseless, powerless, weak.

"Fuck," Owen murmurs against my lips when he finally comes up for air. "The things you do to me."

That *I* do to *him*? Jesus. If it's even a fraction of what he does to me, then we're both doomed.

I whimper as my body hums with the need to fuck. My cock strains painfully against the zipper of my jeans. My balls ache and my skin tingles and I dig my fingers forcefully into Owen's hips to keep myself from throwing him onto the ground and fucking him into it.

A shiver rushes through me.

Owen leans back enough to scowl down at me. "Are you cold?" He doesn't wait for me to answer before climbing off my lap and dragging me to my feet. He grabs the blanket and wraps it around me. "Why didn't you tell me you were cold?"

He shuffles me toward the sliding glass doors that take

us straight into the basement. I roll my eyes at how over-bearing he is, but I don't say anything. This is his way of showing he cares. This is his way of saying he loves me.

Owen manhandles me into the media room and deposits me on our makeshift bed. I grab his wrist to pull him down next to me before he can dart off again.

"Come here." I draw him close, turning so I'm facing him. With his face bracketed between my hands, I stare into his eyes. "Owen."

He cocks one eyebrow. "Yes?"

Then, with my whole chest, with all the feelings springing from the deepest parts of my soul, I say those three little words to him again. "I love you."

Owen blinks, his eyes growing wide and a little watery. His breath hitches and his Adam's apple bobs as he swallows.

"Now you say it back to me. I love you. You can do it. I believe in you."

His brow furrows but his bottom lip quivers. "Fuck you," he murmurs with way more affection than the actual words let on.

"Close! You got one of the three! Let's try again! I. Love. You." I give his cheeks a squeeze for encouragement.

He growls, low and rumbly, a split second before he launches himself at me. I tumble backward and Owen scrambles on top of me. He slips his hands into mine, fingers intertwined, and pulls them up above my head, pinning my arms to the bed.

"I love you, you fucker. Is that what you want to hear? I fucking love you and it's driving me fucking crazy."

He peppers frantic kisses and not-so-gentle love bites all over my face and neck and shoulders. I tilt my head away to give him better access and he latches onto my collarbone. When he licks along its length, it feels like he's licking my cock.

"I love you beyond reason, beyond understanding. I love you when it makes no goddamn sense."

He kisses me, hungrily and desperately, then teasing and playful. My cock strains against the front of my jeans and Owen rotates his ass on top of my groin.

I groan as arousal ripples through me, turbocharged by the love and affection I have for this man. I tug on my hands. I want to touch him. I want to fill my palms with his ass. I want to feel the smooth heat of his skin. But Owen's grip doesn't budge, not even an inch.

I whimper into his mouth, begging, pleading. My hips come off the bed, unable to stay still. Owen growls and drags his cheek against mine. The rough scrape of his beard has my cock pulsing and my body twitching. My vision blurs and my ears ring. A strangled sound escapes my throat.

"Owen," I gasp.

He lifts his head and glares into my eyes. With a squeeze of my hands, he says, "Don't fucking move."

I jerk as his order sends a spike of pleasure through me. My stomach clenches at the pressure building in my groin. Fuck, I need him. I need him so goddamn much it rocks me to the core. How is it possible to want someone so much, to feel like my whole life is wrapped up in him? Like I'll die if he doesn't touch me, doesn't kiss me. Like I can't breathe unless he's looking at me like he hates me and loves me at the same time.

Owen's glare doesn't waver as he cautiously removes his hands. The second mine are free, I flip them around to grip the sheets under me. The grunt of approval he makes sends my heart soaring and a helpless whimper escapes me in response.

He grabs the hem of my shirt and rucks it up to reveal my stomach and chest. But then he doesn't do anything. He just sits his ass on my cock, hands pinning me by the shoulders, and stares at me.

Seconds tick by. Fucking minutes. And still, he just stares like he's trying to memorize every inch of my body.

"Owen, please," I sob. I can't take it anymore. I need him to do something—anything!

Owen's gaze flicks up to mine and he holds it as he leans down. He licks my left nipple, bathing it with his tongue. Then he blows a stream of air right over it, making it pebble so hard it fucking hurts.

"Fuck." I slam my head back and yank on the fabric in my hands.

He does the same with my right nipple and when the cold air hits my wet skin, I nearly buck Owen all the way off. He slams his ass back down, the impact on my jeans-covered cock both painful and delicious. He's killing me. I'm literally going to die and it's going to be Owen's fault.

He draws patterns across my chest with his tongue before sealing his lips around the dip on my sternum. When he sucks, it feels like he's siphoning my soul out of me and drinking it down so I can become a part of him.

Yes. Yes. I want that. All of it. I want to merge with Owen until I don't know where I end and he begins. I want to fuse with him until we become one person. I want to lose myself in him until I don't exist anymore and it's just Owen, Owen, Owen.

Owen charts a path down my stomach, sucking

hickeys into my skin until I'm all pockmarked. He gets to my jeans and makes quick work of the buttons and zipper. When he curls his fingers under the waistband of my underwear, I lift my hips so he can tug all of it down at once.

My cock slaps against my stomach. Hard. Aching. Leaking. The head is so engorged it's red and angry. The veins along the length are so full they look like they might burst.

"This massive fucking cock," he mutters as he gives me long, slow licks along the underside. He trails his lips up and down, concentrating on that super-sensitive spot right under the head before meandering back toward the base. He fucking tortures me. "God, I love this fucking thing."

I'm leaking so much pre-cum it pools on my stomach, in my belly button, runs down my sides. Owen swipes his fingers through it, covering them in the sticky fluid, then shoves them into my mouth.

The taste of my own pre-cum bursts on my tongue, and at the same time, Owen dives down on my cock, swallowing me whole. My cry is muffled by Owen's fingers and I have to concentrate on sucking them so I don't immediately explode down Owen's throat.

That feels so good. So goddamn good. Hot. Tight. His tongue wiggling against the underside. His throat contracting around my sensitive head. His free hand cradles my balls, squeezing just hard enough to create that heady mix of pleasure and pain.

I'm gonna come. I'm gonna come. I'm gonna come. But just as I'm about to dive head-first into the world's best orgasm, Owen abandons me.

I convulse, trapped in this strange place between

coming and not coming. The pressure in my groin is beyond intense. My lungs seize and I can't breathe. But there's no accompanying wash of pleasure, no release, no ecstasy. Like all the side effects of a hard workout with none of the high that's supposed to come with it.

Motherfucker. Holy fucking Christ on a stick. How is this even possible? To like, come, but not come. I hate it. It's the worst feeling in the world. I want Owen to do it again.

"I want to sit on this fucking thing." Owen's voice filters in past the ringing in my ears, actually sounding disappointed and sad.

I grunt, trying to speak, but my tongue doesn't work anymore. I grunt again and blink to clear the haziness in my vision. "D-duffel."

Owen glances over at my bag sitting on the floor. "Your bag?"

"L-lube."

His eyebrows shoot up. "You brought lube to a family weekend at my parents' house?"

I clear my throat. "Not on purpose. There's always a stash in there. I grab them from the giant fishbowls in the locker room at Mars."

Owen stares at me in disbelief. "Your workplace has giant fishbowls filled with lube?"

"Yeah. Condoms too. We take safe sex very seriously. What's wrong with that?"

Owen rolls his eyes as he scrambles off the bed to dig through my duffel. "Your work is weird."

"*Your* work is weird," I shoot back.

Owen turns back to the bed, tossing the packet of lube next to me, but then he stops and stares at the condom still in his hand. He doesn't say anything, but I can read the look in his eyes.

He doesn't want to use it.

The realization slams into me and I almost come just from the thought.

"I got tested last week," I say softly, the words tumbling out in a rush. "Beau and Gavin make us do it every six months. Everything came back negative. And I'm on PrEP."

I hold my breath, my whole body taut, waiting for his response.

Owen's head snaps up and his gaze burrows into me. His chest rises and falls. His jaw works back and forth. "I'm not. And I haven't been tested in a while. I keep meaning to, especially after we…" He waves his hand vaguely in my direction and clears his throat. "But things have been so busy with work, I haven't gotten around to it," he says with a note of dejection.

Every cell in my body rejects his reply. "But you haven't fucked anyone in a while either, right?"

His lips flatten. "No."

"And you always use condoms when you do."

"Yes."

"Then we have nothing to worry about." Not that I would have worried either way. I can't imagine anyone being more careful than Owen. And after everything we've been through, I trust him. With my body, with my heart, with my soul.

I sit up and grab the collar of my shirt to pull it over my head. I toss it to the floor. My jeans and underwear, socks and shoes follow. With the lube in hand, I scoot backward until I'm in the middle of the bed.

Owen's still standing in the same spot, unmoving. His lips are parted and he's watching my every movement like a hawk.

I lay back, pillowing my head in one arm and grabbing hold of my cock with my other hand. With a smirk, I say, "Come on, asshole, what are you waiting for?"

OWEN

I'm paralyzed by how much I want what Everest is offering. That cock. Filling me up. His cum. Painting my insides. Yes. Yes. *Yes.*

Everest is sprawled out in the nest of blankets and pillows, every muscle on display. Wide shoulders, defined biceps, washboard abs. A tantalizing V at his hips that I like running my tongue along. His thighs are impossibly thick. A dusting of blond hair covers his shins.

He strokes himself lazily from the base to the very tip of his long, thick cock. When he squeezes the head, pre-cum leaks out of the slit. He swipes it up with his thumb, brings it to his lips, and sucks it into his mouth.

His lips purse, pillowy and slightly pink. When he pulls his hand away, his tongue slips out, lewd and erotic, swiping across the bottom lip, leaving it glistening.

Jesus Christ, no wonder I hated him so much before. He is sex personified and he knows exactly how to flaunt it, how to use it to manipulate me, to hook me and reel me in.

My clothes go flying, landing on the floor in heaps. At the back of my mind, a voice reminds me that they'll end up wrinkled if I leave them like that, but I can't be bothered to fold them properly at the moment. I need that cock inside me. Now.

I reach for the packet of lube, but Everest holds it out of my reach. He takes my wrist and tugs me forward. I land on top of him, naked chest to naked chest, naked stomach to naked stomach, hard cock against hard cock. He hooks his leg around the back of my knees, trapping me in place.

"Let me," he murmurs, his breath feathering across my ear.

I shudder.

In the weeks we've been having regular sex, I usually prep myself. It's faster, more efficient, less cumbersome. The thought of letting Everest do it instead—of letting him set the pace and take control—it's... My heart pounds in my chest as it struggles with the part of my brain that resists. I don't want to, and yet I yearn for it so desperately it feels like I might die without it.

God. Why does Everest always have this effect on me? How does he always turn me so thoroughly inside out?

"Come on, let me in," Everest whispers again. The earnestness in his voice breaks down the last of my defenses.

Doesn't he know he's already taken up residence inside me? That I'm already his? Every inch of me, every cell, every molecule, every thought, every breath. I have been Everest's, for longer than I'm willing to admit, and I can't fight it any longer.

I nod—just a tiny movement of my chin—and Everest flips us over. He slots himself between my legs, sliding his leaking cock against my balls, against my taint.

"Don't move." His eyes sparkle as he repeats my words back to me.

I scowl at him—loving and hating how our positions have reversed—and bury my fingers into the sheets.

He smirks and lowers his head.

This might be the best and worst thing that has ever happened to me. Everest scrapes his teeth down my front, teases my nipples with his tongue, plants kiss after kiss across my chest and stomach. When he gets down to my cock, he skips it altogether. Instead, he lifts my legs into the air and stuffs a pillow under my ass.

I'm exposed. Open. Laid bare before this man. He devours me with his eyes, the browns darkening to black. His fingers grip the backs of my thighs hard enough that I'll probably have bruises tomorrow, and suddenly I'm craving his marks on my body. I want the evidence of his desire for me. I want to see them and remember this moment, the look of raw hunger on his face, the all-consuming heat in his eyes.

I'm not prepared when Everest dives down, stuffing his face between my ass cheeks. I let out a high-pitched whine as his tongue swipes circles around my hole, as he laps at me before pushing inside. I can't help it. It's filthy. Obscene. Vulgar. And I never want him to stop.

My hand leaves the bed and latches onto the back of Everest's head, keeping him in place, pushing him deeper. His tongue is sure and confident as it works its way steadily into my body. He fucks me with his tongue, lips sealed around my hole.

My cock leaks an entire lake onto my stomach. My legs shake almost violently, still stuck in the air.

Without stopping or even slowing, Everest reaches up, fingers making contact with my lips, just like I did with him. I don't hesitate to open my mouth and suck his fingers inside. I lick them, swirling my tongue around the digits until they are wet and dripping with my spit.

Then Everest brings those same fingers to my hole and pushes one into me. I'm so relaxed from Everest's tongue-fucking that his finger sinks in with no resistance at all, right down to the knuckle. He adds another and that too slides easily inside.

He works his fingers in and out, scissoring them, curling them. His tongue licks everywhere, alternating with his fingers to reduce me into a puddle of pleasure. When he adds a third, I hardly even feel the stretch. Instead, it gives me a pleasant fullness that's not nearly enough. I want more. I need more. I need his cock, filling me up, completing me.

I tug on his hair, but Everest doesn't budge. His fingers don't stop. His tongue doesn't stop. He works my ass like he wants to get his whole fucking hand in there, like he wants to crawl right the fuck inside.

Jesus. It's too much and not enough at the same time. I can't take it anymore and I don't ever want him to stop. I tug on his hair again. He grunts.

I tug harder and he shoves his fingers forcefully into me. His knuckles ram against the outside of my rim and my whole body convolves at the surge in pleasure. He curls his fingers and rubs forcefully on my prostate. White-hot fire rips through me and I slap a hand over my mouth to muffle my shout.

He's enjoying this, the fucker. He's having the time of his life watching me come apart at the seams. I swear I can feel him smiling against my ass cheeks. The vibrations from his chuckles travel right up my ass, hitting me deep in the gut.

"Evvv…" His name comes out as a sob. I can't help it. My senses are overwhelmed with the flood of sensations, and I'm little more than a pile of bones and nerve endings.

Everest lifts his head. The bottom half of his face is wet. His lips are red and shiny. His hair is a mess and his pupils are blown so wide there's only a ring of black. He looks fucking gorgeous.

I grab the back of his neck, yanking him toward me as I sit up, and smash my lips against his. He grunts in surprise, but still manages to catch himself on an elbow when I pull him on top of me.

"Fuck me, Ev," I murmur against his lips. "I need you to fucking fuck me."

But he doesn't. He holds himself above me, gazing down with more love and affection than anyone has ever looked at me with. It steals my breath away. It makes my heart somersault in my chest. It makes me feel strong and mighty, but also small and undeserving.

I've said a lot of nasty things to Everest over the years. I've treated him worse than I've ever treated anyone else. I've been truly, embarrassingly horrid to him, and yet, he still finds it in his heart to look at me like that. Like I'm the best man he's ever met. Like I hung the moon.

Everest swipes his thumb over my temple, catching the tear that escaped the corner of my eye. I squeeze my eyes shut and Everest brushes his lips against my eyelids.

"Shh, I've got you," he says softly, the same way he

comforts Ivy when she's upset. "It's all good. Everything's gonna be okay."

He kisses me then. Not hurried and frantic like before, but rather slow, almost lazily, like we have all the time in the world, like we have the rest of our lives.

"Please," I breathe. "I need you." I open my eyes to gaze up at him, but his face is a blur from the close proximity and the lingering tears. The words bubble up, completely unprompted. They fill me up to brimming and I have no choice but to release them into the open. "I love you."

A smile splits across Everest's face, so bright and full of joy, completely unfettered and unreserved. I can't help but smile too, at how silly and goofy Everest can be, at how much he's grown over the past several months, how much he's changed me at the same time.

I'm a better man because of him. A better partner. A better parent.

"I love you too, O. So fucking much."

We kiss, savoring the taste of each other, enjoying the shape of each other's mouths. The blunt tip of Everest's naked cock touches my hole. And when he pushes forward, I bear down. I take him inside me, slow and steady, inch by inch. He's unrelenting. Unyielding. Forcing me open to accommodate his length and his girth. Remaking me so I'm a mold around him.

When he bottoms out, he drops his forehead to mine. We're both breathing hard. Both shaking with tightly wound pleasure. I wrap my legs around his waist and my arms around his shoulders. He slides his hands behind my back.

We're locked together. As close as any two people can

be. My cock is trapped between our stomachs. We breathe the air from each other's lungs.

We don't fuck. It can't be called fucking when it's this intense, this visceral. I don't even know if this is making love. This is two souls, stripped of every protective layer, vulnerable and delicate, coming together and merging into one. We rock together. Tangle our tongues together. Cling to each other like we're each other's life preservers in this storm called life.

No matter how hard the winds buffet us, no matter how high the waves toss us, we still have each other and we'll save each other. Every single time. I know this with a certainty that surpasses all understanding. There's no reason to it, no logic. But I know it's true, with every fiber of my being, in the deepest parts of my soul.

Everest is so perfect inside me, hitting me at all the right angles, stretching me right to the limit. His body slots against mine like we were made for each other. His mouth is heaven and he kisses me like the devil himself.

The friction on my cock is just enough to keep me on edge, but not enough to push me over. The longer we're locked together like this, the more the pleasure builds. And builds. And builds. Until I can't contain it any longer.

My orgasm bubbles up gradually, eventually spilling over. The waves swell slowly, but they are no less powerful than if we were fucking like machines. They crest, break over me, and drag me to the bottom of the ocean floor. I can't breathe. I can't move. I'm caught in the force of an orgasm so strong I'm sure I'm going to die.

"Fuck, O." Everest sinks his teeth into my shoulder as his body goes taut. Heat fills my passage as Everest comes inside me. His cum. In my body. Shooting deep.

The realization unleashes another set of waves. My balls contract almost painfully. My cock pulses between our stomachs. My ass clamps down hard, trying to milk every drop of Everest's cum.

"I love you. I love you so much. So much. All of you. Everything. I hate it. I can't help it. I don't wanna fight anymore. I love you. I need you. Every day. All the time. I—"

"Shh." Everest's lips cover mine and only then do I realize that I'm the one who's been babbling incoherently.

A sob escapes me. It's too much. It's not enough. I never wanted to fall in love with Everest. I never wanted to bare my soul to him and have him embrace me whole-heartedly. I never wanted to be this vulnerable, this raw, this exposed. But now that I'm here, now that I've come this far, I don't want to go back. I want more. More of this. More of him. More of us.

EVEREST

"Again! Again!" Ivy doggie paddles toward me, eyes bright and smiling a mile wide.

The grandparents have taken off to a country club for the afternoon—Alyssa and Mom for facials and Mark and Dad for a round of golf—which leaves me and Ivy and Owen in his parents' house by ourselves. Ivy couldn't get into the pool fast enough.

I grab her around the waist and hoist her up. "Ready?"

"Ready!"

"One! Two! Three!" I toss her into the air and she lands in the water a few feet away with a giant splash.

She comes up laughing with her whole body, the sound ringing through the air. Up on the deck, Owen's stretched out on a lounge chair in the shade. He's swapped out his typical slacks for a pair of slim-fitting shorts that hit a couple inches above the knee and he's gone full casual by leaving his button-up shirt untucked. He's even rolled up the sleeves of the shirt, revealing the dark hairs that cover his forearms.

With a pair of aviator sunglasses covering his eyes and his iPad in hand, he looks like he's ignoring us, like he's engrossed in whatever journal thing he's reading. But I know better. I notice the tiny shift of his chin, the minute twitch of his brows, the small smile that graces his lips. He's watching us, alright. He's definitely watching us.

My heart does a little flutter in my chest and I dive under the water to scoop Ivy up from below. She squeals as I launch her into the air again.

I've done a lot of really cool things in my life. I've gone to some really awesome places and met the most amazing people. But I've never—*never*—felt anything close to this before.

It's like I'm high on happiness. Vibrating out of my skin with joy. The sky looks bluer than I've ever seen it. The grass smells fresher too. I feel like I could move a freaking mountain. I feel like I could run an Iron Man.

Is this what everyone feels when they're in love? If it is, I don't know why I don't see more dopey people walking around. The world is suddenly more vibrant and alive. Anything—everything—seems not only possible, but actually easy. Shit, maybe I should've tried this love thing years ago.

"Again, Uncle Ev!" Ivy swims back to me and I fake a groan.

"Again?! But I'm tired!" I lean back, spreading out like a starfish to float on the water.

"Please! Please, please, please!" Ivy tries to climb on top of me like I'm an inflatable pool float and I immediately start sinking. With a squawk, I grab ahold of her and right myself again.

On the deck, Owen's act slips a bit. His iPad is lying flat on his lap and there's a wrinkle in his forehead like he's worried about us drowning.

I hug Ivy close to me and pretend to whisper into her ear, but I pitch my voice just loud enough for it to carry to Owen. "Hey, Ivy-bear, you know what? I bet Uncle Owen could throw you *super* far!"

Owen's head tilts just a little bit, like he's rolling his eyes.

"Can he?" Ivy shrieks, pushing off me with her feet like I'm the pool wall and swimming in Owen's direction. "Uncle O! Can you throw me? Pleeeaaase?!" She kneels on the steps at the shallow end and points her deadly pout and puppy eyes at him.

I add my own pouty puppy dog eyes to see if it'll help Ivy's cause. Hell, who am I kidding? I've got completely selfish motives. I want Owen half-naked and in the water with me. I want to see his hair wet and slicked back, sun reflecting off his glistening skin.

Owen's lips flatten into a firm line, but not because he's angry—he's trying to fight off a smile.

"Pleeeaaase?" Ivy pleads again, splashing the water with her hands.

"Yeah, pleeeaaase?"

Owen crosses his arms over his chest, pulling the fabric of his shirt taut across his shoulders. Above his sunglasses, his brow furrows.

"Come swim with us, Uncle O!" Ivy slaps the water to emphasize her point.

"I'm not dressed for the pool," Owen says in his signature dry tone while shaking his head. But there's something in his voice, in the way he's holding himself, that's just begging to be dragged kicking and screaming into the water.

I bend down to speak quietly into Ivy's ear, but I can still feel the weight of Owen's gaze trained on me. It's laser-focused, unwavering, and goosebumps break out across my arms.

"You know what, Ives? I don't think Uncle O is going to come swim with us unless we make him."

Ivy blinks, her long, blond lashes all clumped together with water droplets. "How do we make him?"

"Oh, I don't know. Maybe by getting him wet."

Her eyes grow huge. "Like splash him?"

I wince a little. Owen would *not* appreciate getting splashed. But perhaps something a bit cuter?

"That could work. Or—"

"What are you guys talking about?" Owen's voice cuts in, but I don't stop.

"Or you can go give him a big, wet hug! What do you think?"

Ivy giggles in delight, hands coming up to hide her face from Owen. "Yeah, I can do that!"

Owen sits up straighter and sets his tablet aside, suspicion and mistrust written all across his face. "Everest." He spreads the warning on nice and thick.

We ignore him. Instead, I help Ivy out of the pool.

Owen immediately figures out what the deal is and jumps to his feet. Backing away, he holds out his hands to stave her off, but our Ivy is a force of nature. "Ivy! No! Don't!"

Screaming at the top of her lungs, Ivy launches herself

at Owen, wrapping her little, wet body around him. "Come swim with us, Uncle O!"

Ivy's short, so she only manages to soak Owen's shorts, but the expression on his face is still priceless. Shock and disbelief combined with the promise of murder aimed directly at me. *I hate you,* he mouths silently over Ivy's head.

I burst out laughing and throw myself backward in the water. Oh god, this is great. I love annoying Owen almost as much as I love loving him. It's what makes us work so well. We piss each other off, then we make it up to each other with some fucking hot sex. I never would've thought that a relationship could be like this—I never realized a relationship could be so serious and yet so fun.

"Come swim! Come swim!" Ivy takes Owen's hand and tries to drag him toward the water.

Owen plants his feet, but his shoulders slump in resignation. "Okay, okay, I'll come swimming with you, but I need to go change first. I can't jump in the water wearing regular clothes."

Ivy drops his hand and heaves a sigh. "Fine, but hurry up!"

Owen shoots me a look that says I'll be in trouble later and I suddenly can't wait to see what kind of punishment Owen will dream up for me.

Ivy does a cannonball into the water and I chase her around the pool for a few minutes until Owen comes out again.

"Uncle O!" she yells and I turn to glance toward the house.

Time slows. The world around me vanishes, leaving only Owen striding toward me in slow motion.

He's still wearing his aviators, with a big towel tossed over one shoulder. His swim trunks aren't the baggy surfer shorts I wear. They're fitted, hugging thick thighs and rounded ass cheeks. They sit low enough to reveal his hip bones and a dark trail of hair cuts down the center of his flat stomach to disappear beneath the waistband. His chest is covered in the same dark hair—hair that I've raked my fingers through, that I've licked and swirled with my tongue.

He looks like a supermodel stepping off the pages of a magazine. He looks like a movie star with the sun making his skin glow. He looks… like the man of my dreams.

Owen tosses his towel onto the lounge chair, followed by his sunglasses before approaching the pool. He crouches, then sits, his muscles bunching and bulging as he moves. When his feet hit the water, he hisses at the temperature, lifting himself up by his hands and drawing his legs toward his chest.

For a nerd who apparently doesn't work out, Owen's got an incredible body. And seeing it in the brightness of daylight, not hidden behind carefully tailored clothes or buried under the covers… god, I want to lick every single inch of him.

"Come in, Uncle O!" Ivy calls to him, waving him in.

Owen scrunches up his face. "It's cold."

I slip under the water and swim in his direction. His feet are still hovering in mid-air when I reach up and grab his ankle. I yank, he comes tumbling into the pool.

Ivy squeals and claps her hands, laughing at us.

When Owen surfaces, he shakes his head from side to side. Time slows again. Water droplets fly, catching the late morning sun and creating a glittering halo around his head.

My breath catches. My heart lurches in my chest like it's trying to propel me toward him.

He turns toward me, heat flashing in his eyes. My pulse skyrockets and a shiver of pleasure runs up my spine. He advances on me, gaze focused and determined, like a predator on the hunt for his prey. I push off the bottom of the pool, swimming backward as I scramble to get away.

"Where do you think you're going?" Owen growls. "Get back here."

"Come and get me." I taunt him, laughing out loud.

Okay, listen, I blame it on being high on love. Because, I'm supposed to be the athletic one, right? Like, I teach fitness classes and I know how to surf. So why the hell am I thrashing around like a drowning cat while Owen ducks under the surface and torpedoes toward me like a freaking otter?

He's on me in an instant, grabbing me from behind and putting all of his weight on my shoulders. I immediately sink, but when I try to spin around and grab him, he's gone.

I come up sputtering. "What the heck?!"

Owen's already out of arm's reach, grinning at me like this is the most fun he's ever had in his life. Ivy's propped herself up with a pool noodle under her arms and she kicks the water, sending it splashing into the air. She laughs, the sound high and bright.

Owen tugs on one end of her noodle, pulling her in front of him so he can hide behind her. "Come and get me!" Owen calls to me, throwing my own words back in my face. "Ivy's going to protect me, aren't you?"

"No!" Ivy squeals in delight as I swim toward them.

I try to go around her, but Owen swings in the opposite direction, using the two ends of Ivy's pool noodle to keep her between us.

"Stop using our niece as a human shield!" I shout, trailing after them as Owen leads us around the pool.

Ivy reaches for me with both hands outstretched, laughing. "Uncle Ev!"

"Hang on, Ivy-poo! I'll save you!" I suck in a deep breath and dive. Swimming under Ivy, spot Owen's legs eggbeatering under the water. I tackle them, dragging him down with me.

We wrestle. Sun-warmed skin slides together. Greedy hands grab at waists, hips, thighs, shoulders. Hair floating out into underwater halos, then plastering themselves to our faces when we surface for air. We play like teenagers, dunking each other and tickling each other, grappling until we're both exhausted and out of breath.

"Time out! Time out!" I eventually cry for mercy when it feels like I'm actually going to drown.

Owen smirks at me. "Giving up already?"

"Oh, screw you. So freaking competitive." I turn onto my back, closing my eyes against the bright light of the sun.

"*I'm* the competitive one?" Owen scoffs.

A second later his hand slips into my own. I open one eye to peek at him. He's also on his back, eyes closed, chest rising and falling, half in and half out of the water.

"Me too! Me too!" Ivy abandons her noodle and pushes her way between us.

I give Owen's hand a squeeze and we release each other to let Ivy in. She flips onto her back too and sighs with happiness.

I know how she feels.

I close my eyes, relaxing in the water. The sun is orange behind my eyelids. Water laps against the sides of the pool. Ivy's small hand is inside mine. Everything feels so light, so bubbly, and yet so grounded and solid at the same time.

For so much of my life, having fun was the one rule I lived by. I chased fun from city to city, immersing myself in whatever felt good, whatever gave me that instant high. And when things got boring or tedious or just too real, I left. There's a world of enjoyment out there, why stay in one place and put myself through something difficult and dull when I could be out there instead?

This life I've found myself in for the past few months, the little family Owen and I have created for ourselves, it's so damn domestic. It's traditional and old school and everything I once vowed I would never do.

And yet, here I am.

And I've never been happier in my whole life.

I right myself in the water and tug Ivy to me. She comes without resistance, wrapping her arms around my neck and her legs around my waist. Owen comes too, drifting in close enough to sandwich Ivy between us.

Owen pushes stray strands of Ivy's hair out of her face. His touch is gentle, tender, and Ivy beams up at him.

I catch Owen's gaze, smiling, and he smiles back at me. My heart swells with love and joy and a sense of rightness I didn't know was possible to feel. This is good. This is mine. I don't want to be anywhere else or with anyone else.

"When are you getting married?"

Both Owen and I startle at Ivy's question. Owen recovers first. "Why would we get married, Ivy?"

"Because you're boyfriends. Boyfriends get married."

"Um, well, that's…" I sputter, only realizing now that we didn't actually sit Ivy down to tell her about us. But apparently, we didn't need to.

"Boyfriends don't always have to get married," Owen explains. "I mean, they can. When two people love each other, they can get married, but they don't have to."

Ivy tilts her head as she thinks. "Do you love Uncle Ev?" she asks Owen.

Owen's cheeks flush bright red, and omg, it's adorable. He clears his throat and mumbles something that sounds like, "I do."

"And do you love Uncle O?" Ivy asks me, like she's some sort of officiant in our impromptu mid-pool ceremony.

"Yeah, Ives, I do."

She nods like a decision's been made. "Good. I approve."

Owen and I are silent for a beat before we both burst out laughing. Of course Ivy would dole out her approval like some miniature tyrant. I wouldn't want her any other way.

Life doesn't get much better than this.

OWEN

An afternoon in the pool leaves us shriveled up and chilly. We get Ivy inside, and after a quick shower to warm up, we tuck her into bed for a short nap.

I've got the goofiest grin on my face the whole time. It matches the one Everest is sporting.

A part of me is convinced this whole thing is a dream, a fantasy, and that I'll wake up at any moment because it's too good to be true.

It's the same feeling I get before I step into the operating room, I realize. The spike of nervousness brought on by pressure and the unknown. Do I actually know what I'm doing? What if I make a mistake and lose a life?

But once I've got a scalpel in my hand and bright lights shining down from above, I know exactly what to do. I fall back onto my training, my experience, and more often than not, everything goes smoothly.

I had nothing to be worried about. But that doesn't mean I won't worry all the same.

The second Ivy slips into sleep, I grab Everest's hand.

He gives me an amused look as I drag him downstairs to the bathroom in the basement.

"Not that I'm complaining, but what's happening right now?" Everest asks with a laugh when I crank the water all the way hot and then reach for the drawstring of his swim trunks.

"What does it look like?" I ask, pushing his trunks down and dropping to my knees at the same time.

Everest gasps and sputters when I drag my tongue along the dip that runs from above his hip down to his groin. His hand flies to the back of my head and the other slaps against the wall to steady himself. I smile as I mouth his quickly hardening cock.

"Fuck, O, oh god."

I take his dick between my lips, suckling gently as it grows on my tongue, stretching my jaw and nudging at the back of my throat. My eyes flutter shut as I savor the feeling of him in my mouth, the musky scent, the slightly chemical taste of chlorine on his skin, the way he blocks off my airway, and how I have to fight back my gag reflex.

My head is spinning and my lungs are burning when I pull back. A strand of spit spans from my lips to the tip of his now engorged cock. I take it in my hand, wrapping my fingers around the velvet-clad steel, and give him a couple good, tight strokes.

Then I sit back to admire my handiwork. Everest's body is taut, every muscle on display. His eyes are half-lidded and he's breathing heavily through his mouth. Yes, good, just the way I like him. Hard and desperate and begging.

Pushing to my feet, I undo my own swim trunks and

drop them to the floor. Then I take Everest by his cock and lead him into the shower.

He sighs when I move him under the water. It sluices down his impeccable body like a waterfall and he tilts his head back to submerge it under the spray.

I stand there, mouth going dry and dick growing plump as I watch him. This isn't new to me. I've seen him naked dozens of times. I've touched and licked every inch and yet, this view never fails to take my breath away. He is the epitome of male beauty—strong and muscular with not an ounce of body fat. And those warm brown eyes that are always sparkling and dancing. The riot of curls that can only be tamed by a baseball cap.

It used to annoy the hell out of me that he was so damn handsome, that I couldn't help but be attracted to him. But things are different now. Now, he's mine, his body is mine, and I'm going to wring as much pleasure out of it as I possibly can.

Everest touches himself, running his hands across his chest, pinching his nipples, then down his stomach to wrap around his cock. I follow the movement closely, my own fingers twitching with the need to trace that exact path.

He strokes himself—once, twice—forming a tight ring with his fingers and squeezing from base to tip. A pearl of pre-cum forms at the slit before getting washed away. My knees go a little weak at the sight.

I grab his wrists and pull his hands away from his body. When Everest cocks a questioning eyebrow, my words come out in a growl. "No touching. This is mine."

I run my hand down his front and take his cock into

my hand. "You're mine. Your body is mine. Say it. Say you're mine."

Everest shudders and his cock jumps in my palm. "I—I'm yours. My b-body is y-yours."

I squeeze his cock just forcefully enough for him to rise onto his toes with a high-pitched cry. Then I lean in, lips ghosting over his ear. "Good boy."

He whimpers, trembling so much he almost collapses to the floor. Carefully, I direct him to the wall so he's leaning back on it with his shoulders. Then I reach for the bottle of body wash and pump out a generous amount onto my palm.

Working up a lather, I set my hands on Everest's body, staking my claim on him with every inch I touch, every bump and dip I run my fingers over. This all belongs to me —this beautiful man who I took for granted for so long, this wonderful man who I didn't know how to appreciate.

I was too stuck in my own ways, too preoccupied with being right, too proud to really see Everest for who he is. Kind. Gentle. Fun. A goofball who says and does the dumbest things sometimes. A sensitive soul.

I drag in a stuttering breath, humbled at this gift he's given to me. The gift of himself, of this life, of this opportunity to be truly, deeply happy.

I wash Everest, touching him with a sense of reverence I've never felt before. His hands, threading my fingers in between his. His armpits, lifting each arm to ensure I don't miss a single spot. His legs, digging my fingers into his toughened quads, working my way down to his feet and toes.

Then I tap his hip, turn him around, and work my way back up. I push my thumbs into his calves and Everest groans, his forehead against the tiled wall. I massage his hamstrings, then fill my palms with his muscular ass.

He pushes his hips back as I knead his glutes, running my thumbs down into his crease and over his hole. I pull his ass cheeks apart and his hole twitches, winking at me. Leaning in, I plant a kiss right over the ring of muscle and a high-pitched whine escapes Everest. I sink my teeth into the fleshy part of his ass cheek and Everest sobs.

"Owen, please."

Aw, my poor baby, suffering for me.

I turn him around once more and I'm greeted by his long, thick cock, jutting out in front of him. It's straining toward me, like it can't wait to get inside my mouth.

I glance up past his washboard stomach, past his rounded pecs. His jaw is slack, and his pupils are blown wide. His fingers are spread, flexing against the wall like he's trying to grip it. I lock eyes with him, open my mouth, slide out my tongue, and lean forward.

Everest gasps when I place my tongue on the underside of his cock head. I let it sit there for a moment, enjoying the weight of his dick, and the salty, musky taste of it. I swirl my tongue around the smooth glans and rub my lips across them. I suck on just the tip, moaning when pre-cum pours into my mouth.

"Christ." Everest bangs his head on the wall, his eyes squeezed shut.

I let his cock fall out from between my lips. "Watch me." I want him to see this. See his cock disappear down my throat. Be fully alert and aware of everything I'm doing to him.

He whines before forcing his eyes open. His face is all

scrunched up like it physically pains him to keep watching.

I bring my lips to his cock again and slide down his length as far as I can go. Then I just hold him in my mouth, no swallowing, no bobbing up and down, no sucking. I warm his cock, suckling gently, like I'm a fucking baby with a pacifier.

"Fuck." His hands curl into fists. "Fuck, fuck, fuck," he mutters like it's a mantra that will keep him from exploding prematurely.

I chuckle with his cock still sitting in my mouth. Everest growls and bangs his head against the wall a little harder. "Please, please, Owen, please," he sobs. "I can't take it anymore. Please."

I pull back, letting his dick pop out. Everest lets out a sound of pure frustration and I rub my hands firmly up and down his thighs. He's cute when he's all worked up and needy like this. His chiseled body contracted and tense. Wet strands of hair plastered against his forehead and cheeks. He looks like he's on the brink of falling apart, but I'm the only one who can pull the trigger. The sense of power it gives me is a heady rush that's better than any drug-induced high.

With the thumb of one hand, I lift his cock out of the way and tilt my head down to lap at his balls. Everest's knees weaken and he slides down the wall an inch or two. A broken sob bounces off the shower's walls, a mumble of sounds that aren't fully formed enough to be words.

His balls are so full, heavy, and tender. The scent of them, dark and earthy, fills my senses, making my brain short-circuit. I nuzzle them, lick them, draw them into my mouth to suckle on softly. First one, then the other, then back and forth again. I let them sit on my face, on my cheeks, on my forehead, over my eyes. I worship Everest's balls, love them, obsess over them.

"Owen, Owen, Owen," Everest mutters, his head lolling back and forth. "Please. Please."

I kiss my way from the base of Everest's dick to the tip and then take him back into my mouth. When he hits the back of my throat, I swallow, not stopping until my nose is flush against his pelvis bone.

"Oh god, oh god, oh god."

No more teasing this time. No more slow and gentle. I want his cum filling my stomach. I want every last drop.

I suck like my life depends upon it, wriggling my tongue and swallowing around the head. I cradle Everest's balls in one hand, then inch my fingers backward to press against his taint. His hips buck forward, forcing his dick deeper down my throat. I grunt at the unexpected thrust and suddenly Everest is coming.

He bites his arm, muffling his scream. Cum shoots from his cock, flooding my mouth. My hand keeps working his cock, his balls, milking him for everything he's got, and I swallow as fast as I can, not wanting to waste a single drop.

"Stop. Stop, stop, please." Everest finally pushes at my shoulder as he grows too sensitive.

Reluctantly, I let him slip out from between my lips. Everest grabs my arms and hauls me to my feet. Spinning us around, he pins me against the wall and attacks my mouth. He shoves his tongue inside and licks like he's trying to find traces of his own cum.

I press myself to him. Hard muscles. Smooth, wet skin. Tingles skitter down my arms, up my back, and penetrate into the core of me. I rub myself on him, chasing the sensations that make my nerve endings spark.

My dick, hard and aching, slides against Everest's stomach. The friction goes straight to my balls and they pull up tight against my body. It won't take me long like this. Not with Everest's body covering mine, his tongue in my mouth, and his hands groping everything he can reach.

I latch onto his hips, keeping him still as I hump against him. He tightens his arms around me so that we're plastered together from knees to chest.

I'm close. So close. Right when I'm nearing the peak, I push Everest to his knees. He sinks down, tilting his head back and opening his mouth for me. I shove my cock between his lips and thrust a few times with my hands on the back of his head.

Seeing him kneeling in front of me, unresisting, letting me use him however I want, power and gratitude tumble through me in a humbling mix and suddenly I'm coming. I pull out just enough to spray my cum all over Everest's face, then I push the tip of my cock back into his mouth to feed him the last few spurts.

His eyes are closed. His lips are curled into a serene smile. His expression is blissful, peaceful. When he blinks his eyes open, the love shining from them steals my breath away.

I don't deserve this love or this happiness. I did everything in my power to avoid it, to push it away. Yet, it found its way to me, nevertheless. And now that I have it, I vow to do everything in my power to keep it, cherish it, and never let it go.

Laughter bubbles up from deep inside me, from a place

that used to feel dark and empty and alone. It sounds a little hysterical, a little unhinged. But I don't care. Because that cavern I used to carry around with me has been cracked wide open and Everest and Ivy have been steadily filling it up, one day at a time. I've never felt so full before, so satisfied and complete.

Everest leans his head on my thigh, smiling up at me. "What's so funny?"

I shake my head. "Nothing. Just…" I smooth the hair back from his face. "Just… I love you."

EVEREST

"Great job! You totally killed it today!" I stand next to the studio door and high-five each of the guys in my class as they leave. I'm bouncing on my toes, hyped up on the adrenaline and energy of the class.

Life's been good the past couple weeks since we got back from the Memorial Day weekend at Owen's parents' house. Like, unbelievably good. Like, better than I've ever experienced.

Mars opened up registration for our outdoor summer boot camp classes and they filled up in a couple days. Owen and I finished clearing out Eden and Jeremy's old room and we've unofficially moved in—unofficially because if I think about it too much, the idea of taking over my sister's old bedroom still kind of freaks me out. The school semester is drawing to a close and Ivy's birthday is coming up.

And… that's probably the only dark cloud in this whole situation—Ivy. I don't know what happened. It's like she got body-snatched somewhere between Westchester and Brooklyn. She started out the drive as a sweet kid—kind, well-mannered, and easy-going. But by the time we got home, she'd morphed into this irritable and short-tempered terror. She and Owen are back to arguing almost every day, and this time, I kind of have to side with Owen. Crazy, I know.

But seriously. She gets upset over *nothing*. We asked her what she wanted to watch for movie night the other day and she couldn't decide. When Owen picked something for her, she threw a temper tantrum. I took her grocery shopping last week, and when I said she couldn't buy the entire candy aisle, she had a meltdown in the middle of the store. We went on a family walk one evening, and she threw herself onto the grass, wailing and flailing for no apparent reason. Owen just about died of mortification when strangers started staring.

Both Mom and Alyssa say that this is normal, that kids around Ivy's age go through bursts of being difficult and shit, but then it goes away. It's like they're transitioning from being a *kid* kid, to like being an independent person who wants to do things their own way. I don't know. The whole thing sounds fucked up to me. I just want our old Ivy back.

When the last guy leaves the studio, I start tidying up, putting away my mic, grabbing my phone from the dock on the sound system. I've got an hour to kill before my next class, so I head to the staff break room for a snack.

Donnie and Christian are sitting at the table and nod hello as I grab a bottle of water and a granola bar and plop down on the couch.

I've just bitten into the granola bar when my phone

rings. It's Owen and my stomach sinks. He's at home with Ivy today and he doesn't usually call unless it's an emergency. I quickly swipe to answer.

"Hey, everything okay?"

"Uncle Ev!" Ivy's sob is so loud that I have to pull my phone away from my ear.

"Ivy? What's wrong? What happened?" I shoot to my feet and race for the door. Is Owen hurt? Is that why Ivy's calling me from his phone?

"I don't wanna go swimming!"

I stop in my tracks, halfway across the room. She doesn't want to go swimming? "What?"

"Uncle O's making me go swimming and I don't wanna!" Then thumps that sound like she's stomping her feet on the floor.

"Wha— Uh— I don't understand." Was Owen planning on taking her swimming today? But Ivy loves swimming. Is this another one of her completely irrational temper tantrums?

Ivy's beyond speaking now. All she can do is make crying sounds like she's a wounded animal. I cringe. I hate it when Ivy cries and a part of me wants to rush home and comfort her. But another part, slightly guilty and selfish, wants to hang up and let Owen deal with the chaos for today. I dealt with her yesterday when Owen had a shift at the animal hospital, now it's his turn.

I turn around and drop back onto the couch. Both Donnie and Christian are watching me with concerned expressions, but I just roll my eyes and shake my head.

"Ivy? Ivy-bear?" I try to cut in in between her hysterics. "Where's Uncle Owen? Is he there? Can I talk to him, please?"

She just wails even louder.

I drop my head back and stare up at the ceiling. "Iiivyyy... I can't help you if you don't talk to me. Remember what your therapist said, you have to use your words."

There's a snicker on the other side of the room and when I lift my head, I find Donnie and Christian trying desperately not to laugh. I give them the middle finger, but that just makes them laugh harder.

Ha. Ha. So funny. Neither of *them* has kids they have to raise. Of all the damn people at Mars, how the hell did *I* turn into the first and only parent of the group?

"Ivy?!" Owen's voice filters in, barely audible over Ivy's cries. "What are you— Is that my phone? Who are you talking to?"

There's a fumbling sound before Owen comes on. "Hello? Everest?"

"Yes, hi, what's going on?"

Owen sighs so heavily I can feel the weight of it through the phone line. "Hell if I know," he mutters. The sound of Ivy's crying fades as Owen walks away. "I told her we're signing her up for swimming lessons, like she wanted when we were at my parents' house. And then she just went berserk." There's a pause before Owen speaks again, more softly this time. "I don't know what to do, Ev."

The defeat in his voice breaks my heart. Owen always knows what to do. He prides himself in always having a game plan, always knowing the next steps. And even if he didn't, he would never admit that to anyone—least of all me.

But that was the old Owen and this is the new one. He

trusts me. He actually, really trusts me. It's… humbling. I don't think I've ever been anyone's confidant before. I mean, the guys tell me shit all the time, but not stuff that's like, serious.

"Do you want me to come home early?"

There's another pause as Owen considers the offer. "When are you done?"

The question hits me like a punch to the gut. Owen sounds so small, so vulnerable. His voice shakes a bit, like he's barely holding himself together.

"Technically, I have one more class. It ends at four, so probably four-forty-five? But I can try to find someone to cover for me? If you want me home now?"

Owen doesn't answer right away. The only sound coming across the line is his ragged breathing. I can hear him debating with himself—stay strong, push through, don't give in or accept that he doesn't always have to do everything himself, that asking for help isn't a sign of weakness.

I take pity on him and make an executive decision so he doesn't have to say what he wants out loud. "I'm coming home. I—"

My gaze flicks to Donnie, still sitting at the table. He doesn't even wait for me to ask the question, just nods and silently mouths "No problem."

I jump to my feet and dash toward the staff locker room. "Donnie's going take my class. I'm leaving now."

"No, no, you don't have to do that. It's only a couple more hours. I'll be fine." Owen throws his objections at me, but I can hear the mix of guilt and relief seeping into his words. He feels bad for being an inconvenience, but he's grateful at the same time. That's my Owen—so precious and needy, but too damn proud to admit it.

"Too late. It's already done. Donnie's telling Beau right now."

"Ev…" The way Owen trails off, it's not clear whether he's scolding or whining. It's probably a bit of both.

"Just hang tight. I'll be there as fast as I can." I throw open my locker and start throwing things into my duffel.

Owen sucks in a deep, shaky breath. "Okay, thanks."

"Of course, babe. Love you."

Owen mumbles something that sounds sort of like a "love you too" and then hangs up.

Beau is at the front desk with Sawyer when I run out. "Everything okay? Donnie told me he's taking your class."

"Yeah, I think so? Ivy's just being a pain in the ass and Owen needs backup."

Sawyer shakes his head. "This is why we're never having kids. Preston would never know what to do with them."

"No, he'd just hire an expensive nanny," Beau responds.

Sawyer tilts his head in thought. "Actually, yeah, he probably would."

Beau turns back to me. "Anyway, you go. We're good here."

"Thanks, Beau. I owe you one," I call out as I jog for the door.

I make it home in record time, but the house is silent, like eerily silent, when I walk inside. I can almost feel the tension vibrating in the air.

"We're back here!" Owen shouts from the kitchen.

I brace myself as I head in. What I find there is deceptively calm.

Ivy and Owen are sitting across the kitchen table from each other. Owen's leg is bouncing like mad, even with his hand gripping his knee. Ivy's arms are crossed over her tiny chest, her chin stuck out in the most epic pout as she stares resolutely at a spot in the middle of the table.

Owen meets my gaze, eyes flat and hard before softening into something that makes me want to pull him into the tightest hug.

I move toward him, drawn in by the helplessness I read on his face. I set my hand on his shoulder and squeeze. He takes a deep breath and his knee stops bouncing.

"Hey guys, what's up?"

Ivy lifts her gaze from the table and the glare she shoots in my direction rivals the dirtiest scowl Owen's ever leveled at me. I almost take a step backward at the hostility rolling off her. Who is this girl? What did she do with our Ivy?

"Ivy, do you want to tell Uncle Everest what's wrong?" Owen's voice is tightly controlled.

"No!" she fires back with zero hesitation, and if it weren't for my hand on Owen's shoulder, he probably would've flown out of his chair.

"Ivy," I say before Owen can go off on her, making sure to keep my tone level and calm. "Is this about the swimming lessons?"

Owen huffs an unamused scoff. "That was an hour ago."

Does that mean they've moved on to another argument? How many arguments can they have in the hour since they called me? Jesus.

"So what is *this* argument about?"

Ivy scrunches up her face until she almost looks like she's snarling. The whine she lets out is a little better than a dying animal.

"Where do you want to have your birthday party, Ivy?" Owen demands.

Birthday party? How the hell did they get from swimming lessons to her birthday party?

"I thought we were having it here?" I didn't even know there was another option. We've got a huge backyard and Owen was looking into getting one of those inflatable bouncy castles.

"I don't *wanna* have my birthday here!" Ivy shouts so loud, I do take a step back this time.

Owen's hands are curled into fists so tight his knuckles have gone white. His eyes are closed and… is that a tear gathering on his lashes? Shit. This is… this is bad.

I walk around the table and pull out the chair next to Ivy's. "Ives, hey, why don't you want to have your party here?" I ask gently.

"I just don't!" There's a wobble in her voice that sends up alarm bells.

Owen's on the verge of tears. Ivy's about to break down in sobs. How the hell did we go from a happy little family to this?

"Hey, hey." I put my arm around Ivy's shoulders and thank fucking god she doesn't shrug me off. "It's okay. We don't have to have it here. We can have the party in the park? Or like, a Chuck E. Cheese? There are plenty of places.

"No! No! No!" She bounces in her seat like she's trying to stomp her foot.

"Ivy! Inside voice!" Owen barks at her and I wince. That's going to set her off.

And just as I'm thinking it, Ivy starts wailing.

"No!" Her cry is a knife straight through my heart.

I want to gather her into my arms, cradle her in my lap, and rock her side-to-side until she settles again. But instead, she pushes her chair away from the kitchen table with a loud scrape and jumps to her feet. "You can't tell me what to do! I don't have to listen to you! I hate you! I hate you! You're not my daddy!"

OWEN

I blink.

Did I— Did she—

Then it hits me. Like a sword straight through my gut, twisting, slicing through me.

You're not my daddy.

Ivy's small footsteps reverberate through the house, then the sound of a door opening and the unmistakable noise of the city.

I spin around in the chair, not believing what my ears are telling me.

"Ivy?" Everest is already out of his seat. "Ivy!" He races around the table and out of the kitchen. I'm hot on his heels, running flat out for the foyer.

The front door is standing open and so is the outer door of the vestibule. My stomach drops through the floor and my heart jumps into my throat.

No. No, this can't be happening. This isn't real. This has to be some sort of twisted nightmare.

I smash into Everest at the top of the stoop. "Where is she?"

"I don't know! I can't see her!"

We scan the sidewalk in both directions, but there's no sign of a small blond head. There isn't the pitter-patter of small footsteps pounding down the concrete. No flash of pink from the flouncy skirt she's wearing.

"Fuck. Where is she?" Everest runs down the steps to the sidewalk, hands on his head, a look of panic on his face.

My brain kicks into crisis mode. We need to split up and search for her. She's a little girl. She can't run that fast. She couldn't have gone far.

I reach back to shut the door behind me, then follow Everest down the steps. "You go that way. I'll go this way. Use your phone to stay in touch." I push Everest toward the right and then take off in the opposite direction.

"Ivy!" I check the sunken patios that lead to the garden-level entrances of brownstones. I run up stoops to check every house's vestibules. I zigzag back and forth across the street, screaming Ivy's name.

With every spot I check that's empty, my heart rate kicks up a notch. With every second that passes without finding her, fear squeezes me a little tighter, crushing my chest and twisting my stomach.

This is my fault. She ran away because of me. If I hadn't been arguing with her all day. If I hadn't been so hard on her and just given her some time to cool off instead of… instead of…

Fuck! What if she gets hurt? What if someone kidnaps her? What if we can't find her and she just vanishes into thin air? It'll be my fault. I'll never forgive myself. I won't be able to live with myself.

"IVY!"

At the end of the block, I scan the intersection, looking for any bit of blonde or pink I can find. Which way would she have gone? Left or right? I don't know. There's no way to tell.

My phone buzzes in my pocket and I yank it out, stabbing the accept button.

"Did you find her?" I yell before I've even gotten the phone to my ear.

"No. You?" Everest sounds as panicked and scared as I feel.

Why the fuck would I be asking him if he found her if I already have? "No. I'm…" I spin in a circle, just in case I passed right by her somehow. Still nothing. Where would she go? Where would she feel safe?

"I'm going to check the ice cream place she likes." The idea comes to me almost after the words leave my mouth. "You check the park."

"The park. Right. Good idea. Okay."

I hang up and navigate to my photos app to find a recent photo of Ivy. There's one of her from the zoo, laughing at the camera with a butterfly on her head.

"Excuse me, have you seen this little girl?" I shove my phone in the face of a pedestrian walking past me. "She's six years old. About this high."

The older woman squints at the screen, but then shakes her head, casting an apologetic look at me. "Sorry, I haven't."

I don't wait for her to finish talking before taking off

down the street again. "Excuse me, have you seen this little girl?"

"No, never seen her. Sorry."

"Ivy! Ivy!" I half-walk, half-run, checking every hiding spot I see, making my way toward the ice cream place we often take her to. It's only a few blocks away, but today, it feels like it's in another state entirely.

"Excuse me, have you seen this little girl?"

"Naw, man. Good luck, though."

Fuck. I stop every single person on the street, but none of them have seen any sign of Ivy. And with every "sorry" and every look of pity, I die a little bit inside.

Where the *fuck* is she?

The ice cream shop is at the end of the next block and I hope to god she's there. No, I pray—genuinely, for the first time in my life—to whatever god or higher power that might exist. I'll do anything—*anything*—as long as she's okay.

The windows of the shop are covered with posters, so I can't see inside. I grab the door handle and wrench it open to throw myself through.

"Ivy?!"

Everything in the shop grinds to a standstill as all head swivels in my direction.

"Ivy?" I ignore anyone taller than four feet, weaving around them looking for my little girl.

There! A head of blonde hair in pigtails.

"Ivy!" I grab her by the shoulders, but when I spin her around, it isn't my Ivy. It's another little girl with blonde hair.

Her mom yanks her back from me. "Hey! Get your hands off her!"

"Sorry! I'm sorry! I just—" I scan the rest of the store, but there aren't any more little girls with blonde hair. Ivy isn't here. Why isn't she here?

I pull her photo again. "Has anyone seen this little girl? Her name is Ivy. She loves bubblegum ice cream. We bring her here all the time. Please. If anyone's seen her… Plea—" My voice cracks and I wrap my free arm around my middle, trying to physically hold myself together.

The mom's expression turns from outraged to sympathetic. She leans in to look at Ivy's photo before shaking her head. The three other parents do the same, offering their empty, useless condolences.

I stagger out of the store, struggling to drag air into my lungs. My fingers are numb as I try to call Everest. It takes me three attempts before I manage to hit the call button.

It rings.

And rings.

And rings.

Pick up, goddamn it. Pick up the fucking phone, you motherfucker.

I'm about to hang up and try again when the call connects.

"I found her! I've got her! She's okay!"

"Where? Where are you?" I take off in the direction of the park.

"At the library. We're at the Brooklyn Central Library."

I hang up and run as fast as I can, dodging around other pedestrians and barely slowing down to cross streets.

The library in Prospect Park is *miles* away from our house. How the hell did she get there so quickly? She's just a little girl. Her legs can't possibly move so fast. We were literally seconds behind her.

It takes me fifteen minutes to get to the library and I immediately spot Everest sitting on the steps out front, Ivy snug and secure in his lap.

"Ivy!" I race up to them, practically barreling into them in my haste. I press kisses to the top of Ivy's head, brush her hair back from her tear-streaked face, check her arms and legs for any cuts or scrapes.

Emotions, huge and uncontrolled, ricochet around inside me so hard it feels like I'm going to topple over and burst open. Relief floods through me, but at the same time fear escapes the tightly shut box I've crammed it into. It rushes forward, fierce and unrelenting, plowing down every other thought, every other feeling.

I haul Ivy into my arms and squeeze her tightly to me, not caring if I'm being too rough or if I'm squishing her. I need the weight of her body against mine. I need her scent in my nose.

"Don't you ever do that again! Don't ever run out of the house like that! You can't just run away from us when you're upset. Don't you know how dangerous it is out here for a little girl?"

Ivy's sobbing into my shirt, crying out, "I'm sorry! I'm sorry!" on repeat.

"What if you got hurt? What if a driver wasn't paying attention and hit you? What if a stranger kidnapped you? We wouldn't know where you were. You can't do that to us."

"Owen. Stop." Everest grabs me by the back of my neck and forces me to meet his gaze. "You're scaring her."

I'm scaring *her*? What about me? What about *my* fear?

What about the abject terror coursing through my veins. We could have lost her. We could have lost her and I would never have forgiven myself. We could have lost her and we almost did.

Pull yourself together, Lambert.

I force myself to take a deep breath, though it feels more like a gasp than anything else. My vision blurs as hot wet tears roll down my cheeks.

"Do you have your handkerchief?" Everest asks and I twist sideways so he can pull it out of my pocket. "Never thought I'd be so glad you carry one of these around."

He shakes it out and helps me wipe my tears away. "It's okay. She's okay. We're going to be okay."

I nod, not necessarily in agreement, but more like I'm being given instructions. Yes, I understand—well, no, I don't understand, but I'll take your word for it.

"Come on, let's go home." Everest helps me to my feet with Ivy in my arms. He keeps his hand on my back, guiding me down the sidewalk.

I don't pay attention to where we're going or if there are any oncoming pedestrians or cars. I just let Everest direct me where he needs me to go. My arms stay wrapped around Ivy, as if someone might snatch her from me. She clings to me just as tightly, like she never wants to let go.

I don't remember how we get home. I don't remember going up the stoop or Everest unlocking the door. I'm not fully aware of my surroundings until I'm sitting on the couch in the living room, settling Ivy in my lap.

My cheeks are tight from my dried tears. Ivy's fallen silent too.

Everest comes into the living room, holding two

glasses of water. He sits down next to us with a heavy sigh, his shoulders slumping like he can't quite sit up straight anymore.

"How did you…" My voice is raspy and I can't quite bring myself to finish the question.

Everest glances at me with a sympathetic expression before handing me the glass. I take a quick sip, then offer it to Ivy. She holds the glass with both hands, drinking only a little before giving it back to Everest. She immediately curls herself into me again, the movement soothing some of the terror gripping my soul.

"I was in the park when the library's security guard called me," Everest answers my unspoken question. "Ivy had given him my number."

"Good, that's good." I give the top of Ivy's head a kiss and force myself to loosen my hold on her. She's home. She's safe. She's okay.

"Ives?"

Ivy peeks out at Everest, eyes huge and glistening.

"We were really worried about you," Everest says, sounding more serious than I've ever heard him before. "Do you understand?"

She nods, her hair rubbing against my shirt.

"Why did you run out of the house?" he asks.

She shrugs and tucks her chin to her chest.

Everest glances up at me again, worry marring his handsome face.

For once, I don't want to do the responsible thing—I don't want to have this conversation. I'd rather bundle Ivy up in a million blankets, feed her all her favorite foods, and let her watch all her favorite movies. I'd read her heartwarming bedtime stories and watch her fall into a deep and peaceful sleep.

I want to pretend today never happened, rewind the clock, and start again.

EVEREST

I've never been more scared in my entire life. Not when I watched the movie *It* at five years old. Not when I stared down a ten-foot wave. Not when Eden and Jeremy died and left us with custody of Ivy.

Watching Ivy disappear out that door felt like my heart was being torn from my chest, like the air was being sucked out of my lungs. And when we couldn't find her on the street, I thought for sure I was going to die on the spot.

I swear to god, I almost lost it. Just, go completely fucking hysterical. The only thing that kept me sane and functional was knowing that Owen was with me, that he was in charge, and he would know what to do.

I was in the park, at a loss for how I was supposed to search the whole damn thing. How do I find one little girl among the thousands of people across hundreds of acres?

I dropped to my knees when I saw her at the security desk in the library, and not only so I would be on her level.

My knees just gave way under the flood of relief. My hands were barely functional when I tried to pull out the copy of the court letter that states I'm Ivy's guardian. Thank fucking god Owen makes me carry it around, folded up in my wallet.

Owen was beyond distraught when he finally found us at the library. I've never seen him like that before. I mean, me losing my shit isn't all that usual, but Owen always keeps his cool, always stays level-headed, never freaks out the way I do. So seeing him on the brink like that, barely holding it together... Jesus Christ, that was almost scarier than losing Ivy. Like, I overreact all the time, but if Owen's that close to breaking down, then it's really, *really* bad.

Ivy is so small all curled up in Owen's arms. Her eyes are puffy and red. Her nose is all snotty. Her hair is a wild, tangled mess. She looks so dejected, so miserable.

"Do you remember what you said before you ran out of the house?" I ask Ivy, trying to keep my voice light and non-judgmental. I don't want her to feel like I'm scolding her, but I need her to understand that what she did is not okay.

Owen flinches at my question, his expression looking gutted.

Ivy makes a soft, pathetic sound and squirms uncomfortably in Owen's lap. She definitely remembers. And I'd bet a month's worth of protein shakes that she said it to hit Owen where it would hurt him the most.

"Do you know how that made us feel? How it made Uncle Owen feel?"

She squirms some more, pressing her face into Owen's chest so she doesn't have to look at me.

"It wasn't a very nice thing to say, Ives. You know how

words can hurt us, right? Well, what you said really hurt Uncle Owen. It hurt me too."

She whines, clutching at Owen's shirt, and it makes me feel like I'm the bad guy even when I know I'm not.

Owen's lips are pressed into a firm line, his brows are furrowed, and he's staring at a spot on the floor. Like he's trying to beat back his emotions and keep himself in check.

I rub my hand over the short hairs at the back of his head, then lean in to plant a quick kiss on his temple. His eyes shut and he breathes in a deep, shaky breath.

A part of me wants to pretend that this whole thing didn't happen. Just crack a joke to cut through the tension, then go on with life as if everything was fine. But everything is not fine with Ivy. It hasn't been for weeks now, and ignoring it won't make the problem go away.

Being an adult sucks balls.

"We know something's been bothering you recently, Ivy-poo. You wanna tell us about it?"

She whines again and shakes her head. Owen shoots me a worried look.

"You can tell us, Ivy. Whatever it is, we're not going to be upset. We just want to help, but we can't help if we don't know what's wrong."

Her whine shoots up a couple octaves before she bursts into tears. And not like, little tears either. Huge, body-shaking sobs that seem to come from a place much too deep for someone so young and so small.

Owen and I exchange looks of alarm. Why is she crying like this? What the hell happened?

With Owen's handkerchief, I try to keep up with Ivy's tears, but the cloth is soon soaked all the way through. Owen rubs her back while he murmurs soothingly to her.

Eventually, she breaks. "I'm sorry!" she wails. "I'm sorry! Please don't leave! I'll be good, I promise! I'll do whatever you say. Just please don't leave me behind."

My gaze snaps up to Owen and he looks just as horrified as I feel. What the fuck does she mean? Does she think we're going to leave her?

"Ivy, sweetie, what are you talking about? We're not going anywhere. Why would we leave you?" Owen's voice is thick with emotion. With shock, but also pain at the idea that she thinks we would ever do something like that.

"But I've been bad…" she says through wracking sobs that make it hard to make out her words. "I yelled at you."

I didn't think my heart could break any more than it already has today. But I have zero defenses when it comes to Ivy. Everything she says hits where I'm the most vulnerable. Everything she does affects me to my very core.

"You can yell at us. You can be bad or misbehave. But we're never going to leave you. No matter what you do. We love you," I explain.

"We might get upset or angry," Owen adds. "But that doesn't mean we love you any less."

"We love you *so much*. We always will. We'll always be here." My voice cracks as I fight back a sob of my own. How did this happen? Did we not say it to her enough? Did we do something to make her think that we would abandon her?

Is this why she's been acting so hostile lately? She thinks we're going to leave her, and she's, what, testing us? Pushing us away?

"But— but— Mommy and Daddy left without me. And

now you're boyfriends, so maybe you'll leave without me too."

The admission leaves both me and Owen stunned. Pain lances through me, fueling the grief and fear, until I'm shaking, trembling, and unstable.

It all comes back to that day, doesn't it? Every part of our lives. Every good thing and every bad thing. All our hopes and dreams. All our deepest worries and fears. It all comes back to the day that Eden and Jeremy were taken from us. The day that our lives changed forever.

Will it ever get easier? Will the shadow of that day ever become lighter? Will we ever be free of it?

"Ivy, listen to me," Owen speaks softly into the little space we've created around her. "Your mommy and daddy didn't leave you. They loved you and would never choose to leave. They were taken. From you. From all of us. There's a difference. We would never leave either. We love you just as much as your mommy and daddy did. We want to be together with you. We're a family. Do you understand?"

"But— but— what if someone takes you too?"

Owen and I look at each other, and as much as I want to promise that will never happen, we both know it could. It would be irresponsible to make a promise that we might not be able to keep, that's outside our control.

"We— I—" Owen's mouth gaps open as he struggles with the thing we're both thinking but neither of us wants to say out loud.

"We're going to do our very best to stay with you," I jump in. "We'll do everything in our power to make sure you're never ever alone."

Ivy's sobs slow to hiccups and sniffles. Gradually, she

lifts her head from Owen's tear-soaked shirt. Her face is a disaster, red and puffy and wet. But in her eyes is an awareness and maturity that no child her age should have. It's the realization that we're all mortal, that bad things happen to good people, and sometimes there's nothing we can do about any of it.

I hate that look in her eyes. I hate that this is a lesson she's had to learn at her age. I hate that we're not able to shelter her from this reality for at least a few more years.

I brush back her tangled hair and swipe my thumb across her ruddy cheeks. "We love you, Ivy-bear. More than anything in the world. You're the most important person in our lives. I know we're not your mommy and daddy, but—"

How do I explain this to her? That neither of us wants to replace Eden and Jeremy. That we would do *anything* to bring them back if we could. That we're going to keep doing our best, even if our best will never live up to the real thing.

That this is *so* hard. We're trying, but we're all going to fail and make mistakes. Families are messy sometimes, but that doesn't mean any of us will give up. We're all in this, together, forever.

"But we love you more than anything in the world," Owen finishes the sentence I couldn't.

Ivy watches Owen for a few seconds, as if she's weighing the truth of his words. Then she turns her measuring gaze to me and I try to pour every ounce of love I feel for her into my expression.

"I love you too," she whispers back to us, innocent and utterly precious.

"We're a family," I say. "We're gonna stick together, 'kay?"

She nods. The movement is small, but it feels huge, like we've reached another milestone and graduated to the next level.

Owen tucks Ivy's head under his chin again and I slouch down to rest my head on his shoulder. We sit like that for long minutes, no one speaking, no one moving. The three of us soaking in each other's presence, reconnecting after the trauma of the afternoon.

At some point, I pull out my phone to order pizza, adding extra pineapples because Ivy likes them and Owen hates them.

They've both fallen asleep, holding onto each other like they never want to let go. They're so peaceful, so serene. And as I watch them, I send a silent message up to Eden and Jeremy, wherever they might be.

We've got her. You don't need to worry. Between me and Owen, we'll make sure she grows up to make you proud.

OWEN

We take our time putting Ivy to bed. There's no reason to rush, no need to bundle her off. Instead, we linger, reading her second and third bedtime stories. We lie in bed with her, Everest and I on our sides, facing each other, with Ivy sandwiched between us. We hold her until she falls asleep.

Even then, we don't get up. We stay in bed, gazing into each other's eyes. Everest's browns are darker than normal, filled with fatigue and sadness. It's been a long day. An emotional rollercoaster of a day. And I can't decide if I want to stay with Ivy all night, just to reassure her that we're not going anywhere, or if I want to seek solace in Everest's arms.

Eventually, the cramped size of the bed is too much, and we slowly, reluctantly, tuck Ivy in, Zuzi by her side.

Everest and I go upstairs to our room, and the second the door clicks shut behind us, I crumple like a marionette whose strings have been snipped. All the adrenaline of the day, the steely resolve I had to maintain in order to find

Ivy, the dependable, unwavering strength I had to project, it all falls apart in the safety of Everest's presence.

Strong arms wrap around me, keeping me upright when I would have collapsed to the floor. Everest guides me to the bed and sits us down on the edge. He doesn't speak, doesn't try to comfort me or soothe me. He just holds me, rocking me back and forth as wretched, horrid sounds emanate from deep inside me. My head is tucked under his chin while his fingers card through my hair. His other hand rubs up and down my arm.

Tears that I thought had already run dry spring to my eyes and pour down my cheeks. I don't even know what I'm crying over anymore. We found Ivy, safe and sound. We uncovered the cause of her moodiness, and we did what we could to reassure her that we love her, that we're never going to leave her, that she's the most important thing in our lives. The day started crappy, got untenably worse, but it ended well. We're okay. We'll be okay.

So why am I crying like my heart's being torn out of my chest?

I cling to Everest, to a strength and steadiness that I'd been ignorant of for so long. But he is strong, the way a reed bends in the wind but doesn't break. He's steady like a songbird who will always bring joy.

I lean into him, needing him to prop me up, physically and emotionally, needing him to soothe the wrenching feeling inside. I want to crawl inside him and curl up into a tiny little ball. I want him to protect me from every negative, painful, difficult thing.

How does he do it? How does he go through life unbothered by the weight of the world? He lets it all slide off his shoulders without a care, without holding on to it and letting it drag him down.

I'm so tired. God, I'm *so tired* of being strong and reliable, the one everyone else depends on, who has the answers and knows what to do.

I'm not strong. I don't have the answers. I never know what to do. I only appear to be all those things because I've never had any other choice. But for once, just for one day, I don't want to pretend anymore.

I want to be reckless, wild, audacious, impulsive. I want to let all the spinning plates crash to the floor and break into a million pieces. I want to be able to walk away without feeling an ounce of guilt.

I want to lose myself in Everest and forget everything else. I want him to make the pain go away.

Everest holds me tighter, cheek pressed against the top of my head. "I've got you," he murmurs. "You can let go. Everything's going to be okay. I can be strong enough for the both of us."

Something primal and raw rips through me, obliterating every thought, every uncertainty, every reservation. I surge up, grabbing ahold of Everest's face and smashing my mouth against his. Our teeth bang together and Everest lets out a surprised grunt.

Please, Ev, please. Make me forget. Make it stop hurting.

And as if he can read my thoughts, he kisses me back.

Hard. Furious. Aggressive.

Yesss.

Relief courses through me as my body comes to life. This is it. This is what I need. Sensations to drown out the constant whir of my brain.

His hand goes to the back of my head, angling me for a

deeper kiss. I let him. I relinquish control to him. I surrender.

Everest's tongue plunges past my lips and my head spins. He licks along the roof of my mouth and I whimper. He nibbles on my jaw, sinks his teeth into my earlobe, sucks on the spot where my pulse beats. My head drops back, my eyes drift shut, my mind blanks to everything except the scrape of Everest's teeth, the softness of his lips, the suction of his mouth on my skin.

"What do you want, O? Tell me what you need."

When I don't respond, he pulls back to gaze down at me. His pupils are blown wide. His lips are bruised and swollen. His hair is mussed from my fingers.

I... I want...

The emotions swirling inside me are so big, so complicated, that I can't shape them into words. Desperation claws at my throat, rendering me speechless. I can't breathe. My chest is tight. My stomach feels like it's been ripped to shreds. I gasp for air and fist Everest's shirt in my hands.

His eyes go from frenzied to focused as he hears my silent plea. He grabs my wrists and with a quick twist of his body, he manhandles me back onto the bed. My hands are pinned above my head, and Everest's knee is between my thighs, flush against my rapidly hardening cock.

Leaning down, he bites into that place where my neck meets my shoulder and the sharp sting goes straight to my cock. It pulses, hot and aching against Everest's knee. My hole twitches, hungry to be filled.

Without warning, he pulls away, and I cry out a protest. Rising above me, Everest tears his clothes off, revealing all that skin, all that muscle, primed and pumped and ready.

Naked, he reaches for me. I try to help, but my hands are useless. Everest rids me of my clothes in a blink of an eye, then taps me on the hip.

"Hands and knees."

I don't think. I don't object. I don't question. I simply scramble to obey. With my face buried in a pillow and my ass sticking up high in the air, I wait. I'm open. Exposed.

Somewhere in the deep recesses of my mind, a part of me bristles at letting Everest take the lead. But I smother the whisper of defiance. I don't want to be in charge right now. I don't want to make decisions.

A hand lands on my ass. Loud and stinging. I yelp and jump, more in surprise than in pain. Everest grabs both ass cheeks, squeezing and pulling them apart. A shudder runs through me at the image I must present. Submissive. Vulnerable. At his mercy. The part of me that demands to always be in control roars its displeasure. *Why am I just kneeling there letting Everest do whatever he wants? Why am I so soft, so deficient, so weak?*

A swipe of Everest's tongue right across my hole shuts down my inner critic. My mind goes on the fritz. Everything in my body, every sense, zeros in on my ass and the sensation of Everest's tongue drilling into my hole.

I resist the urge to reach back and push his face more firmly into my ass. I shove my arms under the pillow, gripping hard enough for my hands to ache. I need this. I need him to take me, to fuck me, to make me his. I need to not be me.

Something cold hits my ass, then is immediately pushed into my body by Everest's fingers. He fucks me once, twice, twisting his fingers around, before pulling out again. Then the blunt tip of his thick cock is there, pressing inside, demanding entrance.

I bear down, letting him in. The pressure is intense and unrelenting. He doesn't pause to let me adjust. He doesn't give me time to acclimate to his girth. He just sinks into my body like he owns it, like he belongs there, like I am his.

When he bottoms out, he leans forward to whisper in my ear.

"Hold on tight, 'cause I'm gonna fuck the cum outta you."

His words ricochet around my body, lighting me up from the inside out, before hitting my cock. It throbs where it hangs in between my legs with nothing to rub against. My heavy balls pull up tight, ready to take whatever beating Everest doles out.

His fingers dig into my hips, holding me exactly where he wants me. He pulls out, deceptively slow, until only the tip of his cock remains inside.

Then he fucks me.

Brutally. Savagely. Untamed.

The sound of skin slapping against skin rings in my ears. The impact of his balls hitting my taint reverberates through me. The piston of his cock, tearing through my hole, ignites a fire inside me and I burn.

Pleasure rages, hot and fervent, consuming me whole. The smell of sweat saturates the air. The scent of our sex, of the two of us combined—there's nothing else like it in the world, there's nothing else that reaches so deep inside me, that rocks me to the core.

Everest shifts, changing his angle so the head of his

cock hammers directly on my prostate. I can't stop the scream that rips from my throat and my body curls around the pillow I'm clutching.

It's too much. The pleasure is so intense it borders on pain. Shockwave after shockwave bombard my senses, propelling me to the brink of passing out.

My knees give way, my body collapses onto the bed. Everest doesn't stop, doesn't even falter. He keeps pounding me into the bed, driving into me faster and harder until I can't take it anymore.

I scream into the pillow as the orgasm devastates me. Every cell in my body explodes with pleasure so pure it cannot be contained. Every thought is obliterated from my mind. Every muscle liquified. The orgasm courses through me, unrelenting, fueled by Everest's cock drilling on my prostate.

Then molten heat floods my ass, triggering another orgasm as I accept Everest's cum into my body. It's searing, like it's branding me, marking me. My body is Everest's property. My heart belongs to him. I am his and no one else's.

His heavy weight covers me as I twitch with aftershocks. I want to stay here forever, where there's nothing but the hum of pleasure, where the outside world can't intrude.

EVEREST

Ivy's birthday party sneaks up on us. Or actually, I should say it sneaks up on me. Because Owen is all over that shit.

We'd talked about keeping it low-key, just us and the grandparents, because like, Ivy ran out of the house when she should've known better. And like, as her parents, we're supposed to discipline her, right? Taking away the big, fancy party felt like an appropriate punishment to me.

But nope. This is Ivy's first birthday without her mom and dad, so Owen is determined to make it the most epic birthday party of the year. It's actually kind of out of control.

He ordered a bouncy castle for the backyard, a magician, a balloon person-dude, and a live band. There are two sets of everything—caterers, gift bags, open bars—one for the kids and the other for the parents. I'm not usually one to balk at how much we're spending, but honestly... I'm too scared to ask.

Owen took Ivy shopping for a birthday outfit and they

came home with like, five different options. The little fashion show they put on for me that night was cute, but *five* outfits?! Seriously?

You know what, though? Whatever makes Owen happy. That's been my motto since that day he broke down. It shook me to see him like that, so beaten and defeated, but on some level, I wasn't that surprised. Owen is more fragile than he seems. That's why he hides behind such thick walls all the time. The fact that he's let me inside, that he lets me see him at his weakest and most vulnerable, it's a privilege I will never take for granted.

Owen is up before the sun on the day of the party, phone in one hand and a clipboard with a printed checklist in the other. The living room is already filled with perfectly neat rows of gift bags he prepped last night. I couldn't believe the amount of time he spent arranging the colorful tissue papers so they stuck out of the bags just right.

The bouncy castle people arrive early, and Owen supervises as they set up the unicorn-themed monstrosity in the backyard. The thing is huge, and it even has a blow-up slide attached to the side that kids can access from inside.

Caterers take over our kitchen, kicking me out before I even finish my morning coffee. The band hauls their sound and stage equipment through the middle of the house. I've never seen so many people—so many strangers —in the house like this before, and I kind of don't know what to do with myself.

When the grandparents get here, Mom and Alyssa take Ivy upstairs to get ready. Owen puts Dad and Mark to work making sure all the vendors are staying on task.

Meanwhile, I wander from room to room, trying to stay out of everyone's way.

"Where's Ivy?" Owen demands, appearing in front of me out of nowhere. He's all up in my face like I abducted her or something.

"Uh, upstairs still?"

Owen glances toward the stairs as if that will confirm her location, then checks his watch for the millionth time. His brows are bunched together and his eyes are narrowed in intense concentration. He looks like he's about to go to war, or like he's hyping himself up for a big deadlift.

I grab his wrist before he can dart off to do god knows what else. "Hey, babe, chill." I pull him into my arms and lock my hands together behind his back to trap him.

He glowers at me and tries to wiggle his way out. "I've got stuff to do."

I squeeze him tighter to me until we're chest-to-chest. "No, you really don't. You've already done all the stuff." I look pointedly at his checklist with a column full of bright green checkmarks. "There's only one thing left to do."

His glower deepens. "Let me guess. Chill?"

"Yup!" I lean in to rub my nose against his and despite himself, the tension slowly drains from his body. "This is a party. It's supposed to be fun. It shouldn't give you gray hairs."

"I don't have gray hairs," he mumbles.

"And let's keep it that way." I kiss him on the nose and rock him back and forth as if I can physically shake the anxiety out of him.

"I just want everything to be perfect," Owen confesses quietly.

My love for him expands in my chest. It grows so big it

feels like it's going to burst out of me. "Everything *is* perfect. And even if it isn't, Ivy won't care. Her friends will be here. Her family is here. That's all she really needs."

Owen makes a little choked sound. "Not her whole family," he objects.

I breathe through a bittersweet pang. "You're wrong. They are here. Eden and Jeremy are in these walls. They're all around us. They're with us every day. Especially today."

Owen squeezes his eyes shut and I take the opportunity to steal a kiss. The sneak attack slices through the heaviness shrouding him and he cracks a smile.

"There it is," I say in a lilting, teasing voice.

"There what is?" he asks, skeptically.

"The smile I love."

Owen groans in disgust, rolling his eyes and pushing me away. "Go make yourself useful," he says as he walks away, but the grin on his face is impossible to miss.

Things get about a thousand times more chaotic when the guests start to arrive. Kids scream above the live music, running around the backyard like they're possessed, while parents rush the open bar. Ivy is the center of attention in her fluffy pink dress and sparkly tiara. Her megawatt smile shines brighter than the sun and her bubbly laughter like is magic pixie dust sprinkled over the whole party.

Owen makes me do the rounds with him, welcoming each and every adult, most of whom I've never laid eyes on before. But Owen knows every single person's name and also which kid they belong to.

"Everest!"

I turn to find the most unusual group of people I'd ever expect at a little girl's birthday party—my friends from Mars. Beau and Gavin lead the posse, followed by Sawyer and Logan, then Donnie and Christian.

"What you guys doing here?" I'm stunned as they each give me dude-bro hugs and slaps on the back.

"We wouldn't miss Ivy's birthday!" Logan holds up what must be a giant teddy bear that's probably bigger than Ivy herself. It looks like a mummy that got shat on by a unicorn, all wrapped up in rainbow wrapping paper.

"Owen called the gym and invited us," Gavin explains.

He did? When did he do that? And why didn't he tell me?

"Where's the birthday girl?" Sawyer's bouncing on his feet, already dancing to the live kids' music.

"I'm here!"

I turn just in time to see her running up in a flurry of pink, with Owen right behind her.

"You invited them?" I ask him.

"Is that okay? I wanted it to be a surprise." He looks a little apprehensive.

"Of course it's okay!" I lower my voice. "I thought you didn't like them." He barely acknowledged them when they attended the memorial service for Eden and Jeremy.

Owen shrugs. "I don't really know them."

Gratitude fills my heart at the shy smile Owen gives me and at how far we've come. There's no way he would've invited the Mars guys six months ago. And certainly not as a surprise for me.

"Hi! I'm Ivy! You're Uncle Ev's friends!" Ivy draws our attention back to her and I tug Owen a little closer to me.

Gavin kneels down so he's at her level. "Hey Ivy, I'm

Gavin, and this is Beau." He goes around introducing the guys and they each give her a high five.

Then Ivy spots the poorly disguised teddy bear. She gasps and her eyes turn as big as saucers. "Is that for me?"

"Sure is!" Logan sets it down in front of her.

Ivy tries to hug it, except she's too small to get her arms all around. It tilts over, and Ivy goes tumbling down with it. Logan is horrified, scrambling to help her up. Ivy, on the other hand, is giggling her head off, like this is the most fun she's ever had in her life.

"What do you say, Ivy?" Owen prompts.

"Thank you!" Ivy throws herself at Logan and he hugs her back with a look of awe on his face. I smile—that's how I feel whenever I get an Ivy hug, that I can't quite believe such a beautiful creature exists and that she likes me enough to grace me with a hug.

After Logan is Sawyer, then Gavin, then Beau. She works her way through the group, hugging all the guys and winning them over with nothing more than her charming smile. I can already tell that she's just earned herself six more uncles to spoil her rotten.

"Hey Ivy! Come play in the bouncy castle with us!"

Ivy lights up at the mention of the bouncy castle, and she darts around all the adults to get to her friends, disappearing as abruptly as she arrived.

Owen winces. "Sorry about that. She's a little over-excited today."

"That's okay, it's her birthday," Gavin replies.

"Yeah, she's allowed to be excited on her birthday," Beau adds.

"Thank you all for coming," Owen says. "I'm Owen, Ivy's other uncle."

It dawns on me then. I've never formally introduced Owen to my friends. Not that he was ever interested before this.

"Oh, uh, sorry. I guess you guys haven't actually met before."

"Nope! Way to be a good host, Everest," Sawyer teases good-naturedly and I flash him a discreet middle finger.

"I caught the introductions with Ivy." Owen's hand settles on the small of my back, all casual, like it's no big deal.

The warmth of it, the gentle pressure, amplifies the gratitude already filling my heart. I shift my weight so my arm presses lightly against his shoulder. It's subtle, could almost be accidental, like I didn't notice he was so close. The hand on my back slides around to my waist and squeezes. Holy shit.

My heart goes wild as I suppress a shudder of pure glee. His hold is so possessive, so sure, like I am his and he's staking his claim. In front of family, friends, and half of Ivy's school. There's no way anyone could look at us and not know immediately that we're together, that we belong to each other.

The guys notice it too. Donnie and Christian exchange an amused look. Beau and Sawyer exchange a mischievous one. Gavin smiles at us endearingly. Only Logan's a little clueless, his attention fixed on whatever's happening on the other end of the backyard.

A shriek rings out through the air, a little louder than the rest. At first, it doesn't really register—the kids have been screaming since the moment they arrived. But then I see the look on Logan's face. He gasps audibly, his eyes go wide, and his jaw hangs open in shock.

It doesn't necessarily mean anything. Logan gets surprised by a lot of things. He's a bit of a delicate flower that way. But there's something about the horror in his eyes that makes my stomach drop to my knees. This isn't any old accident. This is bad.

We all turn toward the far end of the backyard, where the bouncy castle is set up. Already, adults have rushed in that direction, and the screaming kids all start crying. Someone must be hurt.

Please don't let it be Ivy. Please don't let it be Ivy.

Owen and I move at the same time. I lead the way, using my bigger frame to shove people out of the way. I don't care if they go flying. I don't care if I trample over some child. I need to get to the front and make sure it isn't Ivy who's hurt.

It's hard to tell what's going on when we get up there. Adults stand in a ring, their children clinging to their legs. Then a smaller ring of adults are crouched down and hovering over someone lying on the ground.

I see pink frilly fabric and my heart stops. *NO.*

OWEN

"Move!" I shoulder my way around Everest, who's now just standing there, frozen. Grabbing some parent's arm, I yank them back then drop to my knees in their place.

Ivy. It's Ivy. I knew it was her the second I heard her scream. When the whole party came screeching to a halt and parents started throwing worried and sympathetic looks in our direction.

She's lying face down on the ground, her beautiful pink dress all rucked up, torn, and stained with grass and dirt. Her sparkling tiara is broken in half, though still stuck in the tangles of her hair. She's not moving.

Somewhere in the back of my mind, raw terror is circling, prowling, waiting to pounce. It's bigger, darker, more menacing than the fear I had when I got the call from the hospital that night. If I let it, it could sink its claws into me and rip me apart, it could devour me and consume me whole.

I can't let that happen. *Keep it together, Lambert.*

A switch flips inside my brain, kicking me into high gear. The rest of the world evaporates as I zero in on the task before me. Evaluate the situation, create an action plan, then execute.

Mom, Dad, Nell, and Graham are around me now and they all reach out to help Ivy up.

"Don't touch her!" I yell and they all snatch their hands away. "I need to check for injuries first."

I hear myself. My voice is steady, sharp, decisive, and in command. It sounds like the voice I use when an animal is brought in for emergency care, or when there's a complication in the middle of a surgery. It's detached and cold, which is completely at odds with the panic winding its way through me. But I need to sound that way, I need to compartmentalize and separate my feelings from my logical, rational mind.

"Uncle O?" The word comes out small, unsteady, and frightened.

"I'm here, sweetie. I'm right here. Shh. Don't move yet. Hold still." Quickly, I run my hands over Ivy's skull, looking for any patches of wetness, or any bumps that shouldn't be there. Nothing—thank god. I move down her neck and find no obvious injuries there either. Okay. Good. "Did you hit your head, Ivy-bear?"

"I— I— don't know?"

"I don't think she did," a parent says from over my shoulder. "At least, she didn't land on her head. Someone jostled her from behind when she was at the top of the slide and she lost her balance. She came down the slide head first, but I'm pretty sure she caught herself with her hands."

The description makes my throat close as my imagination paints the scene for me. Everything plays in slow motion: Ivy at the top of the slide, a shadow behind her, the look of surprise on her face as she tips forward, her hands outstretched in front of her as a scream rips from her throat.

I shake my head to wipe the image from my mind. *Focus on the now, Lambert, don't get distracted by things you can't change.*

"Okay, Ivy-bear, let's try to sit up." I slide my hands under her armpits and hold my breath as I slowly ease her into a seated position.

Her face is scrunched up, silent tears spilling down her cheeks. I can tell she wants to cry out, but she's being so brave. My Ivy, beautiful even when she's all banged up and dirty, injured and in pain. It's all I can do not to scoop her up and wrap myself around her so nothing can ever hurt her again.

"Oh my god, Ivy," Everest comes barging in, finally snapping out of his state of shock. He jostles me in his haste to get to Ivy and does what I wanted to do, lifting her into his lap and holding her close.

"Ow!" Ivy yelps, pulling her arm to her chest.

"Sorry! Sorry!" Everest's face pales as all the blood drains from his face.

I grip the back of his neck and squeeze. The last thing I need right now is for him to pass out on me. "Breathe, babe. Stay calm." Then I tug his arm out of the way so I can get a better look at Ivy. "What is it, sweetie? Where does it hurt?"

She slowly holds out her arm, her opposite hand wrapped gingerly around her wrist. As carefully as I can, I run my fingers from her elbow down her forearms. When I get to her wrist, she hisses, shoulders shooting up to her ears, and lets out a pained whine.

"I'm sorry, sweetie. It hurts here?"

She nods as fresh tears spill from her eyes.

It's only been a few minutes since her fall, but I can already see her wrist starting to swell. Best case scenario, she sprained it. Worst case, it's broken. Broken wrists can be difficult to treat if I remember correctly. They can also lead to a lot of complications. Either way, we'll need x-rays to know for sure.

I scan the rest of her. There's a big, ugly scrape across her chin and her lip is split open and bleeding. I'll need to clean it up to know if she'll need stitches. Dirt and grass stains cover the front of her dress. Her hands bore the brunt of it, though, with more scrapes and cuts along the heels of her palms and some on her elbows.

"Anyone have a scarf, or a necktie, or something?" I stick my hand out without looking up and when nothing lands in my hand, I finally glance around. The backyard is almost empty with the last of the guests filtering out. The bartenders are packing up, and so are the band. The only people left standing near us are Mom and Nell.

"Your friends are ushering everyone out," Nell says, nodding at Everest.

"And Mark and Graham are helping them hand out the goodie bags," Mom adds.

"We told the caterers to leave anything that was already cooked and take the rest with them," Nell finishes.

This stuns me for a moment. Not only did they know what to do, but they also jumped into action so quickly. Without being asked. Without explicit instructions. Our family, our friends, they saw us in the middle of a crisis and they did what needed to be done so we could focus on Ivy.

I've never liked depending on other people or relying on others. I've always thought it would be easier and faster to do everything myself. I like things to be done a particular way and I'm usually better at it than anyone I can ask.

So this phenomenon playing out before my eyes is novel and quite unexpected. An entire support system of people who understand me well enough to know what I need them to do and who love me enough to do it. People who willingly go out of their way to help and who rally around me in my moment of need.

It's not that I've never had those types of people in my life. But I've never let any of them in.

Until now. Until Everest.

Tears prickle my eyes and my throat grows tight with an overwhelming sense of gratitude and relief. I used to think it was simpler to do everything on my own, but I didn't realize how much weight I was carrying on my shoulders. I didn't realize how much sweeter it is to share the burden with others.

"Thank you," I say to no one in particular, fighting back the emotions threatening to overtake me. Instead, I turn back to Ivy. "Come on. Let's go inside."

I help Everest to his feet while he's got Ivy in his arms. Together, we head upstairs to the bathroom where we keep the first aid kit.

Mom appears with a scarf and I carefully tie it into a sling for Ivy's arm. Then I clean up Ivy's wounds, first with water, then with a cotton swab soaked in alcohol.

"This is going to sting," I warn her.

She braces herself and lets out a pained whimper, which triggers a fresh round of tears.

"I know it hurts, sweetie. I'm so sorry. You're being so brave. You're doing so well." I keep up the stream of encouraging words, though if I'm honest, I'm not sure whether I'm trying to soothe Ivy, Everest, myself, or all three of us. "I'm going to put on these bandages to keep the booboos clean. And then we'll go to the hospital so the doctors can take a look at your arm, okay?"

At the mention of the hospital, Ivy's complexion becomes even paler than it already is. "No! I don't wanna go to the hospital. I don't like the hospital." She shies away from me, turning into Everest instead.

Everest winces at her reaction. "Do we really need to?"

I hesitate, caught between my worry about Ivy's wrist and the obvious distress she's in at the mention of the hospital.

"It's just that you know what happened last time we took her to the hospital." Everest gives me a meaningful look. "Do you really want to put her through that again?"

The last time we took Ivy to a hospital, she saw her mom lying unconscious, hooked up to a slew of machines. Her dad was already in the morgue. Her mom would follow soon after.

It's not surprising she doesn't want to go back there. That huge building with strange noises and weird smells. Doctors and nurses walking around in their scrubs and white coats, faces hidden behind masks. Patients and their loved ones in pain, worried, hurting. I don't love the idea either.

But a broken wrist is a serious injury. At the very least,

she'll need a cast. If the bones have shifted, she might need surgery. If it's not treated promptly and properly, Ivy could end up with nerve damage, carpal tunnel, or even lose the use of her hand. We need to know the extent of the injury. We need a doctor to diagnose and treat. It's for her own good. We would be negligent if we didn't. Sometimes, being a good parent means making an unpopular decision. Sometimes, being a good parent means being the bad guy.

My stomach twists as I psyche myself up to put my foot down.

"Owen, what if…" Everest looks like he's just thought of a brilliant, yet horrifying idea. I already know I'm not going to like what comes out of his mouth next.

"What if we take her to your hospital? You can do the x-ray."

"My—" It takes several beats for my brain to process what Everest is suggesting. "What? You want me to take her to the *animal* hospital?!"

"It's perfect! You have x-ray machines there, don't you? And you're a doctor, you know how to treat broken bones."

I push to my feet and back away so I don't physically shake Everest for suggesting such a ridiculous, asinine thing. "Yeah, I'm a doctor for *animals*. You know, like cats and dogs. Not humans!"

"What's the difference? Bones are bones!"

My jaw drops as I gape at him. He can't be serious, can he? Of course there's a fucking difference! It's so blatantly obvious that I have no idea how to explain it to him. "No. What? No!"

"Oh come on. You're always going on about how

you're *Doctor* Owen Lambert. This is your chance to show off your skills!"

"I'm not trying to impress my friends with how much I can bench press!" I yell, throwing my hands in the air. "This is our little girl you're talking about! We should be seeking out the best medical care we can find—for *humans*."

"Boys."

My head snaps around at the sound of my mom's voice. I completely forgot she was standing by the bathroom door. Nell is right behind her, hand over her face, shaking her head. See? Even she knows how absurd her son is being.

"Lower your voices. You're scaring her," Mom says, eyes stern with warning.

My head snaps around again to find Ivy's face buried against Everest's chest. Her shoulders heave as she cries with her arm cradled against her body. Crap.

I drop to my knees and rummage around in the first aid kit for the bottle of children's Advil. The medication should take the edge off the pain until we can get her in to see a doctor—a doctor trained to treat *humans*.

I shake out two tablets and coach Ivy through chewing and swallowing, then washing it down with a glass of water.

Mom puts a hand on my shoulder. "Alright boys, how about we find a compromise between a scary emergency room and an animal hospital?"

EVEREST

Apparently some urgent care clinics have x-ray machines and can check if a bone is broken. Who knew?

Owen takes an obscene amount of time looking for one that has at least a four-point-five star rating, with expertise in pediatrics. All the while muttering about how dangerous a broken wrist can be. He keeps saying things like permanent damage and paralysis and losing her hand.

By the time we actually get there, Ivy's fallen asleep in my arms, exhausted from the excitement of her birthday party, then the trauma of falling down the slide. But I'm more terrified than I was when I saw her lying eerily still on the ground.

Guilt eats away at me. This wouldn't have happened if I was watching her instead of talking to the guys, if I'd been at the bottom of the slide to catch her, if I'd tried to talk Owen out of the damn bouncy castle in the first place. If she loses her hand, it's going to be my fault.

Ivy's body is heavy against mine, her head like a rock

on my shoulder. Her weight is the only thing keeping me from completely freaking the fuck out. It's grounding, reassuring. I'm still holding her, feeling her chest rise and fall. She's still here with us.

That's the thing, isn't it? Life is so fucking fragile and a little girl like Ivy is so fucking vulnerable. No matter what we do, no matter how hard we try to protect her, there's danger lurking around every corner. Today it was a bouncy castle. Tomorrow it could be a falling tree branch. The next day could be god knows what else.

Being a parent is terrifying. Debilitating. How do people do it? How do they walk around without their hearts in their throats, their stomach at their knees, and their insides torn to shreds by fear and desperation? It makes me want to wrap her up in bubble wrap and lock her in her room.

Owen drops into the chair next to mine, perched on the edge like he might jump to his feet to keep pacing around the waiting room. His knee starts bouncing. He usually catches himself pretty quickly, but right now, he's too caught up in his own head to notice.

My hand settles on his knee before I even realize I've moved it. His leg stills under my palm and for a second it looks like the nervous energy is going to burst out of the rest of his body. But then he covers my hand with his own and squeezes.

"She's going to be okay," he says, eyes staring vacantly into the distance. I'm not sure if he's trying to convince me or himself.

"The broken wrist isn't the worst. I mean, it's serious, but it's not the end of the world. It's her non-dominant hand. She's still young. So even if there are complications, she'll be able to adapt."

I don't really know what Owen's talking about, but I don't like the sound of "complications."

"I'm sorry," he blurts out suddenly. His grip on my hand tightens almost painfully. "I'm so sorry. I shouldn't have— If I hadn't, then we wouldn't be here right now. She could still have her party with her friends. I'm sorry. Fuck—I'm sorry."

I feel the anguish in his voice, the guilt and self-condemnation. It's heavy, suffocating, crushing.

Owen shoots to his feet, dragging air into his lungs as if they won't work unless he forces them to. His hands go into his hair as he paces back and forth in front of me. Tension radiates off him, making me feel agitated and jittery. I wish he would sit down. He's making me nervous hovering above me like that.

"I could've done better. I *should've* done better." Pace. Pace. Turn. "Why did I get that stupid bouncy castle? That thing is a goddamn deathtrap." Pace. Pace. Turn. "Oh my god, the other parents, they must think we're incompetent."

"Babe!" The word explodes out of me like the top blown off a pressure cooker.

Ivy stirs in my arms, a furrow forming in her brow as she makes small sleepy sounds. Shit. I didn't mean to wake her.

"Shh, it's okay, sweetie. Go back to sleep," I say, rubbing her back, but a voice calls out before I can soothe her back to sleep.

"Ivy Lambert?"

We all turn in the direction of the nurse. He leads us

down a narrow hallway and into an examination room. It's small, cramped with the exam bed taking up most of the space. There's a tiny table tucked into the corner with a computer and two chairs lined up against the wall. With three grown adults and a little girl, it feels a bit claustrophobic. Suddenly, all of Owen's muttering and talking to himself hits me like a sledgehammer.

What if Ivy's wrist *is* broken? What if it's worse than broken? What if there's permanent damage and she'll never be able to use it again? What if she loses it entirely? All these worst-case scenarios race through my mind as I stand in the middle of the tiny room, clutching Ivy to me so tightly she starts to whimper.

"Sorry, sweetie. Sorry."

The nurse gestures to the bed. "You can set her on there."

Ivy leans into me, grabbing onto my shirt with her good hand, and honestly, I don't want to let her go either. If I keep her in my arms, if I can physically wrap myself around her, then maybe the diagnosis won't be as bad.

"Is it okay if I..." I nod toward the bed and start hoisting myself onto it before the nurse even answers. "She'll be more comfortable if I'm holding her." *And I will be too.*

The nurse smiles sympathetically. "Sure, go ahead. My name is Dustin, and I'm a nurse practitioner. That means I'm qualified to do pretty much everything a doctor can do." He rolls his little stool over to the bed. "So what brings you in today?"

Owen steps up next to the bed, planting his feet and crossing his arms like he's our own personal bodyguard.

"She fell and injured her wrist. We need an x-ray to check if it's broken," he barks with a scowl on his face.

Dustin's gaze darts up to him, a little taken aback, and I nudge Owen with my foot. We don't need to piss off the nurse who's trying to take care of Ivy. What if he gives us a bad diagnosis? I mean, I know that's not how it works, but I'm not taking any chances, okay?

Dustin turns back to Ivy with a cautious expression. "Can I take a look?"

Ivy doesn't move, and a part of me wants to hide her away from this stranger. But that's only going to drag this out longer than any of us want. I rub her back. "It's okay, Ives, you can show him."

Carefully, I help her slip the makeshift sling off and support her arm as she extends it to Dustin. Owen watches like a hawk as Dustin examines Ivy's wrist, now swollen to twice the size of her other one. I'm not a doctor, but it doesn't look good.

Dustin's brow furrows as he turns her wrist over. "We'll have to get an x-ray to know for sure, but from the stiffness of the muscles, I would guess it's broken."

My heart plummets. "Is that bad? I mean, that's bad, right?"

Owen sets a hand on my shoulder and squeezes. I lean into his touch, seeking comfort in his strength. "We won't know until the x-ray images come back," he says.

Dustin agrees. "Yes, that's right. If it is broken, we'll have to see where the break is and if it's partial or complete. There are lots of little bones in the wrist and hand, so if there's more than one break or if bones are displaced, then it'll get more complicated."

I feel the blood drain from my face as I imagine Ivy

with steel rods sticking out of her arm like some sort of cyborg. Ivy starts crying again. Soft, quiet tears that roll down her red and splotchy cheeks. Owen lets out a growl so low it's barely a rumble and steps forward to insert himself between us and the nurse.

"*Or*, it could just be a sprain," Dustin says, trying to sound upbeat while rolling his chair away. "We shouldn't jump to conclusions until the x-rays come in." He stands and pushes the little stool into the corner. "You guys just hang tight in here. I'll let the x-ray tech know and he'll come get you when he's ready."

The door closes behind him and Owen turns to us. He pulls out one of the fresh handkerchiefs he grabbed on the way out the door and dabs at Ivy's cheeks. He wraps his other hand around the back of my neck. "You guys okay?"

Ivy's got her brave face on and she nods, cradling her hand to her chest. I don't feel nearly as brave as she does, but I nod too.

OWEN

They won't let us into the x-ray room with Ivy. I argue with Dustin, the nurse, trying to intimidate him into letting one of us inside. But Dustin stands his ground and eventually Everest pulls me away.

Ivy sniffles, looking so small and vulnerable as she follows Dustin into the x-ray room. She's being so brave, courageous, and strong. I'm so goddamn proud of her and at the same I don't feel worthy to be her parent. I've made so many mistakes already and we hadn't even had her for a year. I don't want to think about all the mistakes I'm going to make in the future, all the ways I'm going to let her down. I just hope I don't fuck her up too badly before she reaches adulthood.

It turns out her wrist is broken—in two places. They look clean, though—I made Dustin show me the images and walk me through what he saw. The bones don't look like they've shifted, so hopefully she'll only need a cast.

We'll have to bring her back in once the swelling's gone down to double-check alignment and maybe get a new cast if the first one becomes too loose.

Dustin lets Ivy choose which color she wants her cast to be. She chooses pink, of course, then he gives us a prescription for pain medication and tells us to schedule an appointment for next week.

By the time we get home, it's long past dinner and all three of us are pooped, barely hanging on by a thread. All I want is to fall into bed with Everest on one side and Ivy on the other.

Except we have guests. The house is full when we step inside, with not only both sets of grandparents but also all of Everest's friends. The grandparents, I understand. But Everest's friends?

"What are they doing here?" I ask Everest in the foyer when I hear all those extra voices echoing out of the kitchen.

He shoots me an annoyed look as he hands Ivy to me. Other than getting the x-ray by herself, she's insisted on being carried at all times. Everest and I have traded her back and forth the entire way home.

"Because they care," Everest hisses at me.

I frown. I didn't mean to imply they didn't care. I'm sure they do. But what does that have to do with loitering in our house all day?

"Hi, how did it go?" Mom leads the procession out of the kitchen to meet us halfway.

Nell's right behind her and she gasps with an excited expression. "Oh my gosh, is that a pink cast, Ivy?"

Ivy gives her a shy smile and nods.

"It's so pretty!" Logan sidles up next to me, holding out his hand. "Can I see?"

Ivy giggles quietly as lets him examine the cast that runs from just below her elbow to halfway down her fingers.

He knocks on it softly with a knuckle. "Whoa! You have an arm of steel!"

Ivy giggles some more and Logan rises in my estimation.

"You guys must be hungry," Mom says, ushering us back toward the kitchen. "We've been keeping it warm for you."

In the kitchen, Donnie and Christian are setting the table for us. I thought they would've just heated up the leftover food from the party, but instead, I find three plates of baked pasta filled with some of the random vegetables I had in the fridge.

My surprise must show on my face because Donnie gives me a knowing smile.

"I tend to stress cook, so I took the liberty of raiding your kitchen."

"That's…" Words fail me as gratitude and the sense of unworthiness overwhelms me. I sit down heavily on a chair, feeling so utterly exhausted. "Thank you," I say, voice thick with emotion.

"You're very welcome." Donnie steps back and lets the other guys crowd in.

"Hey Ivy, can we sign your cast?" Sawyer holds up a brand new pack of sparkly-colored Sharpies. We definitely didn't have those in the house before we left for urgent care, so the guys must have gone out and bought them while we were gone.

Across the table, Everest catches my eye. He cocks a brow, as if saying, "See? That's why they stuck around. That's what it means to care."

Yeah, yeah, fine. He's right. I can admit it. It's nice to have people, and Everest's people are definitely excellent options.

Enticed by the prospect of sparkly markers, Ivy scrambles out of my lap and into her own chair, kneeling on the seat and holding out her arm. "Can you draw me a unicorn?"

The guys stare at each other, a little dumbfounded before Christian holds up his hand. "I can give it a try?"

With Ivy distracted by the guys, Everest and I each grab a fork and dig in. My stomach grumbles as I take my first bite, and I realize I haven't eaten anything all day, not since my morning coffee.

"I assume the cast means it's broken?" Nell asks, she and Mom slide into the seats next to me and Everest.

I nod. "In two places—"

Both Mom and Nell wince.

"But it could've been worse."

"We have to bring her back for a follow-up next week," Everest adds.

"Do you want us to stay a bit longer?" Mom asks. Both sets of grandparents were only planning on staying for the weekend before heading home.

I'm about to decline the offer when I notice the expression on Everest's face. Longing and hopefulness and a general fatigue blanketing it all. *It's okay to accept help, Lambert.*

I sigh. "If it's not too much trouble?"

The surprise on Mom's face is evident. She hadn't expected me to say yes. I guess that says a lot about me, huh?

"Of course not. It's no trouble at all. You know that."

Everest shoots me a smile. It's small, private, just for the two of us. Full of approval and pride. It makes my chest fill with all the good feelings I've become addicted to. I glance around our kitchen, at the people I love most in this world and the people who love us in return. Life can be hard and shit happens. Sometimes we get hurt and sometimes things don't go the way we want them to. But so long as we're surrounded by family and friends who care, everything will work out okay.

The Mars guys don't stay late. Just long enough for them all to sign Ivy's cast. The grandparents retire soon after. Then it's just the three of us.

Everest and I get Ivy ready for bed and stay with her until she's fallen asleep. Then we go up to our room and get ready for bed ourselves.

When we climb in under the covers, Everest scoots up next to me and wraps himself around my body—arm encircling my waist, leg thrown over my thighs.

"I don't know if I'm up for it tonight," I murmur, eyes already closed, mind barely conscious.

"Neither am I. I just want to cuddle." He adjusts the position of his head on my shoulder, pressing his face into the side of my neck.

I sigh, taking in his weight, his steady breathing, the soft puff of air against my skin.

A part of me can't quite believe this is real. This is my life now. I have a partner who likes to cuddle, who brings out the best—and sometimes the worst—in me, who I know will stick by me whether I want him to or not. We have a house, a beautiful daughter, a group of friends who rally around us whenever we need them.

It's like a fairy tale. I never believed in fairy tales. But maybe that's just another thing I was wrong about too.

———

The next morning, I wake to the scent of coffee in the air. My eyes fly open and I bolt upright in bed. I'm alone.

What time is it? Why didn't my alarm go off? Why didn't Everest wake me?

I scramble out of bed and yank open the bedroom door. The fragrant aroma of coffee is stronger now, along with the distinct umami of bacon. Everest is making breakfast? His idea of breakfast is a bowl of cereal with milk. I'm halfway down the stairs before I hear the voices drifting up from the kitchen. Mom and Dad. Nell and Graham. I'd totally forgotten they were here.

Shit. Ivy. Her arm.

I detour to the second floor only to find the door to Ivy's room open and her bed empty, covers rumbled in a messy pile. She must be downstairs with everyone else.

I drag a hand down my face, scratching at my jaw, then comb my fingers through my hair. Jesus. How the hell did I sleep so late? Yesterday was long and exhausting, sure, but I've had longer and more exhausting days before, and I'm not usually one to sleep in.

With a sigh, I make Ivy's bed for her, then head back upstairs to make myself presentable. When I get down to the kitchen, everyone's already gathered, more than halfway through their breakfasts. They all turn when I walk in.

"Good morning." My voice is still hoarse from just having woken.

Everest notices, his lips twitching into a sly smile. "About time. Jeez. Way to sleep away the whole day."

Nell smacks him on the arm and rises from the table. "Grab a seat, Owen. I'll bring over your plate. How do you like your coffee?"

"I've got it," Everest says, following his mom to the coffee maker on the counter.

A warm and fuzzy feeling lingers in my stomach as I watch Everest pour a cup for me. It's not hard to doctor my coffee when I drink it black, but there's something intimate about him knowing how I like it all the same.

He takes the plate from his mom and sets both the plate and the mug down in front of me. His hand glides over my arm and around my shoulder as he steps away. When he sits down, his arm rests across the back of Ivy's chair between us, his fingers brushing against my bicep. It's small, absentminded, almost accidental, but it makes my heart pitter-patter something ridiculous.

"How's your arm, Ivy?" I ask, leaning toward her and into Everest's touch.

She holds it out for me to inspect. The unicorn the guys drew commands center stage in the middle of the cast, with all their names scrawled around it. The grandparents' names are on there too. "It hurt when I woke up but Uncle Ev gave me some medicine and now it's okay."

I take her hand and press a quick kiss to the tiny fingers sticking out at the end of the cast. "Good. Remember to tell us if it starts to hurt again, okay?"

Ivy nods. "Okay! But you won't be here."

I furrow my brow at her strange statement. "What do you mean I won't be here?"

Ivy gasps, slapping her good hand over her mouth. Her eyes are wide, like she's been caught stealing candy from the pantry.

"It's okay, Ivy," Mom says from across the table. "You can tell them."

Ivy beams and even with the scrape across her jaw and the little nicks and cuts all over, she looks brilliant. "You and Uncle Ev are going on a date!"

Me and Ev are what? I glance at Everest who shrugs, looking just as confused as I am, then at Mom who's wearing a smug grin. Nell has a matching one, like the two of them have some scheme up their sleeves.

"Mom?" I don't like surprises. She knows I don't, and yet, the expression on her face has "surprise" written all over it.

"We were wondering, have you guys been on a real date yet?" Nell asks.

Everest blinks, dumbfounded. "A date?"

"Yes, you know, going to do something fun and romantic—alone?" Nell clarifies, putting extra emphasis on that last word.

I scoff. "We've been a little busy lately. When exactly would we have had time to go on a date?"

"That's our point," Mom cuts in. "You went from barely tolerating each other to..." She waves her hand in our general direction. "You completely skipped the hanging out, getting to know each other part in the middle."

"I think I know Everest pretty well, Mom." I shoot her a skeptical look.

"But have you ever had fun together?" she shoots back. "Alone."

Alone? I can think of lots of fun we've had alone, but somehow, I don't think our moms are referring to our bedroom activities.

"So what are you trying to say?" Everest asks, suspicion evident in his voice.

"You're going on a date!" Ivy shouts, bouncing in her seat.

Mom pulls out her phone and a second later, mine chimes with an incoming message. "I just sent you the itinerary. We've planned everything out, including travel time between each location, and reservations have been made under Lambert-Wheeler."

I stare at the detailed itinerary on my phone. Everything's laid out just like Mom said, with address and phone numbers and reservation confirmation numbers. I sputter. "What— No— We can't— But Ivy—"

"Ivy will be fine!" Nell exclaims. "Mark and Graham have tickets to that auto show. And the three of us are having a girls' afternoon. Isn't that right, Ivy?"

"Yup!"

"But—" I try to object again.

"You'll show us where her medication is and any associated instructions. We've got both of your numbers in case there's an emergency. We'll be *fine*." Mom gives me a pointed look, daring me to oppose her.

I turn to Everest for support, because there's no way we can leave Ivy the day after her accident. But I should've known better because instead of the outrage I expect, Everest turns his big puppy dog eyes on me.

"Ev," I scold.

He shrugs and gives me the most adorably pleading look that he definitely learned from Ivy. "Kinda sounds fun?"

Fuck. Guess we're going on a date.

EVEREST

We're going on a date. Which is exciting and weird all at the same time.

Me, going on a date with Owen Lambert, sounds like the craziest thing ever. And if someone had told me about it a year ago, I would've called them delusional.

But somehow, it feels right. We've already hit all the other major relationship milestones. We inherited a house together, moved in together, are raising a kid together. We fell in love. All of it kind of backward. And there's only one thing we never got to do—go on our first date. Things have come full circle and it feels like we're starting over—the right way this time.

I'd be lying if I said I wasn't excited about going on a date with Owen. Okay, I mean, our moms have planned a kayak tour of the East River, a whiskey tasting at a distillery, and a reservation at some fancy restaurant. It's all the things we each like most. But it feels more special because we'll be doing those things together—me and Owen, just the two of us.

We've been through a hell of a lot these last six months. So much pain and grief and heartache, but also unbelievable joy, happiness, and love. We've had explosive arguments and even more explosive sex. We've been at each other's throats and we've been each other's support too. I think we deserve to have the magic and excitement of a first date.

I stretch my arm across the back of the seat, dragging Owen to me as the rideshare drives us toward Brooklyn Bridge Park for our kayak tour. He grumbles and pretends to put up a fight, but when I tug him closer, he snuggles into my side.

"We should've stayed home."

"Stop it."

"What if something happens to Ivy?"

"There are four adults in the house. They'll know what to do. And they have both of our phone numbers."

"What if we don't hear our phones ring? What if we drop our phones in the river?" Owen struggles against me as he works himself up. "What if we're stuck in the middle of the river and can't get back to shore?"

"Then I'll push you out of the kayak and you can swim to shore."

Owen glares at me and I smirk back at him.

"Seriously, babe, you need to chill the fuck out and enjoy the day. They went to all this trouble to plan it for us and it'll go to waste if you're worrying the whole time."

Owen harrumphs, my little grumpy gremlin, but at least he doesn't keep arguing.

His mood improves when we get out onto the water.

Turns out he was on the varsity rowing team in college—which like, of course he did the bougie-est sport ever. His competitive side comes out and he starts showing off, paddling circles around everyone.

Not that he's better than I am—I'm a water guy too, remember? We end up racing each other all the way to Governor's Island, leaving the rest of our tour group in our wake.

"Cheater!" Owen shouts at me when I reach the buoy first.

"Sore loser!" I shout back at him.

He narrows his eyes at me, and before I can react, he runs his paddle across the surface of the water, sending a massive spray right at me. I sputter as water soaks through my clothes and drips off my face. I'm stunned, less from the shocking cold and more from Owen's nerve. He *splashed* me. *He* splashed *me*.

I turn to him and the look on his face tells me he's as surprised as I am. His mouth hangs open, his eyes are wide with disbelief. The second our eyes make contact he starts paddling backward, trying to escape retribution.

"Oh, no, you don't!" I dig my paddle into the water and my kayak shoots forward. When I get close enough, I swing my kayak around and it bangs into Owen's.

The impact knocks him off balance, his kayak rocking precariously back and forth. He throws his arms up in the air to stay upright, but then loses his grip on his paddle and it goes flying across the water.

I burst out laughing, dropping my head back and letting the summer sun shine down on my face.

"Fuck you," Owen shouts at me before realizing we're

in public. He glances around sheepishly at the parents with their kids. "Sorry!"

"Language, language," I scold mockingly.

Owen turns his body to hide the middle finger he flashes in my direction.

Still laughing, I retrieve his paddle and bring it back to him. When he takes it from me, he makes a point of poking me in the leg with it before sticking it back into the water. I give him a wink and blow him a kiss.

His lips twitch like he's fighting off a smile and my chest expands with so much love it feels like I might lift off and float away. Playing with Owen like this, competing with him and teasing him, it's not something I ever thought I'd do. He used to be so stodgy, so stuck up and boring. And I used to push way too hard, taking perverse pleasure in jabbing him right in his soft, vulnerable spots.

But we've found a balance. He's lightened up and I've backed off. The easy give-and-take we have now has been hard-fought, but we did it. And I've never been more grateful for having an enemy like Owen. I've never been more grateful to Eden and Jeremy for sticking us together.

Would we have gotten here if we didn't hate each other so much before? If we'd just been acquaintances, polite and civil but distant, we probably would've worked together just fine, but that would've been all there was.

We needed the animosity. We needed the intense loathing. It's the only way we would've clashed so explosively. It forced us to confront who we were and what we could be—for ourselves, for Ivy, and for each other.

After kayaking, we make our way to the whiskey tasting. As we're waiting for the tour to start, I quietly slip my hand into Owen's. He glances down at our clasped hands, then up at me. For a second, I think he's going to shake me off, but then he adjusts his grip, sliding his fingers between mine. I step in a little closer, pressing my arm against his and my heart does a pitter-patter when he shifts his weight to press back.

During the tour, Owen's at the front of our little group, pestering the tour guide with a million questions, most of which I don't understand. Something about pH balances and types of wood and enzymes and shit. But through it all, his thumb rubs little circles across the back of my hand. It's just a small caress, almost unnoticeable, but it sends tingles of awareness through my whole body. My dick perks up in my jeans, not enough to be obscene, but definitely enough to keep me on my toes and has me counting down the hours until we can be alone again.

The restaurant is across the street from the distillery and they have a partnership where each dish is paired with a different whiskey. Owen scours the menu, consulting his phone for… I don't even know what. I let him order for us while I do my best to distract him under our table. I trap his feet between mine, rubbing our ankles together and running my toe up the hem of his pants. The only sign he's bothered by it is his half-hearted attempts to pull his feet out of my clutches.

He hands our menus back to the waiter with a word of thanks then turns to me, eyes half-lidded and dark.

"What do you think you're doing?"

Resting my elbow on the table and propping my chin in my hand, I give him my most innocent look. "What do you mean?"

He smirks and turns the tables on me. His foot slides up my calf to the inside of my knee. I gasp, my breath trapped in my lungs as it travels up my thigh. Thank fucking god the tablecloth goes all the way to the floor.

Owen presses the ball of his foot against my crotch and my dick roars to life, hardening so fast it's almost painful. I grip the edge of the table and grunt softly as Owen slowly increases the pressure.

His smirk widens into a sultry, evil smile, and his eyes stay locked on mine, unblinking. I don't dare look away. I couldn't even if I wanted. I'm caught in his snare, his amber eyes drawing me in and holding me tight. My pulse races as the world narrows to just me and him around this table. The music flowing through the restaurant speakers, the conversations of the diners around us, all of it fades to silence. My whole body is taut, waiting for something, waiting for him.

"You've been a bad boy today, Everest."

I gulp. Fuck. Jesus. My head spins as all the blood in my body rushes to my cock.

"How are you going to make it up to me?"

I make a desperate sound at the back of my throat. Helpless. Pleading. I'll do anything to make it up to him. Anything. Everything.

"I asked you a question, Everest. It's not polite to keep me waiting." Owen's voice is no more than a rumble that penetrates into my core.

"I— I—"

"Speechless, are we?" He covers my hand with his own, then pries my fingers from around the table edge.

My hand trembles—hell, my whole body trembles—as he lifts it to his mouth. He plants a kiss in the middle of my palm then, then flattens my hand against his cheek. The prickly hairs of his beard send shivers up my spine.

"Are you going to fuck me?" he murmurs, his lips moving against the heel of my palm. "Fill me up with your giant cock and shoot your cum deep into me?" His foot rotates against my throbbing dick.

I nod. It's the only response I can manage without making a complete fool of myself in the middle of the public restaurant.

"How are you going to take me?" Owen's eyes drift shut and his breathing becomes ragged. "Up against a wall? On top of a table? Over the back of a couch?" When he opens his eyes again, they are nowhere near as focused as they were a second ago.

I'm not the only one affected by this. He feels it too. Desire and want. Building slowly but unrelentingly.

"Here we are…"

I snatch my hand back from Owen's grasp and he drops his foot from between my legs. We both busy ourselves with napkins and cutlery as the waiter sets our plates down in front of us.

When we're alone again, Owen sneaks a glance across to me and we hold each other's gaze for a moment.

"Eat fast?" I suggest, no longer interested in a drawn-out meal, even as romantic as this is.

Owen tilts his head in thought before answering. "Take it to go."

He's already flagged the waiter down and given him some excuse about some fake emergency before I even realize what we're doing. Then suddenly we're in a car, heading toward the hotel room our parents booked for us.

The second the door beeps to unlock and I turn the handle to push it open, Owen crowds up behind me, bundling me inside. I barely have time to drop our takeout containers on the table before Owen shoves me up against a wall.

His body molds to mine like we were made for each other. Our mouths fit together like two pieces of a puzzle. I fill my palms with the rounded globes of his ass, and when I squeeze, pulling him up and into me, he grunts, grinding his erection into mine.

Clothes fly across the room and we tumble into bed, too caught up to waste time folding them. I rub my thumb against that spot on his hip that always makes him shudder. He sucks on the spot on my neck that always makes my cock throb. We know each other so well now. We know how to tease and drag things out. We know what drives the other crazy with lust.

Owen pushes me away and I stumble backward onto the bed.

"On your back," he orders, popping open the bottle of lube we packed and squeezing out a generous amount.

I rush to comply, flopping onto my back and gripping the base of my cock to keep the damn thing from exploding prematurely.

Owen straddles my thighs and smirks down at me as he reaches behind himself. His eyes roll backward and his lids flutter. His lips part with a gasp, then a shaky exhale.

I watch as his body goes taut. Dark chest hair smattered against pale skin. A delicious treasure trail running down the middle of his stomach. His cock hanging in midair, a drop of pre-cum gathering at the tip.

He shuffles forward, lines himself up, and impales himself on my cock. Tight heat envelops me and my hips lift off the bed, trying to get closer, deeper.

Owen's body is comfortingly familiar and yet enticingly novel at the same time. A hungry vice around my dick that sends electricity ricocheting through my body like a pinball.

Owen slams himself down on me. The impact makes my vision go white. We're so in sync, perfectly timed as Owen bounces up and down, meeting my every thrust. His cock smacks against my stomach with a wet, obscene sound. A thin stream of pre-cum leaks from his tip. I grip his hips and he grips my wrists. We've got each other, both holding on tight.

Then it clicks.

This is how we did it the first time. All those years ago. At Jeremy's bachelor party. When we still hated each other.

I run my hands up and down Owen's muscled thighs. His eyes focus just enough to meet my gaze. He knows that I know and something inside me cracks open wide.

God, I fucking love this motherfucker.

I think I might have all the way back then too. Why else would I hate him so goddamn much for no reason at all? It had to have been love, twisted and contorted into hatred because I didn't understand it and didn't know what else to do with it. I wasn't ready for him then. I wasn't ready for the all-consuming and soul-transforming love that has turned my life upside down.

But I'm ready now. And I'm going to cherish every fucking moment of it.

Always. Forever.

A sob escapes my throat as I'm overwhelmed by the sentiment. I pull him down for a kiss, needing the intimacy.

Owen's tongue tangles with mine. His hands trail up

my stomach and to my chest. He pinches both nipples until I'm gasping into his mouth. He clenches around my dick and the three points of sensation overload my brain.

I see stars. My orgasm crashes through me as my hips punch up into Owen's body. Wave after wave. Pleasure cresting like the unrelenting ocean. He milks me with his ass, his fingers still twisting my nipples to the point of pain.

Scalding hot cum lands on my stomach in one spurt after another. With each one, Owen's ass tightens around me even more, dragging out my pleasure until I'm nothing more than one big mass of firing nerve endings.

I'm consumed. Spent. Emptied. Yet I've never felt so full and satisfied in my life.

Owen collapses on me, face pressed against the crook of my neck, his still-hard cock trapped between us. His cum is smeared between our stomachs. He doesn't try to move, though. He doesn't roll off to the side or go looking for a towel to wipe up. He lets me wrap my arms around him and hold him to me.

Slowly, our breathing evens out and the sweat cools on our skin. Even then, Owen doesn't disentangle himself from me.

"See? I told you you like to cuddle," I murmur in his ear.

"Fuck you," he says, even as he snuggles closer, tucking his body more securely into mine.

The smile that spreads across my face comes from the deepest part of my soul. "Love you too."

EPILOGUE

OWEN

"We're going to be late!" I call up the stairs while checking my watch for the time.

It's the first day of school and we had grand plans about waking up early and having breakfast as a family. But of course Everest let Ivy stay up way too late last night and then he had a hell of a time trying to get her ready this morning. I can't wait to tell him, "I told you so" when they finally come downstairs.

Footsteps thunder across the second floor landing and down the steps. Ivy first, followed closely by Everest. She's wearing the new clothes we got last week during back-to-school shopping, along with her new backpack—a purple unicorn one because she's graduated from pink, apparently.

"Sorry! I'm sorry!" Everest's light brown curls are a riot on his head and he quickly slams a baseball cap over them, adjusting the brim so it sits above the back of his neck. "I thought we had more time!"

I hold out a bag containing three foil-wrapped breakfast burritos and Everest sheepishly takes it from me.

"Okay, Ives, let's get a photo really quick before we go." I position Ivy by the front door and give her the sign we made two days ago that says "First Day of Grade Two." I snap the photo as tears spring up out of nowhere, stinging my eyes. The photo matches the one Jeremy and Eden took of Ivy one year ago. God, I wish *so much* that they could be here to see this. Ivy, one year older, growing taller, smarter, more sure of herself.

Everest's arm comes around my waist and he kisses the back of my neck. I don't need to say what I'm feeling. I know he's thinking the same thing.

I sniffle and shake away the sentimentality. We don't have time for reminiscing at the moment. We need to get Ivy to school.

"Come on, Ives. Let's go!"

Once we're out the door, Everest carefully unwraps Ivy's breakfast burrito before handing it to her. He doesn't need to do that. She's perfectly capable of unwrapping it herself now that her cast has been off for a few weeks. But it makes him feel better to do little things like that for her, so I only scold him about half the time.

I trail behind, letting the two of them walk ahead of me on the sidewalk. The air is still warm with the lingering summer sun and the trees still have all of their green leaves. In a few weeks, the weather will cool and the leaves will morph into bright reds and yellows. I make a mental note to schedule a day at the park so we can enjoy the colors.

Ivy laughs, head tilted back to smile up at Everest. "Don't be silly, Uncle Ev!"

He bends down to plant a quick kiss on her head and as he straightens, he shoots a quick look back at me. "What about Uncle O? Can he stay with you at school today?"

She spins in a circle, her smile shining brighter than the sun. "No! I'm a big girl! I can go to school by myself!"

Everest and I share a look. Yes, she is a big girl, but she'll always be our little girl. She can go to school by herself, but we'll always be here waiting for her when she comes home.

"But we're going shopping after school, right?"

Everest points at me. "*Uncle O* will take you shopping for a new dress."

"It's *your* friends who are getting married," I shoot back.

Everest rolls his eyes. "Donnie and Connor aren't getting married. It's a commitment ceremony."

"Same thing." I wave off his objection and turn back to Ivy. "Yes, we can go shopping, Ives."

She beams at me and I feel like a freaking superhero.

When we arrive at Ivy's school, we hand her off to her teacher and stand on the sidewalk, waving as she runs inside.

Everest slips his hand into mine, our fingers intertwined. "I love you," he says, seemingly out of nowhere.

I turn, and as our gazes collide, it steals my breath away. "I love you too," I reply, filled to the brim with love so strong it sends me staggering.

He leans in and I meet him halfway. The kiss is short, chaste, gentle. But with a promise of so much more to come.

BONUS SCENE

It took a while, but I finally—*finally*—got Owen to agree to get a Mars Fitness membership… trial. Yes, the jerkwad wouldn't even let me get him a full membership with the friends and family discount. He wanted to "try it out first" to "see if he liked it." As if.

He won't do any of my classes either. Apparently skipping is too hard on his knees—old man—drumming is too loud for his ears, and bungee fitness is too dangerous. Seriously. Ugh.

Instead, he's been using the treadmills and other gym equipment, which I do not approve of because I can't keep an eye on him when I'm busy teaching.

Case in point: I've just finished a class and what do I see the moment I step out of my studio? Some fucking predator standing way too close to Owen, with his hands on Owen's hips. Owen glances back at the fucker and smiles at him.

Fury roils hot in my stomach as I stalk across the main floor. Through the mirrors lining the opposite wall, Owen catches sight of me. His eyes narrow a fraction, calculating, and then he smirks. He fucking *smirks*…

To read the rest of the bonus scene, sign up for Linden Bell's Very Important Reader newsletter here: bit.ly/pumpedbonus.

RIPPED

When Connor walks in on his boyfriend sleeping with his best friend, he finds solace in the arms of older, widowed silver fox, Donnie, in the first Mars Fitness book, *RIPPED*, bit.ly/rippedbm.

THANK YOU

I don't have kids and I'm not a kid person by any means. So I don't know why I decided to write an entire book centered around a little girl! I really hope I did justice to Ivy, especially since I put her through so much. 🩶

If you've enjoyed *PUMPED*, please consider recommending it to your friends. Leave a review for *PUMPED* on social media, your own blog, Amazon, or Goodreads so other MM romance lovers can get to know Owen, Everest, and Ivy too.

If you would like to stay up to date on future Linden Bell books, join the Very Important Reader mailing list and also receive the exclusive bonus scene! bit.ly/pumpedbonus

You can also follow me on:
Facebook - facebook.com/authorlindenbell
Instagram - instagram.com/authorlindenbell
Amazon - amazon.com/author/lindenbell
Goodreads - goodreads.com/authorlindenbell
Bookbub - bookbub.com/authors/linden-bell

ABOUT LINDEN BELL

Linden Bell writes romances that heat you up and make you smile. Her books are low angst, feel-good reads, with no third-act breakups!

For a reading guide to Linden Bell books, check out lindenbell.com/books.

- facebook.com/authorlindenbell
- instagram.com/authorlindenbell
- amazon.com/author/lindenbell
- goodreads.com/authorlindenbell
- bookbub.com/authors/linden-bell

ALSO BY LINDEN BELL

Mars Fitness Series

Where the jocks of Mars Fitness meet the nerds of their dreams.

The Camboy Network Series

When sex on camera turns into love behind the scenes.

9 781739 076399